"Now!"

Upon Mira's signal, Eizenfald
unleashed dragon breath upon the
Protectors. Then Elezina fired
an enormous arrow of light toward
the same point. The attack didn't end
there; every castle-wall cannon,
as well as the cannon-fortress
golems, fired at once.

"Nwah?!"

Mira managed to whip around, but he'd charged out so suddenly, it took all her reflexes just to dodge. Her momentum caused her to trip over her own legs and fall right on the floor.

She caught herself, but her skirt flipped up completely. Rather than fixing it, she whined, "What the heck's wrong with you?!"

"Oh, my bad. Anyway, this is an emergency!"

She Professed Herself Pupil of the Wise Man

NOVEL 11

WRITTEN BY
Ryusen Hirotsugu

ILLUSTRATED BY
fuzichoco

Airship

Seven Seas Entertainment

TABLE OF CONTENTS

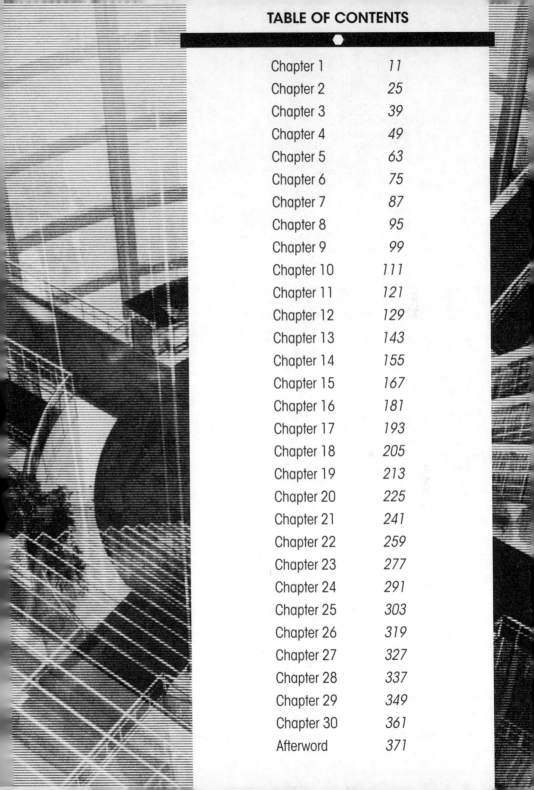

Kenja no deshi wo nanoru kenja 11
©Ryusen Hirotsugu (Story) ©fuzichoco (Illustrations)
This edition originally published in Japan in 2019 by
MICRO MAGAZINE, INC., Tokyo.
English translation rights arranged with
MICRO MAGAZINE, INC., Tokyo.

Seven Seas press and purchase enquiries can be sent to
Marketing Manager Lauren Hill at press@gomanga.com.
Information regarding the distribution and purchase of
digital editions is available from Digital Manager CK Russell
at digital@gomanga.com.

Follow Seven Seas Entertainment online at
sevenseasentertainment.com.

TRANSLATION: Benjamin Daughety
ADAPTATION: Adam Lee
LOGO DESIGN: George Panella
COVER DESIGN: Nicky Lim
INTERIOR DESIGN: Clay Gardner
INTERIOR LAYOUT: M. A. Lewife
COPY EDITOR: Cheri Ebisu
PROOFREADER: Amanda Eyer
EDITOR: Viviane Wishart
PREPRESS TECHNICIAN: Melanie Ujimori, Jules Valera
MANAGING EDITOR: Alyssa Scavetta
EDITOR-IN-CHIEF: Julie Davis
PUBLISHER: Lianne Sentar
VICE PRESIDENT: Adam Arnold
PRESIDENT: Jason DeAngelis

ISBN: 979-8-88843-481-9
Printed in Canada
First Printing: September 2024
10 9 8 7 6 5 4 3 2 1

WAITING IN THE SUBTERRANEAN DEPTHS of the Ancient Underground City was a giant, mechanical abomination, the Machina Guardian. Its body was a full fifty meters long, and its inorganic yet animalistic form constantly whirred with motion—specifically, the rapid movement of its eight metallic legs. It was surprisingly agile for a machine, rampaging whenever any intruder visited its chamber.

Confronting it were countless skeletons and a golem army of all sizes and shapes. They were controlled by one man: Soul Howl, the Great Wall himself.

And now, new forces had joined the battle: Eizenfald—an Imperial Dragon boasting a size equal to the Machina Guardian's—and the seven Valkyrie Sisters. They weren't all. Running through the battlefield was the summoner once known as the One-Man Army, now in the form of a little girl…Mira.

Towers and forts lined the battlefield, courtesy of necromancy. At the very top of the largest one, Mira landed lightly behind Soul Howl and approached.

Before she could speak up, Soul Howl gazed at the battle-field and said ominously, "Eizenfald, the seven sisters... Is it just a coincidence that you're here, Elder?"

He turned to face her with a nihilistic smirk, but his composure instantly shattered into unhinged confusion.

"Huh? Wha—?" Having turned fully around, he let out a confused gasp and gazed at Mira. That was natural, since the girl he saw was entirely unlike the person he'd imagined.

Mira took his confused gaze in stride and waved wryly at him. "Oh, hi. Been a while, Soul Howl." How she'd ended up this way was a bit of a sore subject for her, so she hoped inwardly that he wouldn't press the matter too much.

Soul Howl dashed her hopes instantly. "Sure has, Elder. It sure has. Did you use a Vanity Case? Why? Did Lumi inspire you?"

It was well known among Mira's circle that she'd loved her look as Danblf. Now she was a different person entirely; it would be silly to expect anyone not to wonder why. "Lumi" was, of course, Luminaria—though Soul Howl used to call her "Lumanaria" as a joke. Incidentally, "Elder" was Soul Howl's nickname for Danblf.

"Well, it's a long story. Allow me to share it later," Mira answered firmly, giving Soul Howl no time to speak before changing the subject. Though she said she'd explain the matter, she obviously planned to brush it under the rug as long as possible. "For now, let's prioritize the battle at hand. You need to press on, don't you?"

"So it's not a coincidence that you're here, after all," Soul Howl intuited from Mira's behavior. He looked at her dubiously.

"That's a long story too," Mira replied with a small shrug of the shoulders. "So do you think you can win?"

"Yeah, of course."

Setting the details of Mira's appearance aside for now, the duo looked upon the battlefield again. With Mira's forces having joined Soul Howl's, the battle raged even more intensely.

Eizenfald's blows bore into the Machina Guardian's plating, but the enemy would not fall so easily. It used its many legs to the fullest, taking advantage of any opening to attack. It had already halved the durability of Eizenfald's defensive barrier.

And although Alfina and her sisters fought well, they were plainly struggling against the Machina Guardian's overwhelming defenses.

The impressive Soul Howl continued adding turrets and golems now and then, even as he spoke with Mira. His forces thus remained in perfect condition, save for the hundreds of skeletons the Machina Guardian had culled to only dozens, leaving them unable to fulfill their role as bait.

Soul Howl quickly assessed the situation and decided, "Time for a temporary retreat. Elder...dismiss your summons and fall back to the entrance." It seemed he'd decided to stick with his original scheme regardless of whether he had an ally.

"Hm. Very well."

What was Soul Howl planning? Mira didn't know, but she knew he wouldn't do this without reason. She readily agreed, dismissed Eizenfald and the Valkyrie Sisters, and returned to the entrance.

When Mira looked again, the battle had shifted dramatically. Since the bait skeletons *and* Eizenfald and the Valkyries had disappeared, the Machina Guardian was free to trample the remaining forces. Dozens of turrets collapsed almost instantly, and even the giant golems were helplessly scattered. All that remained was an armored-fortress golem below Soul Howl's feet.

Having destroyed its nearest targets, the Machina Guardian turned its sights on Soul Howl. Its eight legs skittered across the battlefield.

Soul Howl now faced one of the top raid bosses—fighting it alone would be nothing short of reckless. But Mira watched without concern, because she knew exactly what Soul Howl was planning.

The Machina Guardian's leg pierced the thick armored-fortress wall with ease. It repeated this once—twice—more, punching multiple holes in the armored-fortress golem. At once, Soul Howl boarded his Bicorn skeleton and jumped away. The fortress suddenly shone red, and lava spewed from it like an eruption.

The power of the necromantic branch of Internment Arts depended on the size of the golem it was based on. A spell cast using an armored-fortress golem—often bigger than a house—created an explosion of heat that rivaled a real eruption.

Lava instantly engulfed the Machina Guardian. Soul Howl, meanwhile, returned to the entrance, where he jumped off his Bicorn without looking back at the immolated boss and began arranging golems at the entrance again. These golems were the most basic of basic necromancy, only a meter tall at best.

"Is that your strategy for interfering with the raid boss's healing?" Mira asked.

"Exactly," Soul Howl replied.

Just as Mira expected, he was using the method Danblf had once proposed but never put into practice. It seemed Soul Howl would send one golem toward the Machina Guardian every nine minutes and have it self-destruct. That strategy was only possible because they were "laborer mages"—the common term for those that created or summoned minions.

If a certain amount of time passed during which nothing showed hostility toward the Machina Guardian, it would begin repairing itself. But if anything attacked within that time period, the clock reset.

Since the Machina Guardian's wait time to self-repair was ten minutes, Soul Howl could impede its recovery by attacking every nine minutes. The golems lined up here were ready for that task. In other words, as long as Soul Howl kept making golems, he could buy time to rest indefinitely. That made it possible to enter a long-term battle against this raid boss.

"I'm making use of your strategy, Elder. It's going quite well so far," Soul Howl confirmed, lining up five golems. He glanced at the battlefield and muttered, "Only 20 percent so far."

"I'm happy to hear that." When Mira looked to the battlefield, she saw the Machina Guardian—who'd been submerged in lava until moments ago—standing there as if nothing had happened. Its exterior was damaged, however; indeed, the damage Soul Howl had dealt so far was still evident.

"This way. Come with me." Soul Howl promptly walked away.

"It's about dinnertime, no?" It was already nighttime. "How about I give you the dessert I've been saving?" Mira offered as she followed.

"If it's that red fruit, I'll pass," Soul Howl replied, glaring at her. It seemed he already knew about the nameless fruit.

Mira clicked her tongue in annoyance.

Soul Howl took Mira to a large room about half a kilometer from the depths the Machina Guardian protected. When Mira asked why he'd set up camp so far away, he explained that he couldn't sleep with all the booming. She found that convincing.

His camp was in the second-biggest room on the seventh level. It didn't spawn monsters and was often used for final strategy meetings. He must've been expecting a long battle, since there were cooking utensils and more inside.

"So...Elder. You don't mind me calling you that, do you?" It seemed Soul Howl also used a Dinoire Trading sleeping bag. Sitting down on it, he grabbed a random drink from his Item Box and gazed at Mira dubiously. "Why are you here?"

"I call myself Mira now. Feel free to use my new name," she answered, brushing off his gaze as she likewise set out her sleeping bag and sat down on it.

"All that's changed is your appearance. What's wrong with 'Elder'?" Soul Howl seemingly found it much easier to use the same nickname than a new, unfamiliar name.

"Give me a break."

He never changes, Mira thought, before telling Soul Howl about the events so far: how the non-aggression pact's deadline was closing in, how she had visited the Ancient Temple Nebrapolis because it was the easiest part of Soul Howl's trail to track, and how they'd traced clues they found there to locate him. And, finally, how they knew he was after the Holy Grail of Heavenly Light to save the woman frozen in suspended animation.

After accurately yet concisely explaining everything so far, Mira added cheerfully, "I'm relieved that I found you here."

"I see... You came here knowing all that, huh? Good work." He shrugged in exasperation and smirked. It seemed Soul Howl had basically acted for the reasons they'd expected. "You'll help me, then?"

Mira read between the lines: once his current task was done, he'd come home. At the same time, Soul Howl was making an implicit demand—in return, he would need her help.

"Well, I *suppose,*" she replied. If she wanted to resolve this situation quickly, she'd need to help him defeat the Machina Guardian as soon as possible. She laughed dryly at how similar this was to finding Kagura. However, she'd expected this and, in the end, accepted Soul Howl's demand. "Now, before we destroy the Machina Guardian, there's something I must ask. May I?"

It was clear what she would need to do: defeat the Machina Guardian and obtain the item necessary to create a Holy Grail. Avoiding combat was not an option, so only one question was left on Mira's mind.

"What? If it's about the loot, it's all yours, Elder."

"Ooh, you mean it?! How generous! But, er...no, that wasn't it. I wanted to ask why you didn't use advanced spells in the battle earlier." They were about to fight one of the strongest enemies out there, and there was surely no leeway to hold back or let their guards down, so Mira just had to ask why.

"Ah, that? I'm under a restriction right now. I can't use those," Soul Howl replied coolly and smiled, as if to say it was no big deal.

"A restriction? What in the world? *Why?*" Mira pressed him for details. She had never heard of a restriction that would prevent a mage from using advanced spells.

"Well... You saw that girl, right?" Soul Howl asked vaguely. He then explained that the girl in suspended animation, back in the castle he'd once stayed at, had caused the restriction magic.

She had the mark of the Curse of the Underworld, also known as the Demon's Blessing, on her back. Soul Howl had used magic to stop time for her, temporarily severing her from the laws of nature to keep the curse from progressing. That had caused the state Mira found the girl in so long ago.

The spell that made that possible, Otherworldly Stasis, was a Forbidden Art that forcibly warped reality. Its raw power came at a cost: while it was active, Soul Howl couldn't use advanced spells.

"Goodness... You mean to tell me you've been like this ever since you began constructing a Holy Grail?"

The Nine Wise Men had the power to get by just fine with weaker magic, of course. But based on the documents Mira had read, Soul Howl must have fought off many powerful foes so far in the process of making a Holy Grail. That wouldn't have been impossible, given his strength; still, he must have pulled ridiculous stunts to get this far without advanced magic. Even she found it extraordinary that he'd put in the effort to do so.

"It's nothing." He shrugged. "Don't you love challenge runs, Elder? This is the same thing, just...*longer.*"

Successful challenge runs were all the more satisfying thanks to the restrictions one willingly placed on oneself. But what Soul Howl was doing was far, far more difficult. Still, he acted as if it wasn't a problem at all. His resolve to accomplish his goal, no matter the difficulty, shone through.

Sensing Soul Howl's determination, Mira was both confounded and thrilled at the change in her friend. Finally, he was a normal human being. "I see... That girl really is important to you. You've changed; you'd never have fallen for a living, breathing woman before. The passage of time is a truly strange thing." Or so she thought.

Soul Howl frowned in disgust at Mira's words. "No, no, no. Don't be stupid. Who'd love a woman like that? She's an annoying religious *nutcase.*"

"Hrmm...? What are you talking about? Is she not the woman you love? I thought your love spurred you to work this hard...?"

The Demon's Blessing guaranteed its victim's doom. All this time, Mira and Solomon had thought Soul Howl a brave man embarking on a great travail to save his beloved from that awful fate. He'd sounded like the hero of a fairy tale to Mira, and though Solomon wasn't present, he would no doubt have agreed.

"Her? Unthinkable. Of all the women alive, she'd be the *worst* for me." Surprisingly, Soul Howl didn't seem to be denying it out of embarrassment. His disdain was genuine.

When Mira pressed for more, he revealed other details about the frozen woman. According to him, she belonged to a religious denomination that believed the female corpses he'd collected should be properly buried. That denomination's influence had begun to expand ten years ago, and he'd unfortunately run into the girl while he collected more corpses.

She'd managed to sniff out his castle and constantly came to him, preaching that he should return the women to God's side. She'd even tried to cremate them herself eventually. Soul Howl added with an arch chuckle that the woman was too much of a handful for him.

"She sounds like quite a passionate believer," Mira mused. Soul Howl's castle was at the very bottom of a C-rank dungeon. If she went all the way down there to evangelize to him, she must've been devout.

"Oh, please. She's just a thief feigning belief."

Since there were monsters and the like in this world, leaving the city meant risking danger. The laws regarding the treatment of corpses resulting from said danger were lax. There was no legal difference between burying them, stripping them of their gear, or making use of them via necromancy, so Soul Howl was allowed to do as he pleased.

His moral views on this differed from those of Mira and other former players. Given the state of this world, however, there was little that could be done. The bottom line was that there were too many corpses to keep track of. In the midst of that, the denomination the woman belonged to arose.

By cremating a corpse and sending its belongings to relatives, one could at least give closure to those left behind. Even if you died in a deep, remote place, you might still be found someday and delivered home. That hope was her denomination's core dogma. It wasn't for the sake of the dead but for the living left behind.

That denomination's beliefs matched up rather closely with most former players' morals, so Mira didn't feel disgusted at the woman, as Soul Howl did. She was simply impressed by the woman's devoutness. To Soul Howl, though, the woman was little more than a thief trying to snatch away treasure he'd collected over many long years.

"It's rare for you to hate someone so," Mira said. "You've always been very indifferent toward people you dislike."

"Not my fault she's insane. No matter how far I run, she finds me again, and always with a smile." Apparently remembering her face, Soul Howl grimaced bitterly. "Just terrifying," he said, resigned.

"If she bothers you that much, she must really be something." Smirking at Soul Howl's atypical care for a living, breathing woman, Mira went a step further. "And you're going to such lengths to help her. You've *changed*."

It didn't sound like Soul Howl stood to gain anything by helping her, but he must've had some justifications. One was no doubt that he couldn't bear leaving her like that. That was the first thing that came to Mira's mind, after all.

It was natural to want to save someone you'd gotten to know, no matter how you met or how at odds your morals were. Your resolve might waver if they were a genuinely bad person, but this woman was good-hearted. It wasn't hard to understand why you'd want to help someone, even if they were a pain.

Still, Mira knew Soul Howl well, and she was aware that his morals were gray in that regard. He was essentially indifferent to death; whether someone lived was up to them, not him. He wouldn't go out of his way to interfere with the natural process.

Yet Soul Howl had set out on a long, arduous journey to save someone he claimed to *hate*. Mira found it rather odd, but she knew time had a way of changing people.

"I haven't changed," Soul Howl finally replied with a bitter grin, and quietly added, "She was just *crying*, is all."

The woman had come and complained about his necromancy as usual, but she'd lost her usual vigor. She was falling to the Demon's Blessing. Each day, she became more and more feeble, until she finally showed vulnerability to Soul Howl.

"She cried and said she was scared to die," he explained. "I want to say to her, 'Look what saved you—the necromancy you hate so much! Serves you right!'" With that, Soul Howl guffawed, insisting that he hadn't just been moved by her tears.

Then he corrected himself—if all went well, the Holy Grail would technically save the woman. Still, necromancy would play an indispensable role. The magic keeping her alive was necromancy, too, so he insisted it would be no exaggeration to say necromancy saved her.

This had all begun to sound like excuses to Mira. "Ah, of course. Right as always." She was certain now that Soul Howl *had* been moved by the woman's tears.

Life and death alone didn't move him, but if someone begged him for help, he was the kind of guy who'd do everything in his power to save them—even if he complained about it along the way. The woman had cried because she was afraid to die, and that alone had been enough to make Soul Howl act.

He hasn't changed at all, Mira laughed mentally.

She Professed Herself Pupil of the Wise Man

2

"**A**NYWAY, ENOUGH TALK. How about we eat?" Soul Howl casually brushed off the preceding conversation and started preparing food. Collecting the utensils he'd left here and there, he turned away from Mira. It seemed he was embarrassed and trying to hide it.

There was no need to probe further, Mira knew. She refocused and stood up straight proudly. "On that note, I have something better!"

Soul Howl turned and glared with cold eyes. "I said I don't want that red fruit."

"Tsk, tsk, tsk." Mira clicked her tongue and smirked. "It's nothing to do with *ingredients*. I meant better than those utensils of yours." Grinning wider, she instantly summoned the mansion spirit.

A small mansion appeared in the large chamber. Seeing it, Soul Howl exclaimed, "Ooh! Now, this is interesting. New summoning magic, I'm guessing?"

"Indeed. It's an artificial mansion spirit. I only just met it the other day, but it's quite useful." Mira puffed out her chest, expecting praise.

Soul Howl ignored her, however. Interest spurred him to reach for the mansion doorknob. "Huh? It won't open." He pulled and pushed, but the door wouldn't move. Twisting the knob in irritation, he looked back with a frown.

"Hm? That can't be right." Mira ran over and turned the doorknob. It opened with ease.

"You can't open the door unless you're the master?"

"I hadn't tested that, but you may be right."

After that exchange, Mira and Soul Howl followed their scientists' hearts and began experimenting. They learned you just *couldn't* open the door without Mira's permission; a guest couldn't even use the furnishings inside unless she explicitly allowed that.

"What a loyal mansion," Soul Howl mused. Instinctively yearning to refresh himself, he started stripping quickly in front of the shower room and asked Mira's permission: "Okay, I'd like to use your shower."

"Oh, I suppose I have no choice. I deign to permit you entry into the shower," Mira acquiesced, basking in a sense of superiority.

"Yeah, thanks," Soul Howl replied, rushing into the shower room.

Now, as for dinner...I think I'll have him *make it!* Mira laid her special sleeping bag on the floor and plopped down. She was hungry, but she wasn't about to make dinner; that was Soul Howl's greatest skill, after all. Cooking food for two people probably wasn't much harder than for one, so Mira planned to have Soul Howl cook her meals in return for her providing such a luxurious kitchen.

I'll shower while he cooks. A perfect plan! She would come out of the shower nice and clean, with dinner ready and waiting for her. Pleased by this flawless flow of events, she recalled Soul Howl's cooking repertoire and wondered what to demand he prepare.

Just then, there was a voice in Mira's head: *"Umm, hi. Sym? Is this connected? Mira? Miiiraaa? Can you hear meee?"*

"What?!" Mira was getting used to hearing the Spirit King out of nowhere, but the new voice in her mind startled her. Assessing its tone and the words she'd heard so far, Mira realized it was the progenitor spirit Martel. *"That voice... Is that you, Martel?"*

When Mira asked what was wrong, Martel replied happily, *"Oh, hey, Mira! Wow, wow! It really connected!"*

Between Martel's excited squeals, Mira heard the Spirit King. *"Apologies, Miss Mira. Martel said it wasn't fair that only I could talk to you, and she butted in."*

According to the Spirit King, he'd been enjoying Mira's adventures through her senses as usual until he got wrapped up in small talk with Martel. He'd been so distracted, he missed Mira's latest adventure, which made him quite sad.

Furthermore, in the middle of their chat, he ended up teaching Martel to communicate with Mira in addition to other spirits.

However, Martel could only do so while the Spirit King conversed with Mira. That also meant that she could butt in on their conversations at any point.

Martel had been able to talk to Mira from afar during the Fenrir rescue operation because Mira was inside her seal. It was like using a grocery store's microphone. Now that Mira was outside the seal, only the Spirit King could talk to her freely, and Martel was awfully jealous of that privilege.

"Well, it's...fine," Mira eventually responded. *"I'm sure you'll be a reliable help along the way."* Reliable, if a little *noisy*, she chuckled to herself. Still, she now had two veterans of this world to consult if the going got tough.

Hearing the faint sound of water from the shower room, the Spirit King realized someone else was there. *"Miss Mira, it seems somebody's with you. We didn't interrupt something, did we?"*

"Oh, is there somebody? Sorry, Mira," Martel added.

"No problem. He's just enjoying the shower right now. I doubt he'll come out for a while." Mira knew Soul Howl liked long baths; he'd probably take just as long in the shower.

"Sounds like he's a friend of yours, Miss Mira. That must mean you found the person you were looking for—all while I was distracted." The Spirit King knew Mira had been searching for a close friend, and he'd been excited to see them reunite. Yet Martel's small talk had unfortunately made him miss it.

Ignoring his complaints, Martel cut in, *"My! You came all this way searching for someone?"*

"Indeed," Mira replied. *"He's in the process of making a Holy Grail. We tracked his footsteps, and I finally caught him here. That's the long and short of it."*

After Mira's succinct explanation, Martel exclaimed, *"Goodness! Making a Holy Grail? That's incredible."* As a progenitor spirit, she knew all about Holy Grails, and seemed aware of the difficulty of creating one. She was impressed that he was going through such an arduous process all on his own.

"Quite ingenious to think of making one," the Spirit King said, equally impressed. Even he considered the process difficult. *"That friend of yours is a wild card, Miss Mira."*

While Mira listened to them, she hit upon an idea. If these two knew so much about Holy Grails, could she ask whether they truly had the power to erase a Demon's Blessing? It was really only hypothesized that a Holy Grail would do that; they had no clear proof it would work. Soul Howl was trying all this because he had no other options. Would his efforts be rewarded, or...?

"Sooo...I'd like to ask you two something," Mira told them, steeling herself. That prompted her distant companions to say that they'd answer anything they could. Praying that Soul Howl's efforts wouldn't go to waste, Mira posed the question.

"A Demon's Blessing..." repeated the Spirit King.

Mira could tell that he was deep in thought. What if a Demon's Blessing was too much for even a Holy Grail's power? She prepared to hear the worst, but their answers blindsided her.

"What exactly is a Demon's Blessing, Sym?" Martel asked the Spirit King.

"I've certainly never heard of it," he responded curiously.

"What...?" Mira gasped. Her shock was unfathomable. The two apparently knew nothing about the Demon's Blessing, despite having lived as long as this world had existed. *"Come now, you must be familiar with that. The...Curse of the Underworld, or whatever, is also known as the Demon's Blessing. You've got to know it."*

Although Mira did her best to explain, they only replied again that they didn't know what she was talking about.

Then she remembered something: "Curse of the Underworld" and "Demon's Blessing" were names created by players. They were nicknames of convenience; the mark itself had no formal name.

In light of that, Mira explained in more detail to Martel and the Spirit King. The mark would suddenly emerge one day by tearing through someone's skin. It was a six-pointed star surrounded by symbols and shapes, and the characters "XV" were at the center. Those whom the mark appeared on died untimely deaths. When that happened, a demon's shadow appeared beside them.

Mira told them as much as she knew from the instances she'd seen so far. Ultimately, she also told them about the girl at the bottom of Nebrapolis, whom Soul Howl was making the Holy Grail for.

After a moment of silence, the Spirit King gave a surprising response. *"Could it be...the stigmata?"*

In real life, stigmata were unexplainable wounds that appeared on the bodies of the devout. Setting demons of the past aside, the word didn't fit this world's modern demons. However, Martel piped up in agreement at the Spirit King's words.

Nevertheless, hearing the word "stigmata," most would think of a holy figure. The word was more associated with angels than demons, including by Mira.

"Stigmata...?" she asked. *"That word has more of a divine connotation to me..."* Having seen the Curse of the Underworld many times during the game's events, Mira didn't get a holy vibe from the so-called "stigmata" at all.

But the Spirit King and Martel insisted that what Mira was describing must be the same mark.

"To be fair, stigmata might as well be a curse to you humans," the Spirit King muttered, before explaining what it was.

Stigmata were said to be accumulated divine power within the soul that somehow awakened. It was *divine* power—literally the power of a god. As for why such power would lie dormant within a human soul, it wasn't due to a god's whims, consideration, or grace—no, it was mere happenstance.

"Miss Mira, do you remember the night when you saw off my kin?"

"Of course. I remember it well," Mira replied firmly to the Spirit King's nostalgic question, casting her mind back to the great river of light streaming into the sky.

The Celestial Shrine of Nirvana—where the souls had flocked—was adjacent to the divine realm. As such, scant drops of divine power occasionally rained down from it. According to the Spirit King, that spilled divine power could collect in nearby souls, depending on compatibility. Being compatible with divine power might sound lucky to most, but he added acerbically that it was anything but fortunate in these cases.

Simply *having* divine power wasn't a problem on its own. Humans had no understanding of how to manifest it, and it was too much power for them to wield. Instead, it usually lay dormant within their souls. It was only in rare cases that stigmata appeared. In some cases, the power acclimated to the person's soul and blessed them, though it took time. At other times, it blended with the person's mana, allowing them to use the power for themselves.

"Miss Mira, have you heard of people who can perform healing miracles that soothe all wounds and ailments?"

"Healing miracles, hmm...? I believe there were people like that in the Church of Alisfarius." Mira recalled such a quest popping up there. *"That was thirty years ago, though. I don't know about the modern day."*

The Spirit King claimed that divine power was the true cause of miracle healing, and that accumulated divine power would most likely manifest as a healing ability. That didn't make such an ability *common*, though. In almost all cases, people with divine power lived their lives and died before the power manifested. When their flesh released their soul, the power dispersed. It seemed death was a phenomenon so powerful, it could even overcome divine power.

But if one fulfilled certain conditions before death, while the divine power was dormant, the power could awaken and appear as stigmata.

"So you're basically saying that the girl I saw met those conditions?" asked Mira.

"Correct. When the divine power awakens, it changes into a symbolic form. After all, form holds the most significance in a world ruled by material things. That form is the six-pointed star, which is also a symbol. However, the human form is too feeble for it. It tears through the flesh, injuring the victim and eventually killing them."

Awakened divine power destroyed one from the inside, although not by a demon's hand as humanity had thought. It was no surprise, the Spirit King added, that they'd suspect demons first in this day and age.

Now Mira understood that the Demon's Blessing and stigmata were one and the same. But what were the conditions that caused it to manifest?

When she asked, the Spirit King answered that there were two general scenarios. The first was a similar power interfering with the dormant divine power. If something nearby had a comparable power, the divine power would gradually resonate with it until it awakened. In the process, the divine power would swell and put pressure on the soul, causing the host's health to somehow decline.

The other scenario was the opposite: interference by wicked power, the opposite of divine power. When evil power approached, the divine power would abruptly awaken to fight it.

"Hrmm... In that case, one of those two types of power must've been near the girl in Nebrapolis," Mira mused.

"We can assume as much. Neither power is really common, though. I have to wonder how she came into contact with one."

The first situation required divine power—that of a god or something similar, like an angel. Meanwhile, anything that brought impurity and curses held wicked power, including modern demons. Like the Spirit King had said, it wasn't exactly omnipresent.

The chances that a person possessing dormant divine power would run into either and manifest stigmata were extremely low. Yet it had happened. How in the world had the woman met one of those conditions?

There did happen to be a demon back in that castle Soul Howl stayed in...

Just then, an idea sprouted in Mira's mind. She recalled something Soul Howl had said. According to him, the woman he was trying to save had come every day, ranting and raving at him, but her vigor had died down at some point. Shortly afterward, the Demon's Blessing—the stigmata—appeared on her.

When her vitality waned, was that the divine power swelling within her, causing her health to deteriorate? If so, divine power's interference could be the cause.

"I can't be certain, but she might've come into contact with divine power somewhere. She apparently belonged to a budding religious sect. Could an object of worship possibly have influenced her?" Mira wondered.

The Spirit King thought it was unlikely. *"That may be possible, but a power that reaches through the wall of the soul and interferes with the divine power within must be at least as strong as a divine item. I don't know the scale of this 'budding religious sect,' but it would require a minimum of thirty thousand years for an object to obtain such power. Even then, it would need to be a one-of-a-kind object of worship from a sect as large as the Trinity."*

"You make it sound impossible, rather than unlikely." Faith could instill divine power in objects of worship, but that required time and effort. A new sect could never accomplish it.

"That wouldn't be the case if the object had such power already," added the Spirit King.

It wasn't especially rare for religions to take existing items with power or long histories behind them as objects of worship. However, none of those worshippers seemed to end up like that frozen woman.

Furthermore, it was difficult to obtain objects on the level of divine items. That was clear even from the turbulent times players fought over them. Divine items were essentially legendary treasures leagues above the many other categories of items. Rumors often spread of people obtaining or finding one somewhere, but those rumors were always dubious at best—most often lies.

Former top players, including the Nine Wise Men, read countless reports and ran around the continent searching for divine items, but never saw so much as a hint of success. In the end, there were no confirmed reports of anyone obtaining one. Players concluded that divine items were only for NPCs, and that players could only handle items up to legendary status.

Currently, the only known divine items were the three wielded by the generals of the Three Great Kingdoms, which proved how divorced the items were from everyday existence. If a sect had worshipped one, word would've spread across the continent in the blink of an eye.

But what if the sect had obtained something abominable—something *cursed*—and worshipped that? The wicked power within, which opposed divine power as a rule, would've caused the divine power within a soul to awaken at once. But that didn't match the girl's symptoms, which had come on gradually.

These reasons led them to the conclusion that the girl's stigmata had nothing to do with her budding religion. The condition was a gradual awakening of divine power, and only a divine item or something equivalent could cause that awakening.

One of those divine items was *missing. I wonder if it's related...?*

The Hadean Mace, which Mira and company had theorized was used to gouge open a sealed oni coffin, was a divine item. At the time, the dark demon Barbatos had wielded it. The demon's wicked power could have brought on the sudden appearance of stigmata before a gradual awakening took place.

Having reasoned this out so far, another question occurred to Mira. *"By the way, I understand that the Demon's Blessing is stigmata, but why do those who bear it meet such horrible ends?"*

The symbols that emerged, and the demon that appeared upon a victim's death, had led to the curse's menacing nicknames. Yet it came from divine power. Why did it seem so closely linked to demons? That was what Mira wondered.

"The answer to that is probably simple. As I mentioned before, in extremely rare cases, people gain the ability to control divine power."

From there, the Spirit King explained what was behind the demons' rough actions. The stigmata's appearance corresponded to divine power awakening within. Humans couldn't control that state, so that power was released constantly. Demons—with their opposing power—would notice before long.

Even left alone, most stigmata victims would die, unable to withstand the manifested power. But once in a blue moon, someone harnessed that power. Even if they only controlled a fragment, that was still divine power—an existential threat to the wicked power of demons. As such, the Spirit King explained, demons would seek to dispose quickly of anyone they found who had the stigmata.

"I suppose that makes sense."

The Spirit King's theory was that the stigma associated with the divine stigmata came from the fact that it *attracted* demons. That certainly made logical sense, and Mira found her past experiences bore it out.

But that led to another question: why hadn't the woman in suspended animation been hunted down in the same way? Back at the bottom floor of the Nebrapolis, Mira had encountered a demon plotting some evil scheme and defeated it. Nearby, the stigmatic woman sat in suspended animation, yet her body showed no sign of injury.

Hrmm. There must be some secret trick to that suspended-animation magic.

The most likely cause was Otherworldly Stasis itself. It had likely deceived the demon's senses by cutting the woman off from the laws of nature.

Now fairly certain of this, Mira returned her focus to her conversation with the Spirit King and Martel.

"**A**LL RIGHT, if a divine item wasn't the cause, what could it have been?"

Once again, the conversation returned to why the stigmata had awakened.

Mira came up with a wild speculation that maybe the girl was actually someone important who'd been allowed near the Three Great Kingdoms' divine items, but that was rejected on the grounds that a cultist would never be allowed near a national treasure.

She also theorized that the presence of an angel like Tyriel might've been the cause, but that was rejected as well. Any angel would have noticed signs of the stigmata and gotten far away long before it awakened.

Her wild hypotheses gradually quieted down. After some thought, Mira changed her perspective on the issue, realizing that it might all have begun when the girl went to Soul Howl's location.

"In that case, perhaps the cause was specific to that locale?"

Soul Howl was in an ancient temple, Nebrapolis, so it wouldn't be surprising if there was a religious item there. The white castle in Nebrapolis's depths, the large chamber they'd found, the demon doing who-knew-what within—the site was already full of mysteries.

Mira explained this to the Spirit King and Martel and asked for their thoughts. Incredibly, for the second time, they replied that they had no idea what she was talking about.

"'Ancient Temple Nebrapolis'...? I'm afraid I have no recollection of that."

"Sorry, Mira, but I don't know either. I know a few temples in the lands of the Trinity, though..."

"Goodness..."

These two were like walking encyclopedias, but they seemed not to know much about man-made objects. The Spirit King's defense was that, since humanity tended to build all kinds of things in all kinds of places, knowing everything they made would be a Herculean task.

In that case, I'll have to ask someone more knowledgeable, Mira decided. With that, she marched to the shower room. Who would know more about this than Soul Howl, who'd lived in Nebrapolis so long? Perhaps he'd have an idea of what contained divine power.

She called to him, "Soul Howl, I've got a question for you. Do you mind?"

There was no answer; Mira only heard the rain-like pitter-patter of shower water. She yelled louder and knocked on the door. That apparently got through to him, since the shower finally stopped.

"What? You have something to ask?" Soul Howl stepped out and faced Mira, unashamed of his naked body. He was toned and muscular, with scars all over his body—truly, the form of a fighter, though his robes typically hid that. Since Soul Howl was tall, he also had to look down at Mira.

A normal woman might blush at this, but of course, Mira was no normal woman.

"Something's been on my mind. That ancient temple you lived in—was there anything...*divine* in there?" Mira asked calmly as she looked up at Soul Howl.

She wasn't interested in male nudity—far from it. She didn't even notice it. Although the young man and young woman were together under the mansion's roof, one was actually an elderly pervert, and the other was a necrophiliac. Since they knew each other's true identities, there was little room to mistake each other's feelings.

"Divine? That's kind of vague," Soul Howl complained, but cast his mind back. "Let's see..." After a while, he finally answered, "No, there wasn't anything like that. If pressed, I guess I could say that pure-white castle looked kind of divine. Why are you asking, anyway?"

"Oh, it's nothing major. I'm just researching and organizing information. I'll tell you more once I have my thoughts straight. Apologies for the interruption." Mira went back and lay on her sleeping bag again. There, she reflected on the information she'd gained so far.

That white castle had stood tall and proud, as if it belonged there. If push came to shove, she'd agree that it had looked divine. As she remembered her visit to the seamless pure-white castle, part of her began to wonder whether it was made of the same divine mineral she'd encountered the other day.

"Hey, what if the entire castle consisted of divine mineral?"

That substance was produced by the interference of gods, so a castle made out of it could be as potent as a divine item. Perhaps if that castle was made of that stuff, it had been enough to awaken the divine power inside the girl. So Mira thought, at least.

However, the Spirit King's answer was less satisfying than she'd hoped. *"In terms of internal power, that could be enough to give rise to stigmata, yes. But divine mineral is mostly used for sealing, so its power tends to focus inward rather than radiating outward. Even a structure as large as the castle probably wouldn't affect divine power within the soul."*

"Uuugh..." Her idea rejected flatly, Mira groaned and fell face down on her sleeping bag.

Just then, Martel's voice echoed in her head. *"Personally, I'm curious about the place where that demon was working."* According to Martel, that cylindrical hole in the underground chamber was awfully suspicious. Perhaps the demon had stolen, or destroyed, something divine within.

"I see." The Spirit King agreed that, if a demon was involved, something was likely there. *"If there are no surface clues, it must be something deeper."*

After much thought, their consensus was that the cause of the girl's stigmata had likely come from that underground chamber. Unfortunately, they had no more details on that location at this point.

Deciding that they probably wouldn't make more progress on that front, Mira remembered the original reason she'd been questioning the Spirit King and Martel, and brought the conversation back to that. *"So...is it possible for a Holy Grail to stop the stigmata?"* Their discussion on demons, stigmata, and what caused it had all sprouted from that one question.

"Ah, right."

"Goodness, we've gone pretty far off topic!"

Their responses were cheerful; apparently, they'd been enjoying this exchange of ideas.

At that point, the Spirit King calmly stated that it was likely possible. *"As we discussed before, the stigmata are awakened divine power. Once it awakens, you cannot lay it to rest again. All you can do is wait for your body to reach its limit, or for a demon to hunt you down."*

After reiterating that, he explained the potential of the Holy Grail of Heavenly Light. Power that had simply manifested would just run wild, but what if one could suppress that wild power? The Holy Grail of Heavenly Light was the tool to do so. Soul Howl's conclusion was essentially correct, it seemed, yet wrong in one regard: the Holy Grail wouldn't *heal*, but *correct*, the stigmata.

The Holy Grail was the ultimate healing item, acquirable only through an incredibly arduous process. Upon completing that process, one wielded power close to a god's. However, that power wasn't exactly *versatile*; it was focused on healing. Fortunately, that fit the bill in this case.

The stigmata tore through the skin, and because divine power inflicted the wounds, no traditional treatment healed them—not even the most powerful elixirs or holy magic. But the one healing item that shared a common power source with the wounds, the Holy Grail, could close them.

When the physical wounds healed, the divine power would lose its form. Of course, it would never lie dormant again, so it would try to rematerialize. But by pouring the grail's power into it, one could intentionally redirect it into healing, like the Holy Grail itself.

"If divine power acclimates to the body's soul and mana, it may give the bearer any number of blessings and abilities. The downside of using the Holy Grail is that it collapses all those possibilities into miraculous healing."

Divine power was too much for humans to bear, as a rule, but humans were extremely flexible beings. If they learned to control the power, they could master various fields. Using a Holy Grail to adjust divine power restricted the bearer to the art of healing, removing other possible abilities.

"*That's a minor flaw, though,*" Mira said. "*Only the most foolish wannabe hero would throw their life away over such a slim chance.*"

There was just a *chance* of gaining abilities through divine power; it wasn't a given. Most people died under the power's weight, since it wasn't something willpower alone controlled, so taking measures to stabilize it was clearly the wiser option.

Sometimes people bit off more than they could chew. They resisted wisdom and recklessly pushed on. That was all well and good if they succeeded, but tragic when they failed. Only success stories got passed down, though, which inspired those who held foolish ambitions.

The Spirit King had heard of such events playing out countless times, and he sighed, "*Harsh, Miss Mira, but you're correct.*"

Knowing that the Demon's Blessing was actually the stigmata didn't change the fact that it could kill the bearer. Still, discovering that there was a cure for it was a blessing indeed.

At any rate, we know now that making a Holy Grail isn't a waste of time. In fact, it's certain to help. That's a relief to hear. Mira was elated that Soul Howl's efforts hadn't been in vain, but she happened to remember something. *Come to think of it, did he know about that chamber?*

Had Soul Howl even been aware of the mysterious space hidden beneath the white castle? Its proper entrance was underground, and it was well hidden, but he'd lived there long enough and surely had many opportunities to notice it. If he'd reached that chamber, maybe he knew what was inside: something that had caused the stigmata's appearance, potentially.

The cause might be less important now that they knew a solution, but Mira couldn't help her curiosity. Deciding to question Soul Howl again, she stood and moved to knock on the shower room door.

"Something's weird!" Soul Howl screamed as he jumped out of the shower room.

"Nwah?!" Mira managed to whip around, but he'd charged out so suddenly, it took all her reflexes just to dodge. Her momentum caused her to trip over her own legs and fall right on the floor. She caught herself, but her skirt flipped up completely. Rather than fixing it, she whined, "What the heck's wrong with you?!"

"Oh, my bad. Anyway, this is an emergency!" Unbothered by Mira's complaints, Soul Howl started getting dressed, glancing at her in a panic. He stared at her bare panties for a moment and chuckled to himself, but tension quickly returned to his face. "It seems like you've got your own emergency, Elder. Still, mine is more important."

"What? Out with it." Judging that this was a genuine emergency, Mira stopped complaining. She jumped to her feet and stretched.

Soul Howl took a mana potion out of his Item Box, gulped it down in no time, and explained, "All my golems were just blown away at once."

"What...?"

Soul Howl had left fifty golems to attack the Machina Guardian at regular intervals. They were the lowest-level necromancer golems, so it wasn't unusual for them to be destroyed; after all, this floor was for A-rank adventurers. Even so, a Wise Man himself had made the golems. If more than forty of the remainder had been destroyed instantly, that really was an emergency. It was no small feat to destroy that many in the blink of an eye, yet it had happened. How come?

One possible cause appeared in Mira's and Soul Howl's minds: the Mechanized Wanderer.

"Did the Wanderer pass by, you think?" Mira asked.

"Maybe. Still..."

"The fact that they died *instantly* still seems odd, doesn't it?"

The Mechanized Wanderer was a monster that wandered the entire seventh level, mercilessly obliterating all but the monsters inhabiting the level. Besides the Machina Guardian, it was the strongest enemy in the Ancient Underground City. It was the enemy that players least wanted to run into in that dungeon—truly an infamous machine.

The Mechanized Wanderer was a foe that would demand even Mira and Soul Howl attack carefully, but it wouldn't overcome them as long as they were smart. Still, that explanation left them uncertain. Even the Mechanized Wanderer wasn't known to have attacks that could obliterate over forty golems at once.

"At this rate, we won't be able to keep the Machina Guardian from recovering. Either way, we'll have to check."

"Right. I just hope we solve this problem before it starts healing."

No matter how odd this was, they needed to head to the scene—cautiously—before the Machina Guardian recovered from the damage Soul Howl went to such trouble to deal.

4

I N THE LONG HALLWAY before the Ancient Underground City's final chamber, Soul Howl's fifty golems—which he'd set up to charge at regular intervals to keep the Machina Guardian from healing—had all been blown away in an instant.

What could've done that? Mira and Soul Howl sprinted out of the mansion they were using as a base and headed toward the scene, wary all the while of the Mechanized Wanderer.

They rounded a few corners, but a mere two turns before the final chamber, they picked up on something.

"Hey... Do you smell something burning?" Mira had noticed a scent similar to an empty frying pan left on a stove too long.

"Yeah, I noticed that too. What is that?" Soul Howl sniffed and glared ahead. The smell was clearly coming from the location they were heading toward.

Certain that something had happened, they pressed on even more warily, with a discomfort that hadn't been present until now. They turned the next corner without issue. That left just one turn remaining, and Mira and Soul Howl stopped and gazed at the wall ahead.

"Well, this is...something. How could this have happened?"

"I don't know, but it obviously isn't normal."

The seventh level was known for its endless white metallic walls, yet the wall at the corner ahead was charred deep black.

"The only magic fighters here are skeletons, right?" asked Mira. "Are there any nearby?" The black wall, burning smell, and faint heat led her to assume the cause was flame, and the only monsters on this level that could create flame were the skeletons.

Soul Howl shook his head. "No, there aren't." Necromancers could sense undead monsters nearby, and he'd monitored for any on the way. "And I don't feel any residual mana. I don't think it's magic or thaumaturgy at all," he declared, carefully watching the passage ahead.

"Magic" referred to the nine manifestations humans knew and used, while "thaumaturgy" referred to unique powers wielded by monsters, dragons, spirits, and other races.

"Hmm," murmured Mira. "Residual mana...?"

When performing magical or thaumaturgical techniques, mana was always necessary, and using it left residue for a period of time. By discerning whether that residue was present, one could determine whether such techniques had been used.

Perceiving residual mana required a skill called Mage's Keen Eye that hadn't existed in-game—it was a new skill developed over the past thirty years. That meant it was listed in the *Encyclopedia of Skills* Mira had picked up just the other day. She'd prioritized reading about such new skills, so she'd learned of its existence. It wasn't especially hard to learn, either, and she'd already taken the time to do so.

"No, I sense no residual mana," she agreed, trying to act the part of a skilled mage.

It's natural that I can use this level of skill, Mira thought rather smugly as she surveyed the black wall ahead.

"Regardless, we won't know much more until we get closer."

What lay in the corridor beyond the corner? Soul Howl forged an iron golem to take the vanguard, then followed it.

Mira likewise summoned a holy knight, just in case. "The Wanderer doesn't use flames. Has some sort of new breed appeared?"

"A new breed, eh? That's not impossible. I've been to a whole lot of places and dungeons, and I run into them once in a while. Sometimes they're far stronger than average. And the majority are deep inside dungeons like this."

"New breed" was an umbrella term for monsters that hadn't existed in-game. Apparently, sightings of those had increased dramatically over the past thirty years. Mira had fought most of the game's monsters and fiends at least once, so she considered the prospect of new foes exciting. Still, she found herself unhappy this time.

"Suddenly, I can't help but feel like I don't want to go any further..." She shuddered.

This level was home to enemies that even the Nine Wise Men couldn't be careless around. If a new breed far stronger than even the Mechanized Wanderer was here, just how strong was it?

A thousand dark knights wouldn't exactly maneuver well in a hallway... Mira's army summoning was one of her trump cards, but she couldn't use such a force to the fullest in a space this cramped. Eizenfald's giant form wouldn't fit easily either. *Still, I suppose that chamber from before would work fine.*

If necessary, she realized, they could lure the enemy into the large chamber they'd rested in. With that decided, Mira carefully pushed on.

"My word... It goes all the way to the end."

"That's why we didn't sense residual mana. It doesn't seem like anything specific blew up the golems."

Hiding just before the hallway's final turn, Mira and Soul Howl half poked their heads out and saw the spot where the golems had been lined up before. The entire fifty-meter hallway was charred black from ceiling to walls to floor.

"Hrmm. What do you think did it? A new breed, after all?"

"I still don't know. But it's been a straight road to this point, and we haven't run into anything. The culprit must be in the boss chamber."

Gazing at the still-smoldering passage, Mira and Soul Howl beheld their destination: the seventh level's final chamber, which the Machina Guardian protected. If a new breed was in there, they would have to fight both it and the raid boss at once, which would be outright foolish.

"Either way, if something's in there, I'll lure it back into the corridor," Mira declared. "Meanwhile, you can reset your golems. Will that work?"

"Yeah. Good idea. Only if it really is a new breed, though..."

After that quick strategy discussion, the two quickly ordered the holy knight and iron golem down the blackened hall. With heavy footsteps, their servants stepped forth carefully. Mira and Soul Howl watched from behind the same corner.

The two servants passed through the hall without issue, finally reaching the boss chamber's entrance. Things had gone well so far; nothing had lunged out of the chamber just yet. Still, what had happened to the forty-plus golems remained mysterious.

"I'll have the golem go first," Soul Howl said. Receiving that order, the iron golem stepped into the boss chamber. After its second and third steps, Mira and Soul Howl carefully kept an eye on it.

Suddenly, something like a giant spear ran the golem through, and it crumbled to pieces. Mira and Soul Howl watched calmly, then analyzed what had happened.

"That was just the Machina Guardian, wasn't it?"

"Yeah. A leg attack. Still, as far as I can tell, the raid boss hasn't completely healed yet."

The Machina Guardian had obliterated the golem with one awesomely powerful leg. But that leg showed signs of damage, proving that the raid boss hadn't finished recovering. Relieved, the two peered carefully down the corridor, wondering whether they would see anything other than the Machina Guardian.

Just then...

"Hrmm. Is it just me, or is it looking at us?" Mira asked.

"I was thinking the same thing."

The Machina Guardian at the entrance ahead suddenly stooped down. As the duo watched curiously, they spotted the raid boss's torso, which should have been much higher up.

It was hard to see the Machina Guardian, since the holy knight stood at the entrance as well, but it almost seemed to be looking down the passage at them. This was their first time seeing the creature do such a thing. They watched with bated breath, wondering what it meant.

Just as Mira had the holy knight bend over to clear their sight-line slightly, the Machina Guardian's torso suddenly split in two, and the red crystal inside glowed.

"What?! Retreeeat!"

"Whoa! You gotta be kidding!"

The moment Mira and Soul Howl saw that, both screamed, turned tail, and ran. Mira used Shrinking Earth to run as fast as she could, and Soul Howl created several layers of wall-like golems to block the behemoth.

A few seconds later, the Machina Guardian unleashed its attack. Its red crystal gleamed and shot a ray of light that slashed through the corridor ahead. The beam's overwhelming heat burned everything in front of it. This was the Machina Guardian's secret weapon: Ancient Ray.

Intense heat and light swelled explosively, with a bursting sound. The attack easily incinerated the holy knight and sent heat waves beyond even the bend in the passage, destroying many of Soul Howl's wall golems.

Once the Ancient Ray had brought down five golems—each specialized in defense—calm finally returned to the hallway.

Gazing into the eerily silent space, Soul Howl sighed. "Yeah. That would vaporize forty of my golems easily."

"The culprit was the Machina Guardian itself, hrmm? I'm surprised to see it act that way." Mira stared into the corridor, sensing the creeping heat and thickening stench of smoke.

Having turned down two of the hall's corners as they ran, the pair decided to go over what they knew.

First, they'd known of the existence of the Ancient Ray itself. That was why they'd made a quick escape as it warmed up. It was *because* they knew of it that they were so surprised.

The Ancient Ray's power was obviously too much for humans to withstand. It was so strong, even the most defensive of top players, comparable to the Wise Men, wouldn't last a second against it.

Furthermore, the Ancient Ray traveled at the speed of light, so evading it was impossible if one only tried after it activated. To adequately dodge it, one needed the skill to figure out where it would fire based on its warm-up.

"Well, I presume this is another change resulting from the shift to reality. You said you'd only brought down its health 20 percent, yes?"

"More or less. Little things have changed all over the place, I find."

Sitting in front of the further-blackened corridor wall, Mira and Soul Howl laughed together at the ridiculousness of all this.

The Ancient Ray they knew was a weapon of last resort for the Machina Guardian. It was common knowledge among players that the Machina Guardian only started using that weapon once it was under 20 percent HP. Countless raids had proven that. But the Machina Guardian's HP was surely above 80 percent just now. It was far, far too early for it to use Ancient Ray.

But the pair had confirmed with their own eyes that it had. Thus, its most dangerous attack had already unsealed—truly the most troublesome situation imaginable.

"What's more, it reacted to your holy knight," Soul Howl added. "The way it acted when it looked into the hallway... It seems to have been countering my strategy to buy time."

"It did seem so. We understand raid bosses as beings that destroy intruders, then return to a set location. But the Machina Guardian's trying to remove *future* attackers as well."

They looked down the corridor. The Machina Guardian already appeared to be expecting more intruders. In short, it did seem to have recognized Soul Howl's strategy and decided on a counterattack.

"I started here last night, so it learned that in just a day. Things are about to get really rough." Soul Howl had planned to defeat the raid boss over the course of several days. He realized this

necessitated a change in plan, although he didn't show any sign
of giving up.

"For the moment, I say we experiment!" Mira exclaimed.

"Yeah. That's all we can do."

The duo stood with faint smiles and ran toward the charred
hallway.

When Mira or her friends said "experiment," it meant confirming the enemy's moves and special-action conditions. They
did that whenever they encountered a strong foe and were quite
skilled at it.

The first test was to see whether the Machina Guardian's attacks
changed based on whether the target moved. Before, it had *seemed*
to react to the holy knight's movements, but what if it hadn't?

When they peeked from behind the corner, the Machina
Guardian was no longer there. They figured it must've gone back
to its original spot. Upon confirming that, Mira summoned
a holy knight and a dark knight, but sent only the dark knight
into the boss chamber.

When the dark knight charged forth, they saw a similar attack—
but not the same. The dark knight swiftly evaded the approaching
leg stab and struck the foe with its black sword. However, that was
all it managed, as the second stab destroyed it.

"Now, be ready to run."

"Yeah. Let's see what happens."

While the two mages watched with bated breath, the
Machina Guardian moved. As they expected, it peeked into

the passage. They stood by and warily surveyed the boss, ready to run at the drop of a hat.

The holy knight stood closer to the boss chamber. It was unmoving and inconspicuous, but apparently motion had nothing to do with the boss's attacks.

"Retreat!"

"On it!"

Already prepared to scram, they promptly turned tail and fled. Wall golems stood between them and the boss, shielding them from the destructive current that immediately blasted through the corridor.

"Movement isn't the key," Mira noted.

"Doesn't seem like it."

Having completed their first test, they returned to the blackened corridor to begin the second.

"The residual heat is incredible," added Mira. The Machina Guardian was no longer ahead; presumably, it had gone back to its original position. A haze vaguely distorted the space ahead due to the remaining heat from the Ancient Ray's attack.

"It disperses fast, though," Soul Howl added.

"Now that you mention it, it does."

Judging by its appearance and firepower, the Ancient Ray was probably thousands of degrees. Oddly, however, the heat remaining in the corridor was basically bearable.

"This wall seems to hold some secrets." Mira gently touched the blackened wall. She'd found it odd that she hadn't felt any heat come from it when they hid around the corner. Indeed, it felt neither hot nor cold, as if nothing had happened.

"Think it absorbs heat? Well, that'd be convenient for us."

"Indeed. Perhaps that's to be expected of ancient technology."

If enough heat was left to burn them, that would hinder their experimenting. Fortunately, there was no need to worry about that. No doubt those ancient people had used some incredible technology on these walls. That was common in places described as "ancient"; the term "ancient technology" commonly referred to things like this.

"Now, this one should only take a single try."

Thus began the second round of experimentation. Watching the boss chamber, Mira summoned a single dark knight and sent it into the room. Soul Howl poked his head out above her and watched.

The dark knight charged through their field of view until the Machina Guardian loosed an even faster blow at it. The knight evaded and struck the Machina Guardian's leg as it came down, then deftly evaded the next instantaneous leg strike and countered once more.

"Good, good!"

Mira's objective was simply to experiment, but this was where her competitive side reared its head. The dark knight's swordplay and ability to learn were significant. However, it couldn't stand up to the Machina Guardian's overwhelming might; it was struck down before it could unleash its third blow.

"Gnngh..." Mira was saddened by the sight of her dark knight being so cruelly brought down despite its efforts.

"Okay. Now it really begins." Soul Howl poked his head out again, urging her to be cautious. They still needed to be ready to flee at a moment's notice.

Mira gathered herself and focused on the Machina Guardian's actions. They were almost the same as before. Approaching the turn in the hallway, the Machina Guardian stooped and peeked inside.

At the entrance, they saw its torso, covered with thick armor like a tank's. When the torso opened and exposed the crystal—indicating that the Machina Guardian was about to use Ancient Ray—they would need to retreat at once.

What would happen? They kept their breathing low and stayed still for two minutes. Incredibly, the Machina Guardian didn't use Ancient Ray, just returned to its place in the chamber with those heavy footsteps.

"Well, it seems it won't fire if nothing is in the hallway."

"Seems not. But we've confirmed it'll fire if there *is* anything."

If the Machina Guardian identified anything in the hallway to its chamber after something had entered that chamber, it would incinerate it with Ancient Ray. If not, it would go back. At this point, they were certain it followed that basic logic.

"Regarding its ability to learn, though, its first and second attacks were almost the same. I have to wonder how good the Machina Guardian is at learning."

"We know it learns if you repeat the same thing over and over, but it's hard to know just how many repetitions it'll take. As far as I can tell, it's not just once or twice. Either it takes dozens, or it's based on the elapsed time. Its information-processing abilities might take a while to work, after all." According to Soul Howl, the first fifty golems had bought him time without issue. But today, his second day of battle, the guardian was seemingly already hatching a plan.

"Hrmm. That would be reasonable. Either way, we can assume that using the same strategy for long stretches of time won't work."

"No. But based on our investigation, I think leaving the golems around the closest corner would be fine. Not that we can be sure it'll work again."

One corner beyond the blackened corridor, the hallway was still an unblemished white. If Soul Howl left his golems there, they might be able to continue running interference.

Soul Howl sighed, clearly exhausted, and promptly lined up a fresh set of golems. "Good grief. Okay, let's get back to camp."

"Agreed. I'm starving."

Satisfied that they'd bought another day of rest, Mira offered a prayer for the army of golems and left with Soul Howl.

She
Professed
Herself
Pupil of the
Wise Man

5

U PON THEIR RETURN to the mansion spirit, Mira looked expectantly at Soul Howl. "Now, may I leave dinner to you?"

"Ah, whatever. Cooking for one, cooking for two, it's basically the same." Soul Howl was being gruff, but he didn't seem bothered by the request. He evidently liked cooking for others. Looking around the mansion spirit's kitchen, he asked, "Any requests?"

"Hrmm, let's see..." After a moment of thought, Mira seized the opportunity to request something she couldn't cook on her own. "Hamburg steak! I'm in the mood for a big one!"

Since all Mira could do was chop random ingredients and fry thick cuts of meat on a griddle, hamburg steak was beyond her.

"Hamburg steak, huh? I don't know if I have all the ingredients. Still, I'm sure I can manage." Soul Howl checked the ingredients in his Item Box while he grabbed knives and other utensils.

"I have a rather large stock of ingredients. If you need anything, let me know," Mira said, oddly proud, and left her nicest cut of meat in the kitchen as an offering. Her brain was full of nothing but thoughts of eating the best hamburg steak she could.

"Now, that's a nice chunk of meat," Soul Howl noted. "All right, then."

The high-quality meat ignited his chef's spirit, and with that, Soul Howl began listing ingredients. Mira didn't know most of them, so she began simply taking out every ingredient and condiment she had.

"You opening a restaurant?" Soul Howl chuckled as he watched her line them up, then muttered, "Man, you've got everything." He picked out the ingredients he needed. "This one, this one, and that one. Oh, and balsamic vinegar, tomatoes, and butter. I think that'll do it."

Soul Howl arranged his chosen ingredients on the kitchen counter. He'd picked out all kinds of things, apparently preparing to cook more than just hamburg steak.

He'd seemingly finished making his selections for now. Mira put away the other ingredients, but offered as many as he needed, saying proudly, "If those aren't enough, just ask for more."

"I'll do just that. I can't believe how much you've bought, though. I know you don't cook; what in the world were you planning to use all this for?"

Mira had many rare ingredients stockpiled, including several that were very difficult to prepare, with limited cooking methods.

"With all this, I can make anything at my convenience," she replied proudly. She could eat whatever she wanted, whenever and wherever she wished.

Soul Howl cut her down. "Except for the part where you lack the cooking skills."

"Uuugh…" He was so right, she could do nothing but groan in response.

"But, hey, I have to hand it to you," he added, trying to comfort her as he began preparing dinner. As a skilled cook, his handiwork was far more precise and skillful than Mira's.

"Sure, sure. I'll leave you to this, then. As for me, I shall shower and prepare to be fed!" Mira's mood had improved, and she watched with satisfaction for a moment before leaving Soul Howl and stripping in front of the shower room.

"Yeah, yeah. How long do you plan to be in there?" Soul Howl asked while he minced the meat.

"I plan to relax for thirty minutes or so," Mira answered as she tossed her undies aside. She then declared, "Oh, and I like it when there's cheese stuffed inside," before stepping into the shower room.

"Yeah, I know."

From inside the shower room, she heard Soul Howl's murmurs and the comforting rhythm of his knifework.

Mira's dinner was even more luxurious than usual. After chowing down on it, she lay face up atop her special sleeping bag. "Ah, satisfaction…"

"Where do you fit all that food?" Soul Howl chuckled at Mira's bloated belly. In front of him was a golem he'd summoned to use as a table. Its stomach, exposed like Mira's, had many empty dishes atop it.

Even the hamburgers Soul Howl had made with leftover ingredients for tomorrow morning were no more, for Mira had found them and deposited them in her belly.

"You're a pig, I swear," Soul Howl said as he cleaned up the dishes.

"I can eat no mooore." She groaned in pain.

Soul Howl sighed. Was this what had become of Danblf, the great mage he'd once fought side by side with? If monsters attacked right now, Mira would be a sitting duck. However, he knew her at this point; as long as she could summon things, she'd be just fine.

Grinning wryly at the absurdity, Soul Howl began washing the dishes.

"By the way, how are those golems of yours doing?" Mira asked.

"So far, so good." The fifty golems he'd set up to halt the boss's time-based recovery mechanic were doing their jobs quite well thus far. The Machina Guardian had yet to figure out a countermeasure to the position around the corner Soul Howl had picked for the golems.

"Still, the boss is sure to devise a countermeasure by morning," Mira noted. "We'll have to plan our own counter-countermeasure."

"Fair. The longer we take, the more it learns, and the harder the battle gets for us."

Things might be going well now, but that didn't mean this approach would work the next day. Now that they knew the Machina Guardian could learn, they'd be foolish to keep using the same methods. Dragging things out would only disadvantage them.

What were they to do, then? The answer was simple, but difficult.

"I'd like to go in for a quick fight, but between just the pair of us, we lack firepower," Mira sighed.

"That's why I came ready for a long battle," Soul Howl pointed out. "Can we refine a strategy?"

Once upon a time, Solomon and the Nine Wise Men had fought the Machina Guardian. Even the ten of them together had taken four hours to beat it—an exceptionally long time for a video game battle.

Back then, the ten could divide their roles and unleash their maximum firepower. Things were different now, though, and a short battle would be impossible.

"Now that you're here, Elder, things might go a little better." Soul Howl smiled as he put clean dishes into his Item Box one after another. He clearly hadn't given up.

"What's this, all of a sudden? Butter me up all you want; you'll get nothing but lemonade au lait." As easily pleased as ever, Mira stood with a smile and put a cup of lemonade au lait in front of Soul Howl, then drank her own and went back to her sleeping bag.

"The ability to use advanced magic gives us more options, that's all," he replied.

Advanced magic was tantamount to special killing moves that could turn the tables instantly. Soul Howl was quite impressive for coming so far without that magic, but he was seemingly struggling somewhat.

"Indeed, advanced magic's firepower and defenses are indispensable. Given the situation, though, I understand why you must work without them."

Soul Howl couldn't cast advanced magic due to his ongoing use of suspended-animation magic on the stigmatic woman. Stopping that would allow him to use advanced magic, which would no doubt drastically speed up his Holy Grail hunt. But if he stopped, the woman's countdown would continue. And, if they were to believe the Spirit King, that would make the woman a much likelier target for demons. The Holy Grail would be useless if the stigmatic woman died before they could use it.

"What to do, then...?"

"I wonder."

How could Mira and Soul Howl quickly defeat the Machina Guardian, a being that could learn? They racked their brains over the difficult task for some time. Only the sounds of water and dishwashing could be heard in the mansion.

Then the Spirit King's voice reached Mira's mind. *"Say, Miss Mira, he looks like a fairly skilled mage to me. Is there a reason he cannot use advanced magic?"* He'd been busy chatting with Martel since early that morning, so he hadn't heard Mira's discussion with Soul Howl. He only knew about the woman with the stigmata, and the fact that Soul Howl was making her a Holy Grail.

"Hrmm. I suppose I didn't discuss that with you," Mira realized. She explained the magic suspending the woman and its effects.

"I see... I'm amazed that he can get away with bending the laws of nature with such a minor penalty. He must be using a very elaborate spell," the Spirit King analyzed calmly.

Martel's voice followed, squealing excitedly at the apparent love story. *"Aw, he loves her so much. That's wonderful!"*

Mira noted dryly that Soul Howl *didn't* actually love the woman, then explained his real relationship with her, how he loved undead girls, and how the stigmatic woman objected to that. *"In short, this doesn't stem from love or anything of the sort. Just his unwavering sense of justice."* Mira concluded that Soul Howl had no ulterior motives; he also wasn't carrying a torch for the woman, since he only had eyes for the undead. Conviction alone drove him to fight for her life.

The Spirit King lauded Soul Howl, impressed. *"He'd put himself through such tribulations over that? He is truly worthy of the title of hero."*

"He's just bluffing. It's love. I'm certain of it!" Martel was dead set on her romantic theory. Why she was so insistent was a mystery, but to be fair, Soul Howl's rationales *did* sound like excuses on his part. Either way, it was clear he was backed by strong resolve.

Whatever the case, the Spirit King's and Martel's impressions of Soul Howl had vastly improved—though the reasons differed. Perhaps as a result, they took this much more seriously. That led to an unexpected breakthrough when they suddenly made a startling proposal.

"All right, I have an idea. How about I take on the burden myself?" suggested the Spirit King.

"I'd be happy to help!"

The Spirit King claimed he would shoulder the burden of defying the natural laws for Soul Howl so that he could use his advanced magic.

"My word," Mira responded. *"I had no idea such a thing was possible..."*

That would enable Soul Howl to use advanced magic and unleash his namesake Great Wall, which would dramatically expand their options for settling things quickly with the Machina Guardian. Mira's newly devised summoning magic and new contracts would expand the possibilities even further.

Mira, however, couldn't accept the plan quickly. *"That is a very attractive proposition, but I must ask... Will you two be okay?"* Spirits were meant to stabilize the natural world. Wouldn't it be dangerous for them to take on the effects of defying natural laws?

Mira's concerns seemed unfounded, however. The Spirit King and Martel appreciated her concern but revealed a startling truth.

It turned out the Spirit King's current situation had resulted from him breaking natural laws. During the war with onikind, he had used power that disrupted natural law, which led to his losing control of that power. Ever since, he'd been trapped in the Spirit Palace to prevent his affecting the material world.

That came down to the Spirit King suppressing his enormous spiritual power using an even greater power. Letting things become unbalanced would only make it more difficult to control, so he'd been left with no choice.

The Spirit Palace could contain such enormous power, and since it was cut off from the material world, no amount of spiritual power could get through before dissolving into the ley lines encircling the world. That did little more than make nature a bit more vibrant, so taking on Soul Howl's burden wouldn't affect the Spirit King, as long as he remained in his palace.

"I won't know the details until I can confirm them directly, but it also seems Soul Howl's Forbidden Arts contain elaborate techniques to reduce the burden of a spell. Normally, defying the laws of nature would put major strain on the human body, not just prevent someone from using advanced magic."

After the Spirit King lauded Soul Howl once more, Martel followed up emotionally, *"Oh, love's power is so wonderful!"* She was evidently a fan of love stories.

"Anyway, as you know, I'm stuck here either way. Breaking one, two, maybe even three laws of nature won't cause me any grief. Besides, stopping time for one person is trivial compared to the things I used to do." Laughing, the Spirit King said to leave it all to him. Martel was likewise motivated, saying that she'd support them as best she could.

Clearly, they'd both taken a real liking to Soul Howl.

"I think we'll take you up on that offer gladly, then." Accepting their proposal, Mira called out to Soul Howl, "I think I have a viable solution."

"A viable solution, huh? Sure. Let's hear it." Soul Howl, who'd been mulling over a different strategy for a while now, was suspicious of her sudden overconfidence.

"Listen and be amazed: there's a way to unseal your advanced necromancy!" Mira declared, as proudly as if she'd come up with it herself.

Yet Soul Howl didn't react much beyond replying flatly, "If you want me to release my suspended-animation spell, the answer is no."

"I know, I know. I'm saying there's a way to do it while keeping her suspended!" Sauntering over smugly, Mira stood in front of Soul Howl and smirked.

Her confident swagger may have been unearned, but it proved she was serious. Soul Howl knew that well and finally latched on. "Really?"

"Really. However, there's an easier way to tell you than simply explaining verbally. Hold out your hand." Mira puffed out her chest proudly and extended her right hand like a haughty queen.

"Yeah, all right." What was she planning? The necromancer didn't understand her actions but took her hand obediently. A strange sensation flowed forth, revealing to Soul Howl that he'd come into contact with incredible power. "What in the world...?" When he focused, a deep sea seemed to spread infinitely through his mind. Although surprised by the sensation, he noticed two grand beings.

The words of one reached his mind. *"My name is Symbio Sanctius. Due to recent events, I have asked Miss Mira to let me speak to you through her, so I may offer you my aid."*

The voice booming in his head, and the name it gave, shocked Soul Howl. "Wha—?! Where'd that come from? Wait—wasn't that the Spirit King's name...?" He looked around; however, there was obviously nobody there, although the voice had sounded like it came from right next to him. He looked down at his hand, confused by all this.

Another voice then echoed in his mind. *"We heard all about you, Soul Howl! My name's Martel, and I'm the spirit of love! That means I govern your love!"* Martel's voice was passionate, although Mira and the Spirit King laughed together at her new self-styled title.

"All about me? Like what? And what's all this about my love, exactly...?" The mysterious disembodied voices had confused Soul Howl again, but he at least understood they were on his side.

Still, he furrowed his brow, since he had no earthly idea what Martel was talking about.

She
Professed
Herself
Pupil of the
Wise Man

"**A**LLOW ME to summarize."

Hand in hand with Soul Howl, Mira sat and explained the Spirit King Network—which she herself had named, of course. Part of the Spirit King's blessing was the power to link. By doing so, Mira could converse with the Spirit King anytime and request his wisdom and advice.

"As for Martel, allow me to correct her: she's the progenitor spirit of flora, *not love."*

"Aw, Mira, you're such a meanie."

Smiling, Mira explained that she'd recently met Martel and become able to chat with her as well.

"Progenitor spirit, huh? I came across some literature that mentioned those," Soul Howl noted. "They were the first ones after the Spirit King, or something. And you've got *both* on your side...? That's the Elder I know."

The Spirit King was said to be comparable to a god, and this progenitor spirit was second in power only to him. How many people would believe it if they were told someone could chat freely with such beings? But Soul Howl accepted Mira's claims without doubt—partially because she had no reason to lie to him, yes, but also because she was a close friend despite their recent years apart.

Not that either needed to consciously worry about things like that. Sensing the power of Mira and Soul Howl's mutual trust through the blessing, the Spirit King and Martel admired the strength of the humans' friendship.

"Well, moving on. I discussed things with them, and the Spirit King has a proposal," Mira said, leaving the finer details to the Spirit King himself.

He spoke solemnly yet firmly. *"Miss Mira told me everything. Sir Soul Howl, your heroic spirit has impressed me. I would like to take on your burden!"*

After this initial declaration, the Spirit King repeated everything he'd told Mira: why exactly Soul Howl's advanced magic was sealed, that the Spirit King could take on the spell's burden himself, and that doing so wouldn't affect him while he was in the Spirit Palace.

"What? Why would you do that for me?" The proposal startled Soul Howl. Although it would be a chance to keep the suspended-animation spell active *and* use advanced magic, he was also skeptical. It just sounded too good to be true.

In the back of his perplexed mind was Martel's excited voice. *"Isn't it obvious? To reunite two lovers! Soul Howl, we know all about your burning passion!"*

"Two lovers? Who is she talking about?" Unable to figure Martel's comments out, Soul Howl looked at Mira dubiously.

At the same time, Mira casually averted her eyes, muttering, "I don't think she quite understands."

"Oh. I think I get it." It seemed Soul Howl had already caught Mira's drift: Martel thought he was in love with the zealot. "I don't have a problem with the offer, but I told you, this isn't about love or anything."

"I know. That's what I told them. From what he says, the Spirit King views you as a hero—but it turns out Martel adores love stories." The progenitor spirit just wouldn't believe Mira that easily.

Soul Howl accepted this explanation. "There was a girl like that in my class," he replied with a snicker.

"We can't do much about it," Mira said. "Be patient with her, would you? She was alone for thousands of years until I came along."

"Hmm... Then I guess I can't refuse..."

With that, Mira and Soul Howl concluded their conversation, and the Spirit King mentally apologized for Martel's behavior as the progenitor spirit watched the necromancer in obvious disbelief.

Soul Howl brought things back on topic, asking the Spirit King, "Is this really something you can do? There's no risk of the suspended-animation spell cutting out during the transfer, right?" Even if he moved the spell's burden to the Spirit King, the process would be for nothing if it disrupted the spell and allowed time to pass for the woman. This would be Soul Howl's first time trying such a thing, so he was cautious.

"Indeed I can, but there are some limitations. First, I will need to know about the Forbidden Art you used, Sir Soul Howl. The technique, the theories behind it, and the mechanism suppressing the burden as well."

According to the Spirit King, he'd initially need to understand the spell's construction and transfer it to himself, becoming a vessel similar to the caster. Then, he'd need to connect to and harmonize with Soul Howl's mana. Once that link was stable, it could transfer the burden. Even that simplified explanation of the procedure sounded very complex.

"All right, that makes sense. I'll tell you about it." Soul Howl seemed adequately convinced.

He quickly explained the Forbidden Art he'd devised, Otherworldly Stasis. That spell was one of Soul Howl's original syntheses—a combination of multiple spells. It was based in necromancy, with various additional elements of Ethereal Arts and the magics of exorcists and mediums.

While explaining, Soul Howl pulled a bundle of paper out of his Item Box. Countless complex procedures covered the sheets. "As for how I reduce the burden, this is the mechanism. I made synchronized seals and installed them in my wives."

The papers indicated that he had modified the women in maids' clothing on Nebrapolis's bottom floor. Those modifications embedded special magical seals inside them, enabling him to turn them into extensions of himself. Their souls were gone, but their bodies were intact, so the right amount of tinkering through necromancy could make them into vessels to bear some of the burden.

Indeed, Soul Howl had prepared hundreds of them. By doing so, he'd dispersed the enormous burden of defying the laws of nature.

"If you start by making vessels, it might help a little," he added, then described the procedures for the magic seals and how he'd altered the corpses.

One large vessel, or multiple small ones—while the construction and mechanisms differed, the logic was the same, so Soul Howl expected this knowledge would help.

"Hmm... Incredible that you managed to devise such a technique. Now that you've offered so many details, I may not even need to use myself as a vessel as planned. I may be able to create a more perfect vessel."

Soul Howl's explanation, including the advantages and disadvantages of his processes, had proven quite effective.

The Spirit King used Mira's link to analyze Soul Howl's mana wavelength before getting to work on a vessel. This would require Martel's power, too, which meant things would be quiet for a little while.

Before they got to work, Martel hotheadedly demanded, *"What do you mean by 'wives,' exactly?!"*

No doubt she'd give Soul Howl an earful once they were done.

Once she and Soul Howl had finished discussing the process's details, and were left waiting for the Spirit King to do his magic, Mira snatched Soul Howl's bundle of papers up with great interest. "You put a lot of research into these."

They were full of considerations, research results, and hypotheses. It'd be fair to say the papers were a collection of the wisdom Soul Howl had accumulated over many years.

Soul Howl glared at Mira as she skimmed his notes, holding out his hand impatiently. "C'mon, Elder. Show me yours if I'm going to show you mine."

"Ugh, *fine*..." Unable to withstand his constant cheek-poking, Mira took out a notebook. It was her research journal, to which she'd gradually added in her spare time. It was full of as many procedures and thoughts as Soul Howl's bundle of papers.

"Wow. There's a whole lot about spirits in here. Deep, too...as one would expect of the summoner who bears the Spirit King's blessing," Soul Howl muttered as he eagerly paged through Mira's research.

"But of course, but of course." Mira grinned smugly while she likewise consumed his notebook.

Danblf and Soul Howl, like the other Elders of the Linked Silver Towers, were simultaneously rivals and comrades, working diligently for the sake of their country's future. Thus, they'd once shared most of their knowledge, and exchanges such as this one had been commonplace.

Mira, Soul Howl, Martel, and the Spirit King were each absorbed in their own work, so a moment of silence fell upon the

group. All one could hear was Mira or Soul Howl occasionally flipping pages.

Oh ho ho! This is incredible. I was curious before, but this all makes sense. So this is how you synthesize spells!

Synthesized spells, as the name implied, incorporated various spells to create a new one. Mira had heard about them from Cleos, since they were being researched at Alcait Academy. However, he'd been vague, leaving her curious yet unable to follow up with her own research.

Now her knowledge had grown by leaps and bounds. Soul Howl's research documents included innovations far beyond anything the school had discovered.

Soul Howl was among the most passionate of the Wise Men—was perhaps *the* most passionate Wise Man—in this field. His competition would've been Flonne, the Elder of Ethereal Arts.

Mira's eyes lit up at the practical techniques and theories in the bundle of papers. However, while she would be able to comprehend them, it was a difficult feat she couldn't do overnight.

Hrmm. I should at least copy these, she thought, opening her Item Box to search for a notepad and writing utensil. Just then, an item she'd bought at Dinoire Trading a few days earlier caught her eye. *Aha. As I recall, this sheet of paper can copy any text!*

The main intended use of the large sheet of synthetic paper was to copy the intricate magic circles some spells required, removing the drudge work necessary for the spells each time. The spell types requiring special magic circles could serve as potent trump cards, but each had the drawback of requiring preparation ahead of time. All you really needed to do, however, was draw the required magic circles on mana-infused paper. In the past, people who used those spells had typically drawn the circles one by one in their spare time, then put them in storage. Some even made stamp-like templates to mass-produce the circles.

The advent of the copy paper had changed everything. It could easily reproduce magic circles at a low cost. Once someone drew a single magic circle, that was it; they didn't need to draw it anymore. They didn't need to carry around heavy, bulky templates either. In short, the copy paper was a revolutionary product to mages who used magic circles.

Mira tried using the copy paper beloved by magic circle enthusiasts. "Ooh! Now, this is convenient."

The piece of copy paper was huge, so she traced Soul Howl's research notes page by page onto the single sheet, starting at the top-left corner. After a while, the characters began appearing on the copy paper, a perfect facsimile. This wasn't quite the paper's intended use, but it was far more efficient than copying by hand, and Mira smiled at its effectiveness.

Meanwhile, Soul Howl—who'd been engrossed in Mira's research notes—spoke up. "Ah, damn it. I can't remember all this!"

He considered Mira's notes a wellspring of useful wisdom, and he'd tried his best to simply commit them to memory, but they contained so much information he wanted that he'd reached his limit. Resigned, he grabbed a pen and paper to copy them as Mira had.

Before he began writing, he asked with a tinge of hope, "Hey, Elder, mind if I keep your notebook for a while? I'll give it back at some point."

"Of course you can't keep it."

"Figures..."

Mira denied that, obviously, since she still had many things to write in her notebook. She'd show Soul Howl her notes, but even he couldn't abscond with them for an extended period. Soul Howl gave up and decided to start writing, but then noticed what Mira was doing.

"Elder...is that copy paper?!"

His sudden shout startled Mira, who was still copying his notes. At Soul Howl's outburst, Mira realized he didn't have any copy paper and smirked. "Indeed it is. Oh my goodness...how convenient it is! It works for so many things beyond magic circles."

Since she'd just finished writing out his last page of notes, she held up the large sheet of paper onto which she'd copied them perfectly. The copy paper was quick, painless, and low-cost to boot.

Since the copy paper for magic circles was three meters to a side, there was still plenty of blank space left on the bottom half of the sheet when Mira finished copying Soul Howl's research notes. The necromancer reached toward the sheet, pleading, "Elder, share the wealth. I'm begging you. I'll even take that little extra blank space."

"I *suppose* I could. Cutting these sheets is such a pain, though. Why don't I just give you a fresh one?" Mira accepted his request readily, since she knew his pain.

Many spells in all fields required magic circles, so even to Mira, the paper was extremely convenient. It wasn't *as* vital to summoners, given their unique ability to draw magic circles in midair using mana, but this boon would delight magic-users from other fields.

That certainly included necromancy. However, despite knowing of copy paper's existence, Soul Howl hadn't procured such a convenient item on his own. Why? Simple: all the necromancer spells that required magic circles were advanced. Ever since he'd placed the woman in suspended animation, the paper had been useless to him.

"I'm sure you'll need more before long," Mira said before casually handing Soul Howl a whole stack. He wouldn't just need the paper to copy her notes; if all went well, he'd be able to use advanced spells again. It might even be handy soon in the battle against the Machina Guardian.

"Speaking of, I should get ready. Thank you, Elder." Understanding why Mira gave him extras, Soul Howl began copying her research notes.

The reason Mira herself had brought the paper, despite not needing it as a summoner, was special refining. She'd procured the copy paper on the off chance she might need it to make herself stronger someday.

She Professed Herself Pupil of the Wise Man

7

AFTER COPYING Soul Howl's research, cutting up the sheet, and binding it into a notebook, Mira received a well-timed report from the Spirit King.

"Miss Mira, the vessel is complete."

"Ooh. Understood!" she replied, then called to Soul Howl, "I'm told they're done."

"Got it." He stopped cutting his own paper, gathered the pieces haphazardly, and approached Mira. When the summoner held out her hand, he silently took it.

Through their link, Mira and Soul Howl heard the Spirit King and Martel.

"Apologies for the wait," the Spirit King said. *"If it's any consolation, you'll be excited to learn this turned out even better than I expected."*

"We put all of our love into it!"

"I think it'll be great," Soul Howl replied. "What do I have to do?"

"Well, I will now synchronize the vessel we made with your mana. Just feel for when it connects. When it does, infuse your mana as you would while spellcasting. As you synchronize, Martel and I will make adjustments. Don't let go of Mira's hand at any point," the Spirit King instructed.

Soul Howl held Mira's hand tight and closed his eyes to focus. "Okay. Do it."

"Let us begin!" the Spirit King's voice boomed. The marks of his blessing appeared all over Mira. Soon, they traveled through Mira's hand, stretching to Soul Howl.

Mira simply watched. She was nothing but a relay at this point, so there was nothing more she could do besides pay attention and understand what was happening.

The vessel successfully connected to Soul Howl, accepting his mana, and an unfamiliar feeling struck Mira instantly. An odd presence was inhibiting Soul Howl's mana. She could tell instinctively that it was a fragment of the penalty for defying nature—the burden of his spell—which was transferring from him to the vessel.

"It's done. I can tell you're Mira's friend; your control over your mana is incredible." Their attempt to transfer the burden had seemingly been successful. After praising Soul Howl, the Spirit King added, *"This ought to be a good way to kill time."*

"I just hope it works!" Martel sounded happy too.

When asked what he meant by "kill time," the Spirit King explained that the vessel he'd created would allow him to observe the burden he undertook. His research might enable him to find a way to suppress it and return to the material world.

"Goodness me. I have to say, this is all thanks to you, Soul Howl. Without your theories, I would never have come up with this. Thank you."

"I thought I was supposed to thank *you*. If I helped out, though, then that's great." Soul Howl grinned sheepishly. To him, the Spirit King seemed awfully free for someone supposedly confined in the Spirit Palace.

It was worth celebrating the fact that the Spirit King might find true freedom, but that was a different matter. To bring things back on topic, Mira told Soul Howl, "If this worked correctly, your advanced magic should be unsealed. Do you feel a change at all?"

"Yeah. It feels like a weight's been lifted off my shoulders. I think this might just be successful." Soul Howl closed his eyes for a moment, seeming to feel a difference.

"Soul Howl, try an advanced spell as a test for me," suggested the Spirit King. *"I did pull it off you rather forcefully, which may have disturbed your mana. Let's check."* Though this task had ended surprisingly quickly, it was difficult even for the Spirit King, and he wouldn't feel at ease until he saw that Soul Howl's mana was stable.

"Yeah. We *should* make sure." Soul Howl's advanced magic had been sealed away for the past few years, so he assented, ready to regain his sense for it. "All right. Time for a long-awaited reunion."

Standing, Soul Howl held his hand out in another direction. When he did, an enormous amount of mana flowed from his body.

Into this casket I place your memory, a thousand-night tryst in hell.

How long will pass in this hopeless dream, this bleak otherworld?

A boat adrift on dark seas passes through the gate, yearning for warmth.

The ferryman searches alone for light in the darkness.

By his side, a corpse long cold. Your empty, unmoving husk.

Gently do I scoop a single innocent soul from the brine—and to you, I offer a kiss of awakening.

[Necromantic Arts: Hadean Cycle – Martyr's Rebirth]

When Soul Howl activated his spell, mana particles condensed in front of him. They gradually materialized in the shape of a human. A body formed, garbed in clothing and partially protected by armor. Finally, a giant battle-ax appeared in the body's hands.

The figure moved to clutch the battle-ax, then stood there expressionlessly.

Soul Howl looked it up and down. "No problems here," he murmured, relieved.

The burden was gone, and his advanced necromancy had been successful. Through it, he had created a beautiful maiden with vacant eyes. Her pale skin lacked life, and her face betrayed no sign of thought, yet her presence was supernatural. The battle-ax she held, her clothes, her accessories—all of them exuded legendary-tier power.

The maiden's long blonde hair was tied to one side. A tiara adorned her forehead, and her body was covered in light armor reminiscent of the Valkyrie sisters.

"Ooh, incredible!" piped up Mira, who had known the maiden a long time now. "And look how you've customized her." She was amazed by how much the corpse's attire had changed since she'd last seen it.

Flattered, Soul Howl answered proudly, "No duh. She's my top fighter, after all."

The spell he'd cast, Martyr's Rebirth, could be called the pinnacle of necromancy. It relied on another spell known as Martyr's Coffin, which created a coffin, as the name implied. Every coffin needed a corpse to go inside it, of course, and Martyr's Rebirth produced a golem based on the corpse in that coffin.

A powerful person's corpse could bolster one's forces on its own. Even if the golem perished, the corpse itself would be intact, so the wielder could recreate the golem as often as their mana allowed.

That didn't differentiate the spell much from other necromancy, aside from the fact that the corpse remained undamaged. Still, Martyr's Rebirth was potentially a necromancer's ultimate trump card due to its key trait: grave goods. A necromancer placed not just the corpse inside the coffin but various weapons and accessories to function as sacred objects. Those would greatly strengthen Martyr's Rebirth.

Selecting grave goods wasn't simple. There were limits on what you could place inside. Spirit weapons, artifacts, demonic and holy swords, refined equipment, and other items with latent power were forbidden. Essentially, the items couldn't have any special attributes. Their materials were restricted as well.

A simple principle was that you could only put copper, iron, or silver inside.

In this world full of strange and mystical things, those with plain, powerless weapons eventually plateaued. Even a master's skills couldn't overcome that. What you could do, though, was simply power up the items you deposited into the coffin.

That power-up process was vital to necromancers. All they had to do was defeat undead monsters to amass something called "spiritual bondage" within the coffin. Spiritual bondage could power up the grave goods *and* the corpse.

And, once the grave goods had been powered up a little, they could essentially be upgraded. That expanded the range of things you could place inside; you could expand it even further by repeating the process. Essentially, increasing your spiritual rank allowed you more luxurious gear.

When Mira looked at the golem maiden with that in mind, she noticed that everything adorning her was truly luxurious.

"But I can't quite call this perfect," Soul Howl added.

"Hm? You can't?" As far as Mira could see, the maiden looked fine.

Soul Howl, however, claimed that one of her grave goods was a little flawed. Apparently, one item necessary to boost her stats was stuck at the rank-up ready stage. Unfortunately, the Demon's Blessing debacle had begun while he was upgrading her, leaving his work half-done. Now she could only output about 50 percent of her power.

"Hrmm. We can't exactly send her into battle like that." Mira understood the entire process to a degree thanks to one of Soul Howl's lectures long ago, and she grasped the poor situation. The golem maiden would've been a major boon fighting at full power, but unfortunately, it was clear that they couldn't send her into battle against the Machina Guardian for the moment.

Soul Howl didn't seem worried, though.

"Ah, my beloved Irina, how I've missed you." He hugged the golem, his true nature finally showing. "I never thought I'd get to see you again so soon. Oh, Irina, you're just as cute as I remember." He caressed the golem's cheek, madness in his eyes.

When Soul Howl was unable to use advanced magic, he couldn't even cast Martyr's Coffin, let alone Martyr's Rebirth. Therefore, this reunion between the known lover of the undead and his favored first so-called wife had been years in the making.

8

UNSATISFIED BY the temporary copy he'd just summoned, Soul Howl called up the Martyr's Coffin and spoke to the true Irina lying inside. To him, it was a joyful reunion, although it wouldn't look like it to anyone else.

"Your complexion is lovely today," he told Irina's corpse.

Inside the coffin, which was much larger than average, her body was clad in thin white clothes. Her grave goods were next to her. She was still beautiful, and her possessions were all brilliant items worthy of being called legendary.

The only grave good that wasn't beside Irina was the simple hair ornament tying her beautiful, fragile blonde hair to the side.

Soul Howl touched the hair ornament and looked lovingly at Irina, an odd smile on his face. That was enough to make even friends who knew of his odd fetish cringe.

The effect of the ornament—a memento from when Irina still lived—was a percent-based attack-stat increase. It truly was a powerful item, a perfect fit for someone wielding such an enormous axe. Thanks to Soul Howl's efforts and his own growth over time, Irina's power now far outstripped her living strength. She was even tougher than when Mira had encountered her.

Here we go again...

One could generally relate to the pain of being away from a lover, but given who Soul Howl's lover *was*, the only sympathizers would be equally perverted. And while Mira didn't understand Soul Howl entirely, she knew him well enough to give up any hope of redemption.

As Mira watched and wondered when this would end, Martel's voice turned up in her mind. *"Mira...Mira! Who is that woman?"* Since Martel believed that romance had blossomed between Soul Howl and the stigmatic woman he'd gone through so much to save, she perhaps had trouble shrugging this scene off.

"Ah, well... I'm not sure how to explain." Sensing how touchy Martel was, Mira carefully recounted the story of how Soul Howl had met his wife—the story of the end of the Black Lion Mercenaries—as she'd heard it straight from the horse's mouth. *"You see... He really loves the undead. Undead women, anyway."* She concluded by saying that ever since she'd met Soul Howl, he'd called Irina his first wife and doted on her as he now did.

"Oh, so she wasn't a real wife or lover who left him for the afterlife... You're telling me he's in love with a corpse?*"* That must have been a shocking revelation for Martel. It would be for anyone, really. Soul Howl was clearly *special* from the way he so lovingly doted on the corpse.

"Um... Yeah, I think you have the long and short of it," Mira affirmed.

"Loving a woman who will never die..." Martel murmured sadly. Mira knew that even the spirit would have a breaking point, but her lovesick brain wasn't defeated yet. *"The pain of losing someone close to him traumatized him, so he's drawn to a woman death can't take away... Oh, he's had such a difficult journey. But it's going to be all right. Soul Howl's efforts will be repaid. I just know it. The instant that stigmatic girl gets her life back, they'll awaken to true love!"*

Mira just chuckled to herself. She couldn't understand people like Martel who prattled on endlessly about love. The Spirit King had to agree.

Perhaps because he'd been separated from his strange love for so long, Soul Howl doted on her to an unsettling extent. Realizing they were spinning their wheels, Mira called out to him, "Well? How is it? Do you think this will work?"

Soul Howl bid his love adieu, returned her to the Martyr's Coffin, and turned around. "It's perfect. Nothing feels wrong. I'll be able to fight just fine tomorrow."

His batteries recharged thanks to his beloved, Soul Howl's expression was full of confidence—perhaps *too* full.

"Happy to hear it. Shall we devise a strategy to fight the Machina Guardian?" Mira proposed, opening the spirit mansion's door.

The necromancer's new ability to use advanced magic had expanded their range of strategies. He'd gotten stronger during

Mira's absence too; the strategy meeting would be necessary for her to get a sense of that.

"Good suggestion. We don't need to grind that creep down over time. Let's destroy it in one fell swoop."

"Oh ho! Someone's bullish."

"Obviously. If I can use advanced magic, the battle's virtually a done deal. Besides, I'm sure you've got new tricks of your own, Elder." Their foe was a top-class raid boss, but Soul Howl smirked as if it would be no problem at all. The Soul Howl Mira had known wouldn't have been quite strong enough for the Machina Guardian…but this new Soul Howl seemed confident that he'd grown much stronger.

Mira likewise had her own means to turn the tides of battle hidden within. "You're not wrong. Shall we plan for tomorrow?"

She sat on her sleeping bag, Soul Howl found a random place to sit, and they began their strategy meeting in earnest. If even high-ranked adventurers had heard that meeting, they'd think the pair were discussing wild, fantastical dreams.

9

MIRA AND SOUL HOWL outlined their abilities to each other and worked together on a strategy. To react to any conceivable situation, they discussed a vast range of things, all of which they memorized quickly thanks to their past experiences. They devised a rough outline for the Machina Guardian's destruction.

"That ought to do for now," Mira said. "We just need to prepare to react to the unexpected."

"Yeah. Same as usual."

However elaborate their strategy was, there were always unknowns. As a rule, the Nine Wise Men trusted each other's individual decision-making abilities in such situations, so they weren't paralyzed by eventualities their strategies didn't cover. The pretty word "flexibility" simply meant the mutual delegation that full trust in each other allowed for.

"All we must do now is rest well for tomorrow." A little sleepy, Mira yawned and asked, "Incidentally, how are your interference golems holding up?"

"They're doing fine, but we don't know how long that'll last, given this boss's ability to learn. It makes me glad we have a way to finish it off tomorrow."

"Indeed. Goodness, I was amazed it could do that. I'm glad we abandoned any plans for a prolonged fight."

In the game, the Machina Guardian was a truly mechanical boss that followed set action patterns. There were hundreds of patterns, and it executed the perfect one for each situation, so victory wasn't as simple as memorizing things. Since it was basically impossible to study *every* pattern, the usual approach was to prep several strategies that could probably deal with *most* situations. The strategy Mira and Soul Howl had now devised was a derivative of sorts.

But the world was a big place. A dozen people at the top *had* memorized, and could overcome, every single Machina Guardian attack pattern. They were the Twelve Apostles of Nirvana, which was one of the Ark continent's two major nations. Quite a collection of oddballs, in truth.

"Has the Machina Guardian had that function from the start? Or only since things became reality? Either way, it's a pain," Soul Howl grumbled, genuinely irritated. He'd originally believed the raid boss couldn't learn, but perhaps that function worked better as a battle wore on. Fortunately, that wouldn't be a problem much longer.

"Regardless, it can't learn anything if it's dead tomorrow," Mira reassured him. "We have enough plans. Let's give it a good trouncing."

"Fair enough. It'll be a great enemy for me to go all out against for once."

The pair spoke with confident grins—the expressions of mad scientists looking upon a new experiment.

As Mira came out of the bathroom, ready for bed, she suddenly recalled something. "I have some insight that ought to motivate you even more."

Soul Howl, who didn't need much preparation for bed, smirked defiantly atop his futon as he turned to Mira. "Really? If it'll motivate me, it must be a big deal." The way he spoke gave a glimpse of some...*twisted* confidence, but he sat up and urged her to go ahead.

Sitting on her special sleeping bag to face him, Mira explained what she'd heard from the Spirit King and Martel: that the Demon's Blessing was the stigmata, and that a Holy Grail's power was sure to cure it.

"There you have it. It might not be exactly what you planned, but you *can* save her life. Sorry if I stuck my nose into places I shouldn't, but those two approve of your decision." She fell back onto her sleeping bag, not waiting for a response.

"Stigmata, huh? Sounds complicated. Still, if I'm on the right path, that's all that matters."

Soul Howl had spent so long working to save the girl suffering from the Demon's Blessing, but the mark was actually holy, rather than demonic. Moreover, once the stigmata stabilized, she'd awaken new healing powers. He was a little surprised to learn those things, but if they didn't change his overall plans, he had no problem with them.

One realization did make him smirk. "You're saying every time she uses that power, it'll force her to remember that my necromancy saved her, huh?" He lay on his futon and laughed at the thought, then added energetically, "You're right, Elder. That lit a fire in me."

"Good, good. I expected as much."

Soul Howl's efforts to create a Holy Grail were not in vain, and although the situation wasn't what he'd predicted, he was eager to continue. That was all that mattered—or so Mira thought as she stripped and got into her sleeping bag.

Martel's voice echoed pitifully in Mira's mind. *"He's just too shy to be direct about his feelings. I know it."*

Mira could only resign herself to agreeing. *"You're right. Hopefully one day he overcomes that."*

She closed her eyes to sleep.

The next morning, after getting into the shower to wash away her sleepiness, Mira emerged to find breakfast prepared. Today's menu was Soul Howl's homemade sandwiches and soup, along with Martel's stat-boosting fruit. Mira had produced the latter, knowing it would be the perfect dish before the impending battle.

Soul Howl had neatly sliced and plated the legendary fruit. That was much more luxurious than how Mira usually ate it— biting into it whole.

Soul Howl had already finished breakfast. He was hard at work prepping the magic circles he'd need for his advanced necromancy.

"I'm gonna go over the strategy while you eat," he told Mira. "Keep those ears open."

"Mmph." Mira grunted her agreement, cheeks full of sandwich. Silly as she might have looked, her resolve was genuine.

While slightly worried at how unreliable Mira looked, compared to the old days, Soul Howl began reiterating their strategy. It was little more than a quick reminder of what they'd discussed the night before.

"When one of us starts meditating, the other focuses on defense," he said.

"Indeed. Gotta be careful. Meditating cuts all your senses off."

Meditation was among the most useful techniques Mira had learned from the *Encyclopedia of Skills*. The technique was officially called Cerebral Flux, but because the user appeared to be meditating, the pair called it that for short.

There were a wide range of conditions to learn meditation, including spirit-blessing requirements, which made picking the skill up quite difficult. However, all the Nine Wise Men had accomplished those conditions, so they just needed to understand and acclimatize to the technique.

As a result, Mira had learned the skill the very day she read about it in the *Encyclopedia of Skills*, and Soul Howl had done the same during their meeting the previous night.

Though Cerebral Flux was difficult to master, its effect was worth the effort. It greatly increased the speed of mana regeneration. Even someone with a massive mana pool, like Mira, could recover all of their mana in just five minutes.

However, the technique came with disadvantages. Activating it cut off the user's sight, hearing, smell, touch, and pain perception. The lack of pain was most dangerous. In some cases, people "meditating" didn't notice they were being injured until they received a fatal blow. The skill required great situational judgment, especially midbattle.

"For all the risk it entails, the big advantage is that meditation means you don't have to worry about elixir intoxication," Soul Howl noted. "Use it well, and you can maintain maximum firepower without holding mana back. I'm sure that will be essential for all mages."

Laborer mages could mitigate Cerebral Flux's greatest flaw by having servants protect them. Soul Howl was an especially big fan of that strategy, partially due to his elixir-procurement concerns.

Elixirs—items with powerful healing effects—were far more expensive in this world than the original *Ark Earth Online*. But that wasn't the part that concerned Soul Howl, who had plenty of money. The problem was the *number* of elixirs. The high prices mostly resulted from low supply. It didn't matter whether one could afford them if there were none to buy. But elixirs had been especially important to Soul Howl given his travails so far.

"Yes. Meditation ought to keep us from getting into situations where we've ingested too many mana elixirs to use healing elixirs." Mira recalled a story from their gamer days.

"That's a big part of it," Soul Howl laughed in response, no doubt remembering the same incident.

Elixirs above a certain potency caused a problem called "intoxication." Their great benefits came alongside a more-than-commensurate toll on the body, and when a person had too many elixirs, they could become inebriated or even lose consciousness. It was important to plan elixir usage before fighting stronger foes.

Weaker restoratives, on the other hand, could be imbibed endlessly without fear of intoxication...though, now that this was real life, drinking too many often led to a sore tummy or a need to pee.

"Heck, just learning about this made meeting you worthwhile," Soul Howl muttered as he traced magic circles with copy paper.

"Please, that's it...? You must have more to say than that. Aren't you happy to reunite with an old friend?"

"Mmm, I guess. And I appreciate having my—" *Having my advanced spells back.* Before Soul Howl could finish that sentence, he realized something and frowned angrily.

"Something's happened, hasn't it?" Noticing the look on Soul Howl's face was the same as the previous night, Mira presumed the same thing had taken place. "Were your golems destroyed again?"

Her prediction was right on the money. "Yep. Only four were left, but they all just died at once." Soul Howl quickly finished copying his magic circles and prepared for battle.

At the same time, Mira finally forced herself to her feet to finish her final checks. "Has the Machina Guardian learned again, I wonder?" she mused.

"Maybe. We don't want it repairing its weapons, so let's leave early." With that, Soul Howl ran straight out of the mansion spirit.

His interference golems' disappearance would allow the Machina Guardian to heal—repair itself, rather—after a few minutes. The longer it had to repair, the more fully it could restore its destroyed weapons. *That* might make for a difficult time.

"Starting over from the disarming stage would be tough..." Mira muttered.

Of course, she was already aware of that. She quickly cleaned up and dismissed the mansion spirit, then rushed after Soul Howl.

Leaving the mansion, they ran down the hallway toward the final chamber. They turned the first and second corners; upon turning the third, which led to the hallway where Soul Howl had set up his golems, they stopped on a dime.

"My word. *Now*, of all times...?"

"Yeah... Looking back, this happened sometimes."

In the middle of the hallway ahead stood a figure. A mechanical, doll-like creature with a body that looked like scrap metal slapped together, two arms, four legs, and a mask on its face. It wielded handleless blades in both hands.

The creature was a dull lead color all over, and its body creaked as it turned to face Mira and Soul Howl. They weren't used to its appearance—it was now covered in asymmetrical patchwork metal that appeared slapped together—but its eeriness was fully intact.

The roaming boss of the seventh level, the Mechanized Wanderer, had shown up.

"Now that I think about it, this thing *would* have the firepower to destroy a mere four golems at once."

"Yeah. It really picked the perfect time to appear to dash my hopes."

Watching the enemy warily, Mira and Soul Howl wondered what to do.

Mira offered a solution first. "I'll take this one. You prepare the battlefield as planned." She stepped forward slowly, drawing the Wanderer's attention as she summoned two holy knights and one dark knight.

As long as she didn't let her guard down, this fight was winnable. That said, the Wanderer was this dungeon's second-strongest enemy; it was extremely durable thanks to its metal form. But even if the two fought it together, the cramped hallway would make the fight take longer than five minutes.

The problem with that was the Machina Guardian's repairs. According to Soul Howl, eight minutes had already passed since his last golem self-destructed. The Machina Guardian would start fixing itself in no time, so several of its weapons would be in working condition by the time they finished off the Wanderer.

In light of that, Soul Howl quickly agreed to Mira's suggestion. He hid behind the dark knight and holy knights as they leapt into action and darted toward the boss chamber.

With an eerie mechanical sound, the Wanderer likewise pounced, using its four legs deftly. Incredibly, it ignored the approaching knights and swung its two blades at Soul Howl, aiming precisely at the necromancer, although he was hidden.

Soul Howl continued to run, heedless of its attack. He knew what lay in store for the Wanderer when it ignored Mira's knights.

The Wanderer's blades crashed against the holy knights' tower shields, sending sparks flying. Raw power collided and clashed. Instantly, the whirring in the hallway echoed more loudly, and the Wanderer pushed the holy knights back.

What ridiculous force. The Wanderer had combat power beyond A-rank adventurers. Alone, even Mira's lesser summons wouldn't hold it off.

It deflected the shields and ran, turning its back to Mira. Once again, it was going for Soul Howl.

Ignoring me in favor of him, hmm? It prioritizes whoever's closest to the boss chamber. Quickly assessing the situation, Mira ran forward herself.

Up ahead, a holy knight circled the pursuing Mechanized Wanderer and stopped it in its tracks. However, the Wanderer's powerful blow knocked the knight aside and opened its path once more.

As it blindly pursued the necromancer, it was struck by a black blade. That was the sword of Mira's mutated dark lord, a construct reinforced with her mana. Moving with perfect control and freedom, the sword dealt a sure strike upon the Wanderer's thick plating. At the same time, Mira caught up, circled in front of the Wanderer, and summoned two holy knights ahead of her to further shield Soul Howl.

[Mutated Evocation: Holy Lord]

When Mira activated that spell, the holy knights were clad in blinding light from which two mutated spirits emerged. They were pure white, with heavier armor and massive, rampart-like shields in either hand.

The polar opposite of dark lords, these holy lords fully specialized in defense. They were as impregnable as they looked, although at the same time, they were also as sluggish as their appearance implied. The main drawback of holy lords was that they were little more than slightly mobile walls.

But now, in a corridor with limited room to move, the holy lords would exhibit their full potential. They could withstand even blows from high-tier raid bosses. Though the Wanderer was strong, it usually struck many weak blows, so it lacked the raw power to break through the holy lords.

The spirits blocked the way with their giant shields. Mira peeked in the small space between them, too cramped for the Wanderer to fit through, and grinned at a job well done.

She Professed Herself Pupil of the Wise Man

10

"IT'S BEEN A WHILE since I last used this strategy," Mira murmured to herself, summoning two dark knights to her side and promptly mutating them to dark lords.

Meanwhile, the first dark lord clashed with the Wanderer for the second time, reached the limits of its durability, and disintegrated. Given that it specialized in attacking, the dark lord had dealt solid damage, but its low defenses made it fragile in clashes with powerful foes.

After eliminating the nearest obstacle, the Wanderer closed in on Mira. Since it prioritized targets approaching the boss room, it aimed for her this time.

"Hrmm, unsurprising..." Mira muttered. "It may take a while, but it'll break through eventually."

Attacks continued to ring out, and countless sparks flew around ceaselessly. The Wanderer struck the holy lords like a raging storm, attempting to topple their blockade.

It launched flurries of hits, rather than single blows, but each was powerful. Such an intense onslaught would surely overcome a lesser summon eventually—but only if the Wanderer could sustain it. The creature continued to slice at the holy lords' shields, as if those were the only things it perceived.

At that point, countless black swords appeared from the walls, ceiling, floor, and even the air between the shields. The blades struck the Wanderer all at once. Due to its single-minded focus on the holy lords, it reacted too late to the onslaught and sustained deep wounds. However, it managed to evade the ensuing strikes and quickly distanced itself from the swords.

Blocking a path with holy lords, waiting for the enemy to get absorbed in overcoming them, and then obliterating the enemy from behind with dark lords... That was Mira's favorite strategy in a closed space with an enemy who had no way of independently destroying or repelling the holy lords. It worked to terrifying effect. During wartime in the old days, of course, players from hostile countries had shouted abuses when Mira employed that strategy.

"It refuses to approach..." she murmured.

It seemed the Wanderer had already discerned the blades' swing range—about five meters. It waited and watched from just beyond that range. It had no projectile attacks; its only means of attack required it to approach. Still, that also meant it was most dangerous at close range.

The Wanderer moved to strike again. After slowly bracing itself, it accelerated all at once. Its ferocious slashes struck the giant shields, sending up even more intense sparks. Unleashed after sufficient charge-up time, that blow was the Wanderer's strongest attack. It created a deep gouge in the holy lords' iron defenses.

The enemy's next move was awestriking, as well. The dark lords' black blades fell upon the Wanderer, but though they inflicted damage, it wasn't fatal; the creature moved with enough agility to get away with only shallow wounds.

After that split-second clash, the Wanderer retreated again. It knew that staying in one place was disadvantageous as long as those black blades were around, so it employed a traditional hit-and-run strategy. It was acting just like players Mira had faced before.

After the Wanderer landed, it was momentarily immobilized. Six black arms surrounded it as if waiting in ambush, and swung holy swords down upon it. The six blades struck the Wanderer in unison; with the impact, one could hear the sound of metal being crushed.

The six powerful blows, combining partial summoning with the holy sword Sanctia, struck with perfect timing. Mira had waited intently for this moment since the start of the encounter. Gazing upon the horribly battered Wanderer, she muttered to herself, "Hrmm. I must say, I've created one deadly combination."

Due to her lack of skill, Mira couldn't handle Sanctia herself, but the dark knights could use her potential to the fullest. And as befitted a holy sword, Sanctia's strikes were extremely powerful, even partially summoned.

"The fact that I can't fire them off as I like is a bit of a drawback, though," Mira admitted, assessing her experiment's results.

Partial summoning itself consumed little mana, but as a holy sword, Sanctia cost a fair amount. Mira couldn't manifest Sanctia if she tried to suppress the mana cost in the usual way, and partially summoning the holy sword cost about the same amount of mana as a single normal summoning. Still, the element of surprise inherent in partial summoning, and the power of the holy sword, made it more than practical.

Mentally noting those results, Mira smiled, knowing they would help with her next research stage.

As for Soul Howl, how is he doing...? she wondered, turning toward the boss chamber. Just then, there was a jarring sound behind her, like metal plates scattering across the floor.

"What was that?" When she turned back to the Wanderer, there was a harsh impact sound and countless sparks. Simultaneously, the enormous holy lords blocking the hallway fell back slightly.

There was a flash of light. Through the gaps between the shields, Mira saw the Wanderer she knew. It was reminiscent of an old-fashioned android or tokusatsu hero. Gouged metal plates lay on the ground behind it, proof that the holy swords had only cut through its outer plating.

"I see..." Mira murmured. "Reinforced armor, I believe they call that."

Black blades aimed for the Wanderer, but discarding its armor had seemingly made it more agile; it was plainly faster now, and skillfully evaded the dark lords.

It jumped back to put distance between them again. Even when Mira used partial summoning to take advantage of the

Wanderer's landing disorientation, it evaded with a perfect backward somersault, looking even more like a tokusatsu hero.

"It shed its reinforced armor to raise its speed...? Now that's a cliché, if I've ever seen one," Mira murmured, remembering all the mecha anime she'd seen.

In that genre, giant robots often reinforced their defenses and expanded their arsenals using bulky equipment—though the Wanderer's armor had only allowed for the former. When such things became useless, the wielder could release them and regain their original speed. Most protagonists' robots specialized in speed and went on to rule the battlefield afterward, becoming much more fearsome than when they'd had extra armor.

The Wanderer's reinforced armor had worked like that. Its footwork was now lighter, and its speed had dramatically increased, as if it had just taken off training weights.

"Hrmm... Each blow is stronger too."

The Wanderer again accelerated, slashing at the holy lords. Mira watched closely and noticed their shields becoming more deeply scratched. The boss itself wasn't just faster; its attacks were, too, and its momentum contributed to its force. By releasing its reinforced armor, it had powered up like some kind of superhero.

You'd expect it to be weaker *now that there's less weight behind its blows... Well, maybe that goes to show the poor quality of its patchwork armor.*

When she first saw the Wanderer, it had looked deformed. No doubt that had detracted from its speed and balance, leading to weaker slashes. In other words, it was in perfect condition to strike now.

"In that case, second formation!" Mira called.

The Wanderer's blows weren't just fast; they were forceful enough to drive the holy lords back, bit by bit. That proved the enemy was much more powerful now. At this rate, it might *crush* the knights faster than it cut through them.

However, Mira did not fret. She simply peered behind the Wanderer, which stood just beyond the black blades' range. After charging up enough, it leapt forward and unleashed its most powerful blows in the same hit-and-run pattern.

Its attacks required a run-up—a *five-meter* run-up. That was easily within Mira's summoning range.

Its center of gravity low, the Wanderer darted forward. Its blades dug into the giant shields, and sparks flew. Smirking at the sight, Mira began casting her spell.

As the Wanderer evaded the black blades and retreated, Mira made eye contact with it. It seemed to be watching her, no doubt waiting to evade as her spell took shape. The Mechanized Wanderer's reputation as the dungeon's second-strongest enemy clearly wasn't exaggerated.

However, the Wanderer failed to notice one thing: exactly which spell Mira was casting. When it landed, it performed a cartwheel to evade the impending partial summon. However, that summon didn't come. Instead, two holy knights appeared behind the Wanderer, facing the original holy lords.

Realizing Mira's intent, the Wanderer attacked the new holy knights.

"It's too late now, friend." Mira's lips curled into a smirk as she mutated the holy knights.

With the intense impact, sparks flew, showing that the newly mutated holy lords' shields had stopped the Wanderer's blades. "My trap is complete!"

The Wanderer had nowhere to run, ahead or behind. The shields blocked all paths entirely. Having caught the enemy in her clutches, Mira smirked at it from the gap between the shields.

The Wanderer struggled, running at maximum speed to drive its most powerful strikes into the holy lords. It was more ferocious than ever, surely because it understood what was happening.

But the holy lords wouldn't let it through easily. Rather, on Mira's orders, their hulking forms pushed forward. They faced each other as they did so, their intent clear.

The Wanderer's space to move shrank one meter, then two, then more and more. It ran around like a beast in a cage, slashing at the holy lords. Yet the shrinking space left it less room to run, decreasing its attack force as well.

Another meter. Then another. The distance shrank until one could stretch both arms out and touch either holy lord, leaving the Wanderer no space to swing its blade, let alone run.

"Now, the final stage," Mira murmured, giving another order to all four holy lords. They moved once more, surrounding the Wanderer with shields in hand and deftly adjusting those shields to reduce the central space. The Wanderer was flanked on four sides, not just two; its resistance echoed from inside the towering coffin.

"Even the Mechanized Wanderer can't defend itself now." Mira watched quietly and smiled at the panicking Wanderer from the space between the shields. Then she gave her final order.

Two dark lords slowly stepped forth. They stood on either side of the shield "cage," ready to carry out the execution.

The dark lords unleashed countless sword swings that pierced the gaps between the shields, cutting down the imprisoned Wanderer mercilessly. It was like watching a stage magician stab swords into a box.

Initially, the Wanderer's resistance grew louder every time the blades moved. After more swings, it weakened. By the eighth wave of attacks, it stopped.

Mira had the dark lords draw their blades out of the shield enclosure. Looking inside, she murmured, "Hrmm. This fight's finally over? You were a persistent one."

Seen from the outside, the Wanderer was now little more than a shapeless mass of scrap metal. As one giant shield drew back, the corpse tumbled from the enclosure with a metallic noise. It was so mangled, one couldn't even distinguish where its arms ended or its legs began.

Given her plan's success, Mira felt awfully smug. She'd quickly deprived the enemy of freedom of movement and struck the Wanderer down with overwhelming force. "Ah, I'm a military genius!"

"Hm! What a sight. I love your merciless fighting style."

"I prefer such a head-on, full-strength struggle. Power against power, skill against skill. Just wonderful!"

As the voices of the spectating Spirit King and Martel echoed in Mira's mind, the summoner chuckled at the battle's anticlimactic end.

A player defeated by this exact "surrounding" strategy had once told his friends, "I never want to fight Danblf again." Incidents like this were why Danblf had become the most feared of the Nine Wise Men. Mira herself, however, knew nothing about that.

She
Professed
Herself
Pupil of the
Wise Man

A FTER STABBING the Mechanized Wanderer to death, Mira dismissed her dark lords and holy lords and began to make for her true destination. Then the Wanderer's remains shook.

She turned and gazed at the piled remains, realizing something. "Come to think of it... Could it be?" Fishing through the pile, she eventually pulled out a red orb, a black metal fragment, and the swords the Wanderer had swung. "I knew it! That ought to be at least a whole five million ducats!"

Those were the Mechanized Wanderer's three most expensive drops. Blinded by the thought of money, Mira gingerly placed the objects in her Item Box. Then she realized something else. Video game drops were cursed by probability—was that still true now that this was real life?

Back in the game, you obtained materials monsters dropped via butchering. When you defeated a monster, its corpse received a special Item Box slot. At that point, you either took it to a specialized butcher someplace like a town, or butchered it yourself using a learned skill. That would finally turn the carcass into usable materials.

A single carcass generally yielded a couple of materials, although that number fluctuated based on the butcher or player's skill. The materials' rarity was most important, and that depended on proficiency. Clearly, the higher your proficiency, the likelier rare drops were.

Now, anyone who'd played a similar video game had probably thought the same thing if an enemy's rarest drop by far was its horn, but the player got something else: *Just cut off the horn!*

The video game medium itself made probability a limitation. Now that this was reality, Mira realized she could in fact essentially "cut off the horn." The result of this revelation was all the loot she'd located amid the wreckage: the Wanderer's red orb power source, the black metal from its vital machinery's protective plating, and its blades, undamaged despite its frantic fighting.

In short, drops that had been rare long ago could apparently be obtained consistently now, as long as no conditions actually *required* luck—for instance, things randomly forming inside the body.

"In that case, the Machina Guardian..."

The Machina Guardian could drop ten unique items. The drop from each part of the machine differed in rarity, but even the most common among them was very unusual.

If Mira could sort through the Machina Guardian's remains, as she had the Wanderer's, maybe she'd obtain even its rarest drop.

Based on what she'd heard in-game, its drops included things she'd never even seen before.

As I recall, Soul Howl did say I could have all the loot. *Yes—of course he did!*

Happy to have received his word, Mira smiled and darted toward the boss chamber, full of vigor and excitement.

Although obtaining rare materials from monsters was easier now, a realistic limitation accompanied this change: if you wanted a monster's hide, you had to defeat it without damaging the hide. In a video game, you merely defeated a monster to obtain its parts, but that aspect was much more complicated now. You needed a discerning eye to know which parts you could obtain as drops, but the summoner charging forth only knew the materials' names and descriptions.

When Mira arrived at the boss chamber, she surveyed the room and murmured in satisfaction, "Oh ho. Things are ready, I see." It was an entirely different battlefield from the one she'd witnessed yesterday.

For one thing, there was a giant castle gate about fifty meters from the entrance. A wall ran from either side of it to the end of the room, perfectly separating one half from the other. One look at the great walls revealed their awe-inspiring weight.

Furthermore, the walls were equipped with countless artillery batteries. Golems operated them in perfect unison; indeed, they had fired ceaselessly for some time now. It was like a castle siege, which proved that Soul Howl was following the previous night's strategies. Admiring the growth in his power, Mira used Air Step to run to the castle wall's highest point.

Landing on the towerlike top of the rampart, she met up with Soul Howl. "Is all well?"

"So-so," he answered, peering at the Machina Guardian below. "It seems to have learned more, as you can see. We can assume head-on bombardment is useless now."

Beyond the huge walls, in the main battlefield, stood the enormous Machina Guardian. Its many legs easily fended off the cannonball barrage—not blocking the cannonballs but parrying them entirely. No doubt it knew direct impact would detonate them. It repelled the endless projectiles deftly, delicately, and surprisingly quickly. The cannonballs missed their mark and crashed into the ground, sending pillars of flame upward with loud explosions.

Unlike the previous night's scattered turrets, the ones on the castle walls were strong enough to blow away even A-rank monsters. Yet amid the explosions and swirling flames, the Machina Guardian shook their attacks off and watched them quietly. It was an eerie sight.

"Even if you fire all at once?" Mira suggested as she gazed upon the raid boss.

All four of the Machina Guardian's legs were deflecting cannonballs, so as far as she could tell, its reaction speed was limited. As someone who believed strength lay primarily in numbers, she wondered whether a simple simultaneous volley would do the trick. Surely the Machina Guardian couldn't fend so many cannonballs off at once.

"Good question. Firing everything in one volley *could* deal some damage."

However, according to Soul Howl, he'd already done that twice. He explained the battle from the start to now. Since the turrets had been in use until last night, the Machina Guardian had figured them out. From there, Soul Howl figured it wasn't a big leap to the raid boss learning to deal with castle-mounted cannons. That said, he'd noticed its limited reaction speed and tested simultaneous volleys.

"Those did deal damage. Seemingly a lot. The problem is what happens afterward."

Gazing at the ceaseless cannon fire, Soul Howl explained that a simultaneous volley meant simultaneous reloading as well. The Machina Guardian was hoping for that moment exactly.

"I tried twice, just to make sure. There's the result." Soul Howl pointed out a part of the wall visible from their vantage point. A large dent had indeed been gouged in the sturdy-looking castle. If the Machina Guardian kept attacking that spot the same way, it would soon obliterate it. "Anyway, I've taken two Rampages from that thing. That's a sample size of only two, but I still know it's guaranteed to Rampage if I try again."

"Rampage" was an attack the Machina Guardian sometimes used. It was among its strongest moves—second only to the laser beam they'd seen last night—and could blow away even a holy knight in a defensive posture with every defensive buff possible cast on it. As long as there was a risk of the Machina Guardian using Rampage, it would be best to avoid simultaneous volleys. Losing the castle walls, which played a major role in their strategy, would be disastrous.

"Anyway, at this point, bombardment is basically useless," Soul Howl emphasized. "That's the bad news. As for the good news, look at the wall damage itself. What do you think, Elder?" He'd told Mira things were "so-so," so the battle hadn't initially sounded good at all. Yet strangely, the necromancer was full of confidence.

"Hrmm. Indeed, this structure seems to be working well. If that's all the damage it took from two whole Rampages, it must be extremely tough," Mira said, impressed, as she gazed at Soul Howl's damaged great wall. It had withstood two blows from the Machina Guardian, a testament to its sturdiness. "I've heard of giving golems special traits, but what you've done to your castle golem is outrageous."

The castle golem was the source of Soul Howl's title, the Great Wall. It was one of the highest-level necromancer spells, and extremely versatile, although it had to be positioned very carefully. As the name implied, the spell summoned an enormous golem as big as a castle. That structure was a fortress meant for fighting. It was outfitted with various weapons, including over a hundred cannons.

Those were meant to be operated by human hands, but Soul Howl had created golems to act as cannoneers and run his fort without other humans' help. As a result, he could force people to conquer *his* castle before they besieged a real one. Players who attacked the Palace of Alcait often stared at the castle golem in amazement, then burst into stunned laughter.

The giant walls towering over and dividing the battlefield were simply part of the castle golem. One advantage of golems like this was that they could be used in parts, so they were surprisingly helpful in closed spaces.

Mira gazed at the castle golem's slowly recovering wall and recalled what she'd heard from Snake, an Isuzu Alliance elite. The magical item "mystic dagger" could extract special souls from undead monsters and attach the resulting traits to golems, giving them various buffs. That was rather new technology in the field.

"You said you planned to add Sturdy this time, didn't you?" she asked Soul Howl. "It seems your castle golem can do justice to nearly any upgrade now."

"Nah. It just happened to be a good match for Sturdy. When I added Fleet-Footed and Leap, they were useless." Soul Howl had apparently tried various things before his advanced magic was sealed. He recalled his experiments with a wry chuckle, adding, "Frankly, I didn't know what would happen this time either."

He'd never had an opportunity to test a Sturdy-affixed castle golem's limits. However, now that he had a perfect test subject—a large-scale raid boss—he'd figured out just how good the combination was. Since it was much stronger than he'd expected, he confidently declared that he could engage the boss *and* defend their side. That would be a considerable advantage. Hiding behind the castle golem's sturdy wall, he and Mira could safely "meditate" via Cerebral Flux.

"I suppose I'll be relying on your castle golem as usual," Mira said wryly.

Soul Howl's castle golem, which was key to their defense, had often served as their base and shelter when fighting big bosses.

"Yeah, but the offense is all yours." Soul Howl was in a great mood, probably because he had access to advanced necromancy again. Elated, he began using his magic to replenish ammunition, creating special castle golem weapons. "I ought to mix some time bombs in with the contact-based explosions," he muttered to himself as he had transport golems carry the ammo.

Mira chuckled at the smirking Soul Howl and jumped back down behind the castle gate.

12

IN FRONT OF THE CASTLE WALL, Mira summoned Eizenfald and the seven Valkyrie Sisters, then quickly explained things to them. "We'll be fighting that big thing from yesterday."

"Leave it to me, Mother!" Eizenfald was in a better mood than usual, no doubt because his dear mother had summoned him two days in a row. He seemed ready to jump into battle at any moment.

"The Sisters Seven live to serve," the Valkyries replied solemnly. Eagerness burned in their eyes. They were impatient to fight such a powerful foe—save for the youngest sister, Christina. She teared up as she remembered yesterday's battle.

"Next, we'll need support personnel," Mira murmured as she formed the Mark of the Rosary.

Eizenfald's ultimate fighting strength, the Valkyrie Sisters' ultimate adaptability—those two resources were indispensable for large battles like this. Still, Mira summoned supporters for them too. One after another appeared Leticia, spirit of song; Wasranvel, spirit of stealth; Pegasus; First Pupil Cat Sith; and Garuda.

As soon as she appeared from her magic circle, Leticia began humming. "Master! I finished part two of 'Ode to My Master'!"

"It's been a while since you last called on me. I see we have... quite the impressive lineup." Wasranvel's smile faltered somewhat when he saw Eizenfald, the Valkyrie Sisters, and Leticia.

Meanwhile, Mira's First Pupil was more energetic than ever. "We got a big battle on our paws!" There were some new faces, but Cat Sith quickly grasped the situation, hopping around with a sign that read THERE'S A THIN LINE BETWEEN BRAVERY AND RECKLESSNESS!

As for Pegasus, it stood by Mira as calmly as ever. Garuda loomed alone in a corner silently, simply awaiting orders.

Mira surveyed the group. "Today will be a difficult battle. I'm counting on you all." The summons tensed up, and there was an anxious air, although Leticia and First Pupil's attitudes didn't exactly suit the mood. "Now, the time to summon my main force has finally come."

She quickly set up summoning points in a number of spots behind the gate. She already had enough firepower to burn down a city, but that wouldn't be adequate against the Machina Guardian.

Mira and Soul Howl were fighting this raid boss alone, so they couldn't hold back. It was time for Mira to pull out all her firepower—her ultimate strength-in-numbers gambit. With Hermit's Cursed Eye actively taking in surrounding mana, Mira activated her evocation. At the same time, the Spirit King's blessing glowed all over her.

It was similar to, but not the same as, her usual One-Man Army summoning.

A chain of countless magic circles extended, linked to Mira's front. They weren't for the holy knights or dark knights she loved. The circles, numbering a thousand, revealed her new fighting force: an army of knights neither dark nor holy.

"Good. They turned out quite well." Mira smiled, satisfied at her new army.

This evocation was unique to Mira. It made the most of the Spirit King's blessing and the knowledge she'd gained from Soul Howl's notes on synthesized spells.

She'd used the Spirit King's power to link before, in the spirit mansion, making the location more convenient by rendering the kitchen, shower, and other facilities usable. In the process, she'd wondered if she could use the power on other things. Soul Howl's notes had confirmed her suspicion.

The result was this army of ashen knights. The knights—perhaps worthy of the title of "knights-errant"—carried shields in one hand and black holy swords in the other.

Mira had linked dark knights and holy knights; the ashen knights wielded the traits of both, while also having boosted vitality. By adding the holy sword Sanctia's power, she had greatly improved their potential. Wielding holy swords, they were especially strong offensively.

Mira's new summoning technique went far beyond the framework of armor spirits. The ashen knights' power rivaled that of advanced summons...yet because they were just armor spirits, there was no limit to their number.

However, they weren't forces she could use anytime she wanted. They required the Spirit King's blessing *and* the holy sword Sanctia, making each ashen knight's mana cost eye-watering—again, rivaling that of an advanced summon.

Still, because the ashen knights qualified as lesser summons, Mira could generate a great force of them without wasting time casting. She could think of plenty of situations in which that would be handy.

"Alfina, I'll trust you and your sisters to lead this army and decide when to let loose. Form ranks, please." Mira looked back at her troops, feeling a real sense of accomplishment.

This was likely the sisters' first time seeing the ashen knights, but the Valkyries could tell at a glance that the knights were unfathomably strong. Honored by Mira's willingness to entrust such a force to them, Alfina kneeled to her with heartfelt gratitude. "Yes, Master!"

Under Alfina's command, the sisters split the army into squads.

As the Valkyrie barked orders, Mira turned to her First Pupil. "Now, I have the usual important mission for you. I trust you know what I mean, First Pupil." She handed over four pebble-sized magic stones.

"I'll do a purr-fect job, Ringmeowstress!" Cat Sith respectfully accepted the stones, swiftly changed into a ninja-like outfit, and struck a shinobi pose. Behind it was a sign written in flashy colors: UNDERCOVER ASSET.

He knew exactly what Mira meant by "important mission." After all, he'd done this same job every time Mira needed to use her full power. Specifically, his role was to place those specially prepared magic stones on the four corners of the battlefield.

A four-point formation around the battle was the most effective layout; it put everything inside under the effects of the Bound Arcana. While there was a limit to the formation's maximum size, Mira's power could cover the large square that would house this battle just fine.

The Bound Arcana could only be positioned near the caster, but using the clever First Pupil allowed Mira to quickly set them up at a distance. It wasn't a flashy job, but it was a vital one.

"This battle will be more dangerous than usual. Help him for me, please," Mira told Pegasus, cradling the cat in her arms before putting him on Pegasus's back. In the game era, all Nine Wise Men had usually been together for these battles. Now, there were only two. She felt a little uneasy about letting her First Pupil run around alone, so she decided to rely on Pegasus's mobility.

"Finally, I have my own trusty steed!" The cat scampered happily across Pegasus's back.

Pegasus frowned for a moment, but when Mira stroked its mane and urged it to protect her little friend, it neighed eagerly. Then, it turned to the cat on its back and neighed at him. No doubt

Pegasus was asking whether First Pupil really knew his mission and whether he'd really be okay.

The cat puffed his chest out proudly, replying, "I've done this dozens of times. Leave it to me, paw-tner!" He actually *was* quite experienced, and the quality of his work proved that.

After dealing with her adorably small—yet reliable—pupil, Mira turned to Wasranvel and Garuda. "Next up..." she began as Alfina returned, having just divided Mira's army into seven squads. "Good timing. At this point, I should inform you all of the strategy."

Mira explained the gist of the plan to defeat the Machina Guardian to her personal army.

"Open the gate!" she yelled at Soul Howl, backed by a force big enough to fell a small country with ease.

After a moment, there was a dull, heavy sound as the enormous gate opened. Through the widening gap, she saw the battlefield ahead. The sounds of cannons, which had been muffled to this point, now reached her directly.

The artillery's suppressive fire was seemingly becoming less effective, though. The Machina Guardian was much closer now than when she'd first surveyed it; its parries were also more refined. The fact that it was reacting faster, allowing it to get closer, proved it was continuing to learn. Based on the angles of the cannons aimed at it, it might've assaulted the gate if Mira took much longer.

Now, though, everything was ready. Mira stood before the fully open gate and glared at the Machina Guardian head-on. The cannon fire all stopped at once.

As if waiting for that moment, the Machina Guardian leapt forward. Every single cannon fired in unison; it was a simultaneous volley, able to deal real damage to the raid boss. The Machina Guardian reacted quickly, but more than ten shots struck home, causing fiery explosions.

Using that as her signal, Mira loudly ordered, "Charge!"

The army waiting behind her finally leapt into action. There was a moment of silence while they reloaded after the volley, but there was no opening for the boss to take advantage of, now that her army could charge.

Eizenfald was the first to move. As the Machina Guardian attempted to prepare its Rampage once more, dragon breath tore through the smoke. Light surged forth, and hot wind swirled. The attack traveled in the blink of an eye, creating an intense, dazzling explosion in the distance.

Eizenfald's powerful dragon breath pushed the raid boss all the way to the chamber's back edge. He'd singlehandedly moved the Machina Guardian, a giant being with awe-inspiring power. That took unbelievable force, but the shocking thing was that this wasn't even Eizenfald's full power—after all, he was subject to summoning magic's limitations.

Soul Howl smirked from above at how the dragon had surpassed his strength of long ago. "Don't fire that off at such close range, you fool," he laughed.

Under cover of the blast, the ashen knights rushed onto the battlefield, led by the Sisters Seven. They spread out in perfect unison like an army of battle-hardened elites, surrounding the Machina Guardian. Together, they prevented the raid boss from attacking the wall again, bringing the battle into full swing.

After confirming that the Machina Guardian was fully focused on the ashen knights, First Pupil held fast to Pegasus's back and pointed his sign toward the corner. OUR SUCCESS RIDES ON THIS MISSION! it read. "Begin the meow-ssion!" he exclaimed.

"I'm counting on you, friends," Mira said. Her feline pal responded elatedly, while Pegasus nodded solemnly before heading to the battlefield. "Next..."

Leaving the rest to them, Mira looked back at Wasranvel and Garuda, who were waiting inside the gate. When they nodded to her silently, she took Leticia back with her to Soul Howl's location atop the wall.

There, she asked, "How do things look?"

Below, her army had encircled the Machina Guardian, thanks to Eizenfald drawing aggro—that is, the enemy's attention.

"Well enough so far. You called those ashen knights your trump card, right? I've seen them cross swords a few times. They're plenty strong," Soul Howl answered, never taking his eyes off the battlefield.

The ceaseless cannon fire finally calmed now that the battle had begun in earnest, but he watched for opportunities to fire nonetheless. That helped distract the Machina Guardian from

Eizenfald and the sisters, supporting them and occasionally suppressing the enemy's movements.

"Indeed. I knew giving them holy swords was a good idea. Now I can focus on bolstering their defenses."

The Machina Guardian was one of the raid boss "tanks." Heading into this battle, their biggest concern had been whether they had the offensive power to cut through its plating. After all, its learning ability made them want to avoid a long fight.

When they'd taken it on long ago, Luminaria, Flonne, and Meilin could fill that offensive role just fine. Unfortunately, none of them were present, so Mira and Soul Howl had to use the tools at their disposal to make up for that.

They couldn't match the full force of Solomon and the Nine Wise Men, who held the record of defeating the boss in under two hours. Still, they wanted to defeat it within the day. That was when Mira hit upon something: holy sword Sanctia.

"Leticia, I'd like you to play 'Serenade for a Dear Knight.'"

"Request received!"

Next to the roof overlooking the battlefield was a wide scaffold. Leticia skipped gleefully to its center. It was only natural for her to stand in the middle of that unnaturally large scaffold, since it was a stage prepared just for her.

It would be close to impossible for enemies to stop Leticia's songs, since the castle-wall cannons shot down any who approached. That was evidence of Mira and Soul Howl's strong teamwork after fighting together for so long.

Onstage, Leticia began playing a song infused with mysterious power. It resounded across all corners of the battlefield, empowering those she considered allies. The song's inherent buff was Damage Reduction.

"Now, we just wait and watch for a while."

"Yeah. Let's hope things go as planned."

As the Machina Guardian sustained damage, its patterns and attack methods changed. The laser beam they'd seen last night made that most obvious. Normally, the Machina Guardian attacked with that once it had taken 80 percent damage, but the previous night, it had used the laser to wipe out everything in the hallway.

In light of that, Mira and Soul Howl decided to start off watching from afar.

Mira used Far Sight, a skill she'd learned from the *Encyclopedia of Skills*, to look at the battlefield from a distance and send orders to Eizenfald and the Valkyrie Sisters. Soul Howl used the same skill—which he'd learned from Mira—to set his gunsights more carefully and provide supportive fire.

The Machina Guardian's attacks had weak and strong versions—weak versions had little windup, while strong ones had more. Focused entirely on defense, Soul Howl easily spotted the strong moves' windup phases and suppressed them with cannon fire. As a result, none of the Machina Guardian's attacks were able to destroy the knights in one strike.

Two hours after the battle began, things were going mostly as planned. Mira and Soul Howl recognized that the enemy's movement patterns and attacks suggested that it had taken at least 40 percent of its health as damage. So far, the Machina Guardian had done nothing unexpected.

The boss's expanded repertoire of attacks increased the casualties in the mages' army, but only among the ashen knights on the front lines. Each time the knights took damage, Mira repaired them. She couldn't replace the ones destroyed entirely, but she kept losses to a minimum. That consumed her mana quickly, however, and she was forced to hide behind the wall and recover her mana with Cerebral Flux each time.

The First Pupil and Pegasus did their job with aplomb, filling the battlefield with the maximum effects of the Bound Arcana. However, the effects only lasted thirty minutes, so they had to replace the magic stones regularly.

Their efforts bore fruit, bolstering Eizenfald, the seven Valkyrie Sisters, and the ashen knights. With their defensive barriers repairing automatically as well, this was even more advantageous in longer fights.

Still, the Machina Guardian's blows were powerful. When one of the mages' allies took a direct hit and shattered as a result, healing was pointless. They had to be careful. That much was well within their expectations, though. The plan now was to continue until the Machina Guardian sustained more than 50 percent damage.

"Rampage really is a thorn in our side," Mira complained.

"After three Rampages, I'm amazed you still have so many soldiers."

Kicking its eight legs, the Machina Guardian jumped overhead and barreled downward, creating a massive explosion below. That Rampage culled a portion of Mira's army. Getting hit by Rampage directly would've vaporized even fully kitted-out top players, so ashen knights didn't stand a chance against the attack. The previous three had already eradicated 40 percent of the knights.

Had this been an army of dark knights exclusively, it would probably have been obliterated long ago. Even Rampage's shockwaves were strong enough to blow them away, after all. The fact that 60 percent of the ashen knights remained was only thanks to their added holy knight defenses.

"Thorn though it is, I love the opening it presents."

"Same. We can knock the raid boss down 2 percent while it recovers."

The Machina Guardian's Rampage ended with a powerful explosion, disabling the enemy in the process. It took only five seconds to right itself, but that was ample time for Mira and Soul Howl to aim.

On the battlefield, Alfina commanded the ashen knights to fall upon the Machina Guardian all at once. She and her sisters were prepared to perform a powerful joint attack. Just before the Machina Guardian could right itself, the ashen knights would strike, then scatter like ants. At that moment, Alfina would unleash a spear of light created by her and her sisters.

The spear's flash was followed quickly by a boom. Its power didn't equal Eizenfald's dragon breath, but the attack still dealt the Machina Guardian considerable damage. To rub salt in the raid boss's wounds, there was then another volley from the castle wall.

"Ooh!" Mira piped up. "I think we're past 50 percent!"

"Yeah. Finally time for phase two."

Having seen the spiderlike Machina Guardian's eyes turn from blue to green, the mages looked to the battlefield to figure out where its gaze was pointing.

The Machina Guardian jumped up forcefully, and its back suddenly burst—no, opened up. Several objects flew out, descending upon the battlefield one after another.

"There they are."

"All according to plan."

Five enemies had appeared: Mechanized Protectors. Each looked a lot like the Mechanized Wanderer defeated by Mira. They appeared when the Machina Guardian's damage surpassed 50 percent, and they were powerful foes, rivaling the Wanderer itself.

This was the same as usual. Even halfway through the fight, the Machina Guardian had yet to do anything unexpected. Carefully confirming that, Mira surveyed the battlefield and assigned sections of her army to deal with each Protector.

The five Protectors each used a unique weapon. All the Valkyrie Sisters were currently armed with swords, but each possessed their own favored weapon to respond to various situations. Mira quickly sized up their targets and assigned the Valkyries to advantageous fights. Eldest sister Alfina and second sister Elezina would stay to fight the Machina Guardian, while the third sister onward would fight Protectors.

The Valkyries' leadership was superb, and the army was split back into squads in no time. They encircled the Protectors, gaining an advantage before the new enemies could move.

To people strong enough to challenge the Machina Guardian, Protectors were equivalent to the Wanderer: they could be beaten solo, as long as you didn't let your guard down.

If left unattended, however, Protectors would cooperate and cause casualties you couldn't ignore. Furthermore, if left unchallenged too long, they could even fuse to become a *more* troublesome foe. As such, they had to be taken down individually.

13

"**S**URROUNDING THEM sure makes things easy," Soul Howl chuckled.

"Doesn't it? Fine work, if I may say so myself," Mira boasted.

A mere five minutes after the Protectors had appeared, the five had been reduced to just one.

The Protectors' greatest strengths were cooperation and fusion, but the ashen knights' encirclement negated those. However fast the Protectors were, they couldn't break through the holy-knight-enhanced defenses of the ashen knights. The Valkyrie Sister in charge of each squad would hardly let that happen.

As a result, each Protector was forced to fight a Valkyrie alone—and was defeated. Most of the sisters finished their work and returned to the battlefield; the only one stuck fighting was, perhaps unsurprisingly, the youngest sister, Christina. She was in a deadlocked battle with her Protector, which shot pebbles wildly from its arms.

"It's firing too many!"

Those pebbles were this Protector's weapon. Christina could defend herself using her shield, but the closer she got to the Protector, the harder reading its attacks' trajectory became. Furthermore, both the Protector's arms could fire from different angles, making it impossible to evade the projectiles from both arms at once. Christina was stuck waiting for an opening from just barely far enough away to defend herself.

"Aww! My sisters are already done. What do I do? I'm gonna be in so much trouble!" Christina realized that, if she struggled here, she was sure to get a scolding from Alfina later.

If Christina had used the ashen knights waiting around her, she could surely have finished this in no time. The reason she *didn't* was that her sisters hadn't. If they knew she alone had relied on the ashen knights—on Mira's power—her training would surely become more intense, which was her chief worry.

The same would happen if she kept wasting time, though. Desperately wanting to avoid special training, Christina resolved herself.

"I hate it, but it's my only choice..." she murmured.

Shield at the ready, she raised her sword behind her. It was then that her shield turned into light that enveloped her. She'd wanted to show off this new technique in a more fitting, flashier situation. As she rushed forth, however, she screamed an even more heartfelt desire: "I don't want special traiiiiining!"

Christina's new technique was truly like a ray of light. She deflected incoming pebbles as her sword traced a bright arc through the air, then sliced the Protector in half with just one swing.

"...Phew. It's all right! I think I made it in time! Surely...!" Christina turned from the felled Protector to the Machina Guardian. Confirming that nothing major had happened in her absence, she repeated herself, as if praying, and took her ashen knights back to the front line.

Spotting that instant burst of brilliant light, Mira piped up excitedly, "Ooh! That was a new move, wasn't it?"

"And it killed a Protector in one blow," added Soul Howl. "Not bad."

"Sure wasn't, sure wasn't!" Mira replied. Soul Howl's words improved her mood, especially because her eyes had been glued worriedly to Christina's fight the whole time. Now Mira glowed like an old man who'd just seen his granddaughter praised.

In fact, Mira was so gleeful, she couldn't help complimenting Christina's work. "Very good. That skill was fantastic."

"Th-thank you!" Either surprised by the sudden compliment, or simply not expecting to hear Mira's voice, Christina sounded oddly nervous.

The battle raged on, and damage increased over time. Mira and Soul Howl took turns hiding behind the wall to recover mana with Cerebral Flux, throwing out powerful spells whenever they could, but Mira's army was finally under 40 percent of its original size. To make up for that, Soul Howl erected dozens of cannon-fortress golems on the field to support the Valkyrie Sisters and their army from more varied angles. Issuing them all orders left him extremely busy.

About an hour after the Protectors had appeared, the Machina Guardian's eyes turned from green to gold, and it unleashed a Rampage, sweeping everything around it away. Seeing that, the mages prepared for the next phase.

"Ah. It's down to forty now."

"Next up's the leg gimmick, right?"

First off, Mira ordered her full army's retreat. The five seconds after a Rampage were an ideal opportunity to deal a lot of damage at once, but Mira abandoned that opportunity and told her troops to fall back.

Her army reacted swiftly. Under Alfina's leadership, the squads distanced themselves from the Machina Guardian without breaking rank. Eizenfald also backed off, keeping a close eye on the raid boss. There wasn't a moment's hesitation in their movements; despite this ideal chance to attack, they all promptly obeyed Mira's orders. That proved their absolute faith in her.

Mira's troops watched the Machina Guardian cautiously from about fifty meters away. The raid boss recovered from Rampage's recoil. Immediately, the second set of back legs on either side of its body fell off. The limbs were giant, measuring twenty meters long and three across.

"There they are!"

"This is just sad."

Before the eyes of Mira and Soul Howl, ten Protectors burst out of each fallen leg. The twenty Protectors gathered beneath the Machina Guardian. This group would be more difficult to deal with, since they started close by. Many raids had wiped out on this phase back when strategic information was less plentiful.

Now, though, they knew all that information. Mira and Soul Howl had been through this situation many times.

"Now!"

Upon Mira's signal, Eizenfald unleashed dragon breath upon the Protectors. Then Elezina fired an enormous arrow of light toward the same point. The attack didn't end there; every castle-wall cannon, as well as the cannon-fortress golems, fired at once.

All these attacks engulfed the Machina Guardian as well, creating a massive explosion of flames that shook the very air. Light spread instantly, followed shortly by a boom and heated wind. It was such an awesome torrent of destruction, it might've vaporized anything nearby.

Even amid this, Leticia continued to sing. Despite the noise, the sound still reached all ears clearly. Truly, the power of the spirit of song was amazing.

"C'mon, Elder. Can't you do something about her?" Soul Howl complained.

"...She has her own free will," Mira replied dismissively.

In front of them was an apocalyptic scene, but Leticia seemed wholly ignorant of it. "Okay, here comes my next song!" she announced gleefully before singing again. She didn't exactly fit in a raging battle.

Mood aside, though, the fight was going well. When the light and smoke cleared, the mages saw the Protectors were greatly damaged.

"Three left, hm? How stubborn."

"Nothing we can do about that. However much we focus our firepower, we can't reach Lu-man—uh...Lumi's raw power."

"Fair. Maybe we should be satisfied that we insta-killed seventeen of them."

When the Machina Guardian's health went under 40 percent, twenty Protectors emerged. After much trial and error, players had determined that the ideal strategy against them was to blast them with as much firepower as possible while they were gathered together.

There were many methods, but the most reliable was for a sorcerer to use wide-range magic. When the Nine Wise Men had cleared this boss, Luminaria naturally played that role. The spell she'd used was explosive magic, and it required the longest cast of all the ultimate sorcerer spells. It obviously obliterated all the Protectors in one blow.

Their current focused attack was nothing to scoff at, but it still couldn't compare to Luminaria's power. Amazed again by her comrade, Mira quickly analyzed the situation and gave her next order.

In that instant, amid the faint remnants of the blast, another figure danced behind the Machina Guardian: First Pupil, heroically riding his trusty steed Pegasus. "I've been waitin' all my nine lives for this chance!"

He'd gotten so used to his job setting up the Bound Arcana, he'd had time to play games with Pegasus. When he appeared, some kind of win-loss record was written on his sign. Of course, First Pupil's losing streak was staggering.

"Eat this!" Under his new orders, Cat Sith hurled another of the stones Mira had given him—a blasting stone—as hard as he could, seemingly letting off steam.

Stuck dealing with Alfina and the rest of the army facing it, even the Machina Guardian couldn't immediately react to Pegasus's sudden speedy charge from behind. The blasting stone the feline threw slipped past the raid boss and directly under the Protectors, who were too scared to move after the sudden bombardment.

Immediately, the power within—wind—was unleashed. Gales rushed from the point of impact and blew the remaining three Protectors away.

"Good. It looks like it worked." Having confirmed that, Mira gave another order.

The third, fourth, and fifth sisters acted swiftly. The blasting stone's wind had launched the Protectors a distance away from each other, leaving them unable to cooperate. The sisters' ranks surrounded them quickly to keep them separated.

Victory was finally coming into view. As their forces felled each Protector, Soul Howl looked upon the battle and muttered, "So far, so good."

"Indeed. All that remains is to beware..." *Beware the laser beam.*

Before Mira could say it, the Machina Guardian moved unexpectedly. It began stomping on the ground—another Rampage. But on closer inspection, nobody was in Rampage range. Pegasus and First Pupil had already returned to the castle wall, and most of the sisters were fifty meters off. Even the ones dealing with the Protectors were a good eighty meters or so away. What was the Machina Guardian planning?

As Mira ordered her army to be wary of any unexpected movements, the raid boss's intentions became clear. Far up ahead, it stomped its legs and raised itself so that its abdomen faced them. Then its remaining legs grabbed the remains of its two severed ones and hung them in front of its abdomen.

The moment he understood, Soul Howl hid behind the castle wall. "You can't be serious!"

"That's its plan?!" Ordering the Valkyrie Sisters to switch to emergency defenses, Mira rushed to summon a holy knight in front of Leticia. After promptly mutating the knight into a holy lord and maximizing its defenses, she fled behind the wall as well.

A few moments later, there was an intense explosion in the Machina Guardian's abdomen. This attack, launched so soon after Rampage, could have destroyed even the strongest shield. It blew away the legs hanging in front of the raid boss's abdomen, and the resulting debris flew around like bullets due to the power of the explosion. Fragments of various shapes and sizes became hail upon the battlefield.

Using Rampage for the detonation had made the explosion even more powerful. Despite being far away, Eizenfald, the Valkyrie Sisters, and the mages' army were still in the blast radius. Despite their defensive postures, they still took considerable damage.

The damage to Eizenfald was especially great due to his giant form, leaving his protective barrier at less than 10 percent. The sisters were able to dodge some of the shrapnel, but given the sheer quantity of it, they'd nearly lost 30 percent of their barriers by the end. Surprisingly, Christina's skillful shield use reduced her damage to only 10 percent. She looked awfully smugly at her sisters, who'd taken three times that damage.

The real problem was Mira and Soul Howl's army. That attack alone had cut it in half. Christina's squad had sustained the most casualties by far; their numbers had fallen to below ten.

Christina turned around to face them confidently, but the tragedy before her left her speechless. "No way..."

As for the third, fourth, and fifth sisters' squads, which had split off to deal with the Protectors, they'd sustained damage as well. To add insult to injury, the explosion had destroyed those Protectors, although those individual fights would've been an opportunity for the sisters to prove themselves to Mira, their master.

"Dumb Christina gets all the glory, showing off her new moves! I'm getting stronger too!"

The three muttered similar complaints, giving the destroyed Protectors another slash each for good measure, then returned to the main battlefield.

The Machina Guardian's attack had even reached the sturdy castle wall in the distance. The debris had gouged countless bullet-hole-like marks in the wall, and even the holy lord's ultimate defensive posture had left its shield heavily damaged.

Behind it, Leticia continued singing as if nothing had happened at all, looking carefree. Without the defensive buffs her songs provided, the damage would've been much worse. She'd courageously continue singing, no matter the circumstances; that was the spirit of song Mira knew.

Or at least, that's what she bragged to the Spirit King.

"It's a little earlier than expected, but it's time to begin the operation." Mira returned to the roof of the wall, which was now broken in places. From there, she looked at the battlefield, grasped the situation, and swiftly gave out orders. Meanwhile, she used the summoner skill Benevolent Touch, which healed Eizenfald's protective barrier in exchange for a large quantity of mana.

Eizenfald's position directly fighting the Machina Guardian was important in this long battle, and it was surely a difficult task.

"It will be difficult, but I'm counting on you," Mira urged him gently and lovingly.

"Leave it to me, Mother!" Eizenfald replied with genuine eagerness. He was seemingly enjoying this fight; he even asked to try a few things. Mira replied that he could try whatever he wanted.

She gazed at Eizenfald, who'd begun using the draconic magic he was learning from the Great Elder Dragon in the capital, then called back the leader of the squad that had lost the most troops: Christina.

She
Professed
Herself
Pupil of the
Wise Man

14

I'VE DECIDED you'll lead the stealth-drop squad. All right?"

"Eep...! Um, yes, I graciously accept this mission."

During the initial strategy discussion, Mira had decided that the first leader to fall under ten squad members would receive this special mission. In other words, she was giving this role to the most unworthy leader—one who couldn't so much as protect her unit—and the job went to Christina.

Realizing this, Christina gritted her teeth for the coming punishment. "Um... So, if I remember right, we draw everyone's attention..." As she prepared, she thought about the mission she'd received. When she *really* thought about it, it was a rather conspicuous job, she realized. "Does this mean I'm...the *star*?"

Christina's preconceptions based on *why* Mira had assigned her the task made it hard to tell, but when she thought about it, she was about to become the main character of this battle.

"Ooh! This is getting fun!" Once Christina started fantasizing, she couldn't stop. Imagining herself saving the day, she rushed to prepare.

Mira looked back to the battlefield and watched Eizenfald dance bravely through the air, keeping the Machina Guardian's eyes on him. "Goodness, that air defense laser is a pain."

Despite his size, Eizenfald flew skillfully around the area. One might call him the ruler of the sky, and he indeed dodged the machine-gun-like barrage of antiair lasers with aplomb.

Small lightning bolts rushed from him at times. That was draconic magic; he'd only begun to learn it, so despite its grandiose name, it wasn't especially strong. A single claw swipe would be about ten times more powerful. Still, draconic magic was stronger than intermediate magic, so it had terrifying potential.

That said, it wasn't enough to restrain the Machina Guardian. At times, Eizenfald's aggro level dropped so low that the boss turned its attention to the surface troops.

As for those troops, the ashen knights under Valkyrie command kept striking the Machina Guardian's legs. At times, they even leapt and struck its torso. It wasn't easy to get through such thick plating, but each knight dealt damage slowly but surely.

Then a laser barrage similar to gunfire rained upon them. Having quickly noticed it was coming, the Valkyrie Sisters twisted out of the way in time.

"Impending cleave!" Alfina called out to all forces. In this drawn-out battle, she'd learned to perceive the meaning of the

Machina Guardian's slight movements, so she could predict its next move and give orders.

The sisters quickly repositioned their ashen knights and took defensive stances. Then the Machina Guardian's giant leg tore horizontally through the air. The sisters escaped it easily with graceful leaps, but that was only possible due to their powers. The ashen knights lacked the Valkyries' agility, forcing them to block. With a mighty sound, the boss's attack blew them back. Most of the ashen knights landed on their feet, and the troops quickly reformed.

The Machina Guardian's swing combined height and distance, so dodging it was no simple feat. Often, player tanks defended themselves rather than trying to dodge and potentially taking more damage. But the attack's great impact immobilized the target for a while, subjecting them to the machine-gun volley of lasers. That was one of the boss's behavioral patterns, at least. Before the Machina Guardian could take the opportunity to aim at the ashen knights, though, Eizenfald's ferocious tail swung down, and Soul Howl's bombardment tore into the boss.

That painful attack from an unexpected angle threw the Guardian off-balance. The Valkyrie Sisters and ashen knights seized the opportunity to attack. It might lead to more casualties on their army's side, but this was a perfect way to deal major damage.

Observing her plan's smooth fruition, Mira lavished herself with praise. *Without the combined offensive and defensive prowess of my ashen knights, you couldn't pull this off. Ah, what a genius I am.*

Thanks to the Bound Arcana, her ashen knights would recover as long as they weren't destroyed in one blow. If the Machina Guardian attacked like this multiple times in a row, Mira would need to change her strategy; for now, though, the ashen knights were healing enough that this was a good source of damage.

Confirming the situation and providing backup fire as necessary, Soul Howl checked in with Mira. "It's almost time to strike, right? My gut feeling is that it's about to hit 30 percent."

"Indeed. I think it's about time to bring her out," Mira replied, then ordered Christina—who'd finished prepping behind the castle wall—into battle.

"Got it!" Christina replied before leading her squad to the fight.

Mira watched the Valkyrie head off, then turned her eyes to the main battlefield and ordered Eizenfald to fight on the ground for a while, focusing on defense.

"Understood, Mother!" he replied cheerfully, weaving through antiair lasers to land. When the Machina Guardian tried to strike during his landing, cannon fire from the castle walls stopped the boss just in the nick of time, giving Eizenfald plenty of leeway to defend himself.

The battle remained at a stalemate for a while after that. The Valkyrie Sisters intermittently attacked and retreated before the boss could counter. Eizenfald didn't use big attacks, instead maintaining a distance and attacking with smaller dragon breaths to keep the boss focused on him. Unlike before, they fought cautiously, but that was necessary to keep the Machina Guardian in check—all part of Mira's new plan.

"Okay, she's in position. Let us begin." Having confirmed that Christina's squad was on standby, Mira signaled Soul Howl, then ordered Eizenfald and the Valkyries to attack full-on.

Immediately, every cannon on the castle wall fired at once. The shots slipped past the Machina Guardian's legs as it tried to defend itself, striking its body one after another. Explosive flames burned wildly.

Amid all that, the Valkyrie-led army sprang into action. They abandoned defense for an aggressive attack, focusing on striking down one leg. The Machina Guardian swung a leg to try and stop them, but Eizenfald's tail deflected it, temporarily neutralizing the limb.

That didn't last long. Aiming lasers at the ground, the Machina Guardian fired madly. Its aim was poor due to the smoke still wafting around, but it had no shortage of targets, and shot through multiple ashen knights. It culled one-third more of the army.

Still, the sisters succeeded in destroying the leg. The Machina Guardian staggered. Now perceiving the sisters as a major threat, it focused fire on them.

While the boss was fully focused on the ground below, Mira ordered Christina, "Okay, now!"

Christina's ashen knights suddenly appeared above the Guardian in a total blind spot—the most unexpected sucker punch possible. Garuda had carried them, and Wasranvel had kept them imperceptible, making this the perfect stealth-bombing ambush.

Falling from above, the ashen knights stabbed their holy swords into the Machina Guardian's back. One even cut another of the boss's legs off in the process.

Their seven swords pierced the boss one after another. When they pulled the blades out, sparks flew, and smoke rose from the wounds. The momentum of their falls contributed to their force, enabling these blows to deal the most damage yet to the Guardian. The attacks pierced into its depths, rendering its movements unstable. It lurched even farther sideways, as if unable to bear the pain.

Then the "main character" made her appearance. After gathering more than enough mana, Christina finally leapt down, turned her shield into a foothold of light, and accelerated instantly. Despite being the youngest, she was still a Valkyrie. Therefore, her speed was many times greater than the knights', and her sword much sharper than theirs could ever be.

"Go!" Christina cried, penetrating the armor despite its overwhelming toughness.

Eizenfald, the Valkyrie Sisters, and the ashen knights on the vanguard had created the perfect opening for Christina. Mira had given her a vital role, but this wasn't a tall order for her; she sliced heroically through the enormous, powerful foe that lay before her.

Then, with a shrill metallic sound, the sword in the ecstatic Christina's hands snapped right in the middle. "Nooo! My six-time-hand-me-down swooord!"

Swung with such speed that one expected it to slice the Machina Guardian's torso in half, the blade had broken. Christina lost the resistance it provided, and her momentum sent her falling right onto her face.

"At a time like *this*?!"

The youngest sister glared at the sword angrily, more upset that she'd missed her big chance than by her fall itself. She'd felt the attack succeeding until the antique sword, passed down from Alfina on, had snapped cleanly in the middle.

She looked up to survey her attack's results. "Huh?"

Christina could see the gleaming red crystal inside the Machina Guardian's opened torso. Indeed, what she'd felt about the attack had been accurate. Despite breaking her sword, she'd dealt deep, significant damage to the Machina Guardian.

That was precisely what triggered Ancient Ray, the Machina Guardian's trump-card attack, which surpassed even Rampage's raw power. The Machina Guardian always used Ancient Ray when it hit 20 percent health, and always aimed at whoever had earned the most aggro.

Christina had just torn through the Machina Guardian's torso, so the boss naturally targeted her, though her sword had just broken. Instantly, destructive light engulfed the Valkyrie.

SHE PROFESSED HERSELF PUPIL OF THE WISE MAN

"That was a massive hit! Well done, if I may say so myself!" Mira called proudly as she watched the Machina Guardian unleash Ancient Ray.

"Yeah, great job. Its eyes turned red and started flickering right away. I didn't think it would go that well," Soul Howl said, impressed, as he watched things unfold.

When the Machina Guardian's gold eyes reddened, that meant damage had exceeded 70 percent. When they flickered, that proved damage had gone beyond 80 percent. If Christina had completed her attack, she might even have finished off the boss herself, but the immense force put the sword through too much strain.

Christina, who'd just barely missed her chance to shine as MVP, froze thunderstruck in a curled defensive posture next to Mira.

Despite the accident, the stealth-drop team had dealt more damage than Mira anticipated. She thanked the team's leader, Christina, putting a hand on her shoulder. "A shame that the unexpected happened, but you did well, Christina."

Christina raised her head in surprise and looked around. When she spotted Mira, she gasped in confusion. "Huh? Master? Um, what just...?"

"I used Shepherd to Refuge. That was close, wasn't it?"

Shepherd to Refuge was a summoner skill that allowed the user to instantly return a summoned target to their side. Mira had used it to relocate Christina immediately before Ancient Ray hit her.

When she explained as much, Christina finally realized what was going on. Gasping, she uncurled and kneeled before Mira. "I'm sorry I couldn't finish it off..." The Valkyrie hung her head sadly at her failure to accomplish the major role entrusted to her.

Mira simply praised her. "Please, you did well. Quite well." This operation had merely been an attempt to shave off 10 percent of the boss's HP—in a way, a slapdash experiment to see how well the strategy would work. Christina had achieved even greater results, which deserved praise, not shame. "You charged up quite a while, I noticed. Was that a new skill? What impressive power."

The final blow Christina had unleashed had drawn a trail of light behind it, tearing through the Machina Guardian's torso. No doubt it was a derivative of the Christina Slash the Valkyrie had shown off not long ago. Mira was happiest to see one of her partners growing.

At first, Christina was taken aback, since she'd thought her sword breaking meant she failed. However, she started to comprehend that she wasn't being scolded; she'd actually succeeded, and Mira was openly praising her for it.

Christina's vigor gradually returned. "I made it just to help you, Master! Your praise honors me!" she announced, taking this opportunity to show off to Mira.

Christina's sword of light was actually a skill she'd happened upon totally by accident. She'd condensed her mana during training to *look* like she was trying really hard while actually slacking the whole time. She didn't *tell* Mira that, of course, despite thinking of all the bitter, painful training she'd been put through.

"Is that so? Really, I can't thank you and your sisters enough."

When Mira expressed gratitude again, Christina replied with a very smug grin. "Please. We're just doing what's right!" It was true that even Christina did everything necessary to help Mira. She just *also* used her wits to survive the overly harsh training she was forced to undergo.

"Now, Christina, we just need to press on a little longer. I'm counting on you." Mira offered Christina a summoned holy sword Sanctia to replace her broken one. Christina had a shield as a secondary weapon, but couldn't fight with that alone, and Mira thought it might be fun to give a Valkyrie a holy sword.

Christina and Sanctia... Sounds like a good match to me!

The swords the sisters usually wielded were true works of art. Your average famed sword, holy sword, or demonic sword couldn't hold a candle to them. Even the antique blade Alfina had passed down through the family was far superior to the average sword. That was why Mira had neglected to try this until now. Since Christina's sword was broken and useless, it was the perfect opportunity to have her use Sanctia.

Even clumsy Christina was a first-rate swordsman. What would happen if she swung the holy sword? Mira gazed at her, eyes burning.

Christina interpreted Mira's gaze as expectant. The thought that her hopes were pinned on Christina, not her sisters, filled the Valkyrie with a sense of superiority.

"Thank you so much!"

A gift of a sword from her beloved master? Though this unexpected turn of events surprised her, the elated Christina sheathed her broken sword and accepted the gift reverently.

She
Professed
Herself
Pupil of the
Wise Man

15

FAR AWAY ON THE FRONT LINES, the heavily damaged Machina Guardian rampaged wildly, as if some limiter had been removed, while the leg the ashen knights had severed spawned Mechanized Protectors. As Eizenfald held off the raid boss itself, Mira quickly ordered the sisters to deal with the smaller spawns.

Even while Alfina worked to support Eizenfald, her eyes were glued to Christina, who ran in from behind. *She had Master's help, so things turned out fine, but...* She knew Christina had only escaped danger thanks to Mira's emergency Shepherd to Refuge. That just made Alfina's eyes sterner. *How shameful for her to let her guard down to the point that our Master needed to step in. I'll have to give her more special training to avoid such a thing ever happening again.*

The sword breaking had been an unexpected accident, which was all the more reason one needed to react calmly and swiftly if that happened. Yet, right in front of the enemy, Christina had simply stared at the broken sword. Then she'd turned and goggled at the *enemy,* leaving herself defenseless. That was Alfina's assessment.

They'd come here through Mira's summoning magic, so a direct hit from Ancient Ray would only destroy their barriers and forcefully dismiss them. It wouldn't actually hurt them, just return them to their location pre-summoning. Still, Alfina couldn't forgive Christina for reacting in a way that put her so close to "death."

Perhaps I should teach her to use her shield as a weapon. Alfina, capable of simultaneously supporting Eizenfald and worrying about her sister, decided that—once they returned to Valhalla— she'd teach Christina to fight after losing her means of offense.

While the other Valkyries ran around finishing off Protectors, Christina gleefully returned to the front line. "I'm back!" She ever-so-confidently reunited with her ashen-knight platoon, looking up at the Machina Guardian again. It was rare for her to be so enthusiastic about battle.

Right away, Alfina chastised her. "Christina, have you no shame? How could you leave yourself so open to attack that Master had to rescue you?"

"S-sorry. I'll be more careful!" Christina replied, showing her willingness to reflect on her actions. It was so natural, one would think she *had* genuinely been careful.

That was merely because Christina was used to paying simple lip service as a "genuine apology" to shut Alfina up and keep her from complaining.

"Goodness, Christina... Fine." Alfina had a feeling that she wasn't being genuine, but they were in the middle of a battle. "We can't have you fighting without a sword, so use this."

Admonishments could wait; instead, Alfina offered Christina her second sword. When she did, she finally noticed that Christina *already* wielded another sword.

"Wait! That blade..." Shock suddenly colored Alfina's eyes. She knew exactly what the holy sword Sanctia was. "Christina, why do you have Master's holy sword?!"

A special holy sword only *Mira* could summon—that was Alfina's perception of Sanctia. She'd only seen the dark knights and ashen knights use it, but she'd been able to tell how the sword itself propelled and bolstered their attacks.

The holy sword Sanctia was undergoing growth. Alfina's only dream was that she'd get to wield it when it reached its zenith. Yet Christina was armed with the growing sword here and now. Shock was apparent on Alfina's face—shock she'd never shown since the day Danblf disappeared from the world, thirty years ago.

"Um, she lent it to me to replace the broken one..." Christina explained quickly, chilled by Alfina's unusual reaction. To avoid incurring Alfina's wrath, she did her best to emphasize that Mira had just let her borrow it for the time being.

For Valkyries, receiving a sword from their master was an extreme honor. But this particular instance wasn't as grand as Alfina assumed; Sanctia was more serving as an offhand substitute. Still, to someone who'd only used her sisters' hand-me-downs, it was special. Yet Sanctia was something Alfina could never so much as ask to get her hands on, prompting Christina to emphasize that there wasn't any special meaning behind her use of the sword. The younger Valkyrie was certain that experiencing Alfina's long-held dream first would mean Alfina tasked her with harsher training than ever.

Knowing Alfina, she'll tell me to get stronger and stronger until I'm worthy of the sword. I'm just sure of it! Christina was in a better mood than ever at having received the sword, but her mind had raced to wring out an answer, and to clumsily emphasize that it wasn't anything special.

"I see. Well, be careful next time. I won't let you act shamefully while wielding our Master's holy sword."

"No, ma'am! I'm very aware!"

Quickly finishing their conversation, the sisters jumped back into the fray on the battlefield, which they'd left to the other Valkyries and Eizenfald.

I think I got her off my back... Christina mused.

It wasn't rare for Christina to slack off during battle, but it was a different story when it came to Alfina, who was devoted utterly to her master. It would perhaps be understandable if Alfina were distracted for a moment, but it was normally unthinkable for her

SHE PROFESSED HERSELF PUPIL OF THE WISE MAN

to leave a mission from Mira unattended. She'd never make her attachment to the holy sword obvious by neglecting the battlefield while others fought. Still, that attachment was perhaps proof of just how special the sword was.

Standing before the Machina Guardian and Protectors, Christina gazed at her sword and smirked to herself.

"I'm gonna finish these things off!"

Backing off to a safe distance, Christina raised the holy sword. Sneaking away to take a break midbattle was one of her special skills, but it seemed she'd use a different skill this time. She clutched the brand-new sword, wholly unused by her sisters. Then she gathered her mana—a feat she was better at than anyone, thanks to her endless slacking—into the holy sword.

A moment after, the mana emitted a blinding flash rivaling the sun's brightness, turning Sanctia into a three-meter-long sword of light.

Everyone watched the sword with bated breath as it radiated overwhelming divinity. However, one person—Christina herself— was unusually shaken by the change. "Huh?" *What?! What's going on? Something changed!* Had the sword Mira gave her transformed because she'd done something wrong?

Worried, Christina looked up at the sword of light. *It's so cool...* She felt like a real-life hero right out of a storybook.

As she fantasized about her glory, Christina heard the thing she feared most: a sharp warning from Alfina. "Christina, dodge!"

Either out of instinct or genuinely taking Alfina's advice, Christina reflexively jumped. A hairsbreadth away, a beam of light struck the place where she'd just stood. The Ancient Ray shot burned the floor black.

When Christina looked up, she saw the Machina Guardian aiming at her again. At the same time, its thick leg reached out to strike. Having dodged, the Valkyrie was still in midair, leaving her no way to evade the massive blow. *I'll use my shield as a foothold... No, it's not fast enough!*

Just before the Machina Guardian's swing struck her, there were several explosive sounds. A slight delay caused the boss's leg to sail right by her.

"Whoa, that was close..." When Christina landed, she jumped further back and took a sidelong glance at the leg that had just crashed into the ground. On its inner side were countless new bullet marks. It seemed the cannons on the castle walls and towers had diverted the strike's arc by force. Soul Howl boasted terrifying precision.

Christina's relief was short-lived. The Machina Guardian continued to target her. Its vertical strikes, horizontal swings, and laser volleys all ignored the other sisters, Mira's army, and even Eizenfald in favor of Christina.

"Why does it want me so baaad?!" Christina dodged frantically in every conceivable direction. Due to her single-minded focus on evasion, the holy sword's light faded, and it returned to its normal state.

The Machina Guardian continued to follow Christina obstinately.

Its concentrated attacks utterly ignored the biggest threat, Eizenfald, who boasted far more offensive and defensive power than the Valkyrie. Had Christina's stealth attack been that effective? Overall, Eizenfald should have been the most obvious threat to the Machina Guardian. After all, Mira had the dragon attack to maximize his aggro levels.

But here, at the very end, things had gone awry. This was something they'd never seen in the Machina Guardian.

Observing it, Mira asked her companion, "Say, Soul Howl, what do you make of that?"

"Must be because of that sword of light from before. Condense mana that densely, and anything would be wary," he answered matter-of-factly. Even from a distance, he could tell that the sword of light's power was awe-inspiring.

"So you think so too."

Mira had also guessed that the raid boss noticed Christina's massive concentration of mana, so her opinion aligned with Soul Howl's. She decided to share a strategy she'd just hit upon with Soul Howl and the Valkyrie Sisters.

"Understood." Alfina and the other sisters immediately took action. Eizenfald got to work, too, though more slowly.

"No more! Please! Come ooooon!" Christina ran for her life.

Unfortunately, either she'd reached her limit or the Machina Guardian was learning how she dodged. It got closer and closer to her. When one attack finally grazed her, the raid boss unleashed a stabbing blow sure to strike her no matter what. Christina fended it off with her shield, then jumped as far back as she could.

"Nice! It worked." She'd mitigated the attack's impact while putting distance between them.

At the same time, Eizenfald descended from above to cut the Machina Guardian off from Christina. He swung his powerful tail, hitting his mark perfectly. The Machina Guardian's sights were set on him again, and they resumed their kaiju-like battle. Meanwhile, the sisters fighting the Protectors had moved their battles far from the main battlefield.

"Now, Miss Christina, you may focus to your heart's content," said the spirit of stealth, Wasranvel.

He was at the back of the battlefield, next to Christina, whom he'd hidden after her retreat—decreasing her aggro levels and changing the Machina Guardian's priority target. That wasn't as strong as total concealment, but with so many people on the battlefield, it was effective enough to distract the boss.

Having Wasranvel calibrate aggro was another strategy Mira had thought of during her travels.

"Yes, sir!"

Christina readied her sword and gathered mana within it. At the same time, Wasranvel perfectly concealed the mana's flow. Their plan to defeat the Machina Guardian proceeded smoothly in the corner of the battlefield.

On the front lines, the boss was about to cross the 10 percent health threshold. With that transition, its attacks became even more ferocious. It fired its laser machine gun mercilessly and used Ancient Ray much more often.

Especially vicious were the Ancient Ray attacks it launched immediately after knocking targets off-balance with a leg sweep. It was no overstatement to say half the battle's difficulty would lie in this final stretch.

Eizenfald and the Valkyrie Sisters fought defensively. Now was the time to hold steady. The boss became even harder to deal with when its health went below 10 percent, so preserving *their* health was vital.

Mira planned to watch for an opportunity to deal nearly 10 percent damage at once. Christina was doing part of the prep for that, and Eizenfald was warming up a dragon breath to help out.

The Valkyrie squads dispersed, focusing on evasion as they maneuvered. Eizenfald continued to fight off the Machina Guardian, taking some attacks head-on and parrying others. One by one, the sisters defeated their assigned Protectors, then took on the task of scattering the Machina Guardian's attacks.

The battle pressed on with minimal damage, but that didn't mean they could let the raid boss attack as it pleased. One strike of its massive leg had enough force to destroy an ashen knight.

Its individual laser machine-gun shots were less strong, but rained down ceaselessly, slowly but surely racking up damage.

Given that the mages' side was waiting for preparations to finish, they were doing a fantastic job buying time. However, there was a curveball during that preparation period.

While Mira awaited the perfect time to activate the summoning spell that would provide the necessary last push...

While Soul Howl prepared special ammo for the final volley...

While Eizenfald used draconic magic to neutralize the laser machine gun...

While Alfina destroyed the Machina Guardian's joints...

While her sisters finished a defensive formation...

While Christina's charge was approaching completion...

While First Pupil and Pegasus placed a new round of stones...

It happened.

There was a sound like an alarm. It was harsh—no doubt meant as an emergency alert—and there was something eerie about it. That wasn't all; red lights in the corners of the large chamber began flashing.

"What is this...? What's happening?!" Mira demanded.

"I don't know, but I don't like the sound of it," Soul Howl replied.

They'd defeated the Machina Guardian countless times in-game, and they had the entire player base's collective knowledge. But they had no recollection of that alarm. This late in the game, the mages were facing something new.

What in the world was going on? They braced themselves to be ready for anything, but the siren's meaning quickly became clear: it warned those present to conduct an emergency evacuation.

Instantly after it sounded, sparks flew from the Machina Guardian's giant form. As its plating flew off, its actions and appearance changed drastically. Intense metal creaks came from the raid boss. They sounded like mechanical shrieks, as if the beast itself were screaming. The noises caused its actions to become very noticeably different.

"This...is just like Rampage."

"Yeah, that's exactly what it is."

Mira and Soul Howl voiced what was apparently the most apt comparison to the Machina Guardian's current state: Rampage Mode.

"I can't believe it still had such secrets hidden up its sleeve," Mira grumbled.

Up to this point, the boss had used many attacks outside its usual windows. It had fired Ancient Ray before crossing the necessary damage threshold, used Rampage despite lacking the required conditions, and so on. This Rampage Mode, however, was wholly new. Being as cautious as possible, the mages swiftly got to work responding to the maneuver.

Meanwhile, the Machina Guardian abandoned self-defense entirely and crushed everything in reach. It didn't perform any of the defensive maneuvers it had used against Eizenfald and Alfina. It replaced those with more ferocious moves than ever, meeting all the mages' attacks with desperate counterattacks. To the Machina Guardian, offense was now the best defense.

Most annoying of all was its laser machine gun. The shots' individual power hadn't changed much, but it fired many more than before, as if firing a shotgun at the rate of a Gatling gun. Unlike shotgun ammo, each shot had the full force of a laser. The machine gun had become a vicious cannon that could blow away summons' defensive barriers in an instant. Worse, it never stopped firing. Its aim was a mess, making its fire impossible to concentrate, but the range and overwhelming quantity of its shots meant it rained lasers all over the battlefield.

Thus, casualties popped up everywhere. Over half the golems positioned throughout the battlefield were destroyed, and the laser machine gun was culling the army of ashen knights in real time.

Worst of all, because the lasers rained *all* over the battlefield, they exposed the hidden Christina and Wasranvel in no time.

"Eek!"

"Well, this is tricky!" Wasranvel managed to dodge, putting up a shield to block the lasers, but he struggled against their endless number and range.

Christina deflected the lasers deftly with her shield, but unfortunately, her focus on defense caused more than half the mana she'd condensed into the holy sword to disperse. "Aah! All the mana I gathered..."

Left with nowhere to run, the pair scurried behind a defensive wall they spotted towering over the battlefield. Soul Howl's necromancy had created the structure; it was quite sturdy, so it wouldn't break down too quickly under laser fire.

They'd secured their safety for the time being, but Christina just stared sadly at the holy sword, aware that she wouldn't regather all that mana any time soon.

16

AFTER SETTING UP a rampart around the battlefield, Soul Howl fixed his eyes on the rampaging Machina Guardian and noted his initial priority. "First things first—that laser battery has to go."

The hail of lasers even reached the castle wall where he and Mira stood, slowly carving into its surface. It would take some time before the lasers dealt the castle real damage, but the mana cost to defend against them had increased drastically. Things would only get worse at this rate.

"Mm, indeed. There's little we can do until that's dealt with."

The bigger problem was that the lasers engulfed the whole battlefield. Christina and Wasranvel weren't the only ones hiding; the lasers forced the other Valkyries and their army of ashen knights to take shelter as well.

The battle was like trench warfare now, subject to endless fire from above. Their forces couldn't move safely due to the laser attacks' wide range.

Amid it all, only Eizenfald could withstand the barrage. While the lasers did strike him, his draconic magic provided armor that reduced the damage each shot dealt. The lasers cut away his barrier little by little, but since it could be reapplied once more, he'd endure for some time.

Of course, the Machina Guardian wasn't *only* attacking with its lasers. If it focused all its attacks on Eizenfald, especially in Rampage Mode, even the dragon couldn't last long.

Mira judged that if the one tanking the majority of the damage fell, that would likely lead to a party wipe. She decided to use her trump card. "It's a little earlier than intended, but now is the time."

Even faced with a battle turning disadvantageous, Soul Howl answered with excited eyes, "Agreed. Do it."

Mira was about to summon a special being—made even more special by Soul Howl's love of edgy things. Under Soul Howl's expectant gaze, she faced forward and alerted Martel that she was ready.

"Yep! All ready here too!" Martel confirmed, as Mira expected.

With that, Mira finally unleashed her spell.

When the Bound Arcana deployed by First Pupil and Pegasus changed into the Mark of the Rosary and resonated, it drew an even bigger magic circle on the battlefield. It was time to summon a being known to all with even a vague interest in myths and legends: Fenrir himself.

At twilight's end, the advent of night eternal.

When even the gods sleep at the dying of the light and the brink of the abyss,

Eternal darkness rules, and all becomes an illusion beyond recollection.

What remains but wavering chaos, a sea of dead stars, and a vacant moon atop a throne of corpses?

Seeker of dawn, breaker of chains, fling open the gates of violence upon the heavenly tower.

Now is the time of change. Now is the era of a new beginning.

My friend, feast upon the end itself.

Words flowed from Mira's mouth and transformed into power, spurring the magic circle into action. When the light reached its apex, the gate had already begun to open.

[Mythical Evocation: Fenrir]

A black hole widened like an endless void in the earth below, and Fenrir appeared as if crawling from its depths.

With bluish-black fur like the night sky, golden eyes reflecting his divinity, and silver claws that metallically reflected light, Fenrir appeared with an aura befitting his legendary status, instantly displaying his overwhelming power.

When the ceaseless hail of lasers touched his fur, they appeared to vaporize. It seemed Fenrir had already come up with a countermeasure thanks to Martel sharing the situation with him—total nullification. What more could one ask for?

"So that's Fenrir..." Soul Howl muttered. He didn't sound impressed; he sounded more...befuddled.

How could one blame him? The legendary Fenrir summoned by Mira was a puppy.

Although he was the size of an adult dog, he wasn't the giant wolf one expected upon hearing his name. At a glance, he hardly seemed like a reliable ally.

"He still lacks a lot of his power. Some things happened when I first met him," Mira told Soul Howl. Now that she thought about it, she remembered that she hadn't told Soul Howl about that encounter. She brushed that off, adding, "Cute as he is, I assure you he's strong enough to go toe to toe with Eizenfald."

"Well, if you say so. Offense is all yours, Elder." Either way, now wasn't the time to dawdle. Putting his full faith in Mira, Soul Howl went back to focusing on defense.

He followed the ever-changing laser angles and the Machina Guardian's movements to create walls and control golems to obstruct and impede the boss. Without Soul Howl's golem defensive line, the Machina Guardian would've wiped out even Mira's army twice over by now. Thanks to the golems, the rampaging boss's range of motion was very limited for the time being.

"You leave it in good hands." Mira nodded firmly, then informed Eizenfald and Fenrir right away that their first priority was the laser cannons.

"Understood, Mother!"

"Right. Understood."

Both leapt into action. Eizenfald charged and held the rampaging Machina Guardian back by force. Even a being of the dragon's power would struggle to continue that for long, so Eizenfald was doing little more than creating a small opening. They'd have had no way to take advantage of that opening before, but they certainly did now; there was an ally who could do just that on the battlefield.

Fenrir used the opening Eizenfald made for him to maximum effect. He ran like a speeding bullet, leapt forth like an arrow, and destroyed a laser cannon with a single swing of his claws. He didn't stop there; he jumped off the restrained Machina Guardian's legs to neutralize two more cannons.

"Little guy's stronger than he looks," Soul Howl muttered to himself.

Hearing that, Mira turned smug, as if she were the one he'd complimented. "Of course. He is *the* Fenrir, after all!"

Using Eizenfald and Fenrir's combined powers, they'd escaped danger. This was the duo's first time working together, but they'd done quite well, destroying the cannons one after another.

However, that didn't mean the Machina Guardian was finished. Incredibly, it revealed yet another new attack. The boss's open abdomen fired beams of light that engulfed large areas; where the beams struck, they created pillars of flame.

"Were those Ancient Rays?"

"I think so."

Each shot was less powerful than an Ancient Ray, but still deadly. Ancient Ray could blow away the most powerful tank player in an instant; this attack merely took an entire second to deal equivalent damage.

The Machina Guardian began firing these beams, which Mira and Soul Howl would call "Diffused Ancient Rays." Getting hit by those Diffused Ancient Rays could be lethal.

Eizenfald and Fenrir positioned themselves on either side of the Machina Guardian, kept their distance, and aimed for the remaining laser cannons.

"Eep..." Even as she quivered at the battle's heightened intensity, Christina resumed gathering mana. Wasranvel's power hid her presence, and Soul Howl had placed many layers of defensive golems in front of her.

Christina found herself a bit happy to receive such VIP treatment. Perhaps as a result, her sword gleamed even brighter than before.

Behind the castle walls, fully separated from the fierce battle, a single cat watched the rain of fire with fearful eyes. It was First Pupil.

"I'm just glad that happened while we were over here..." he sighed, relieved.

Pegasus and Garuda, who waited next to him, nodded. However, this moment of relief wouldn't last long, for Mira gave them another order. She said she needed the Bound Arcana redeployed in order to summon Fenrir.

"When this war's over, I'm gonna propose to the girl I love!" First Pupil gallantly boarded Pegasus and departed for the battlefield again, bearing a sign on his back that simply read KAMIKAZE. Garuda saw them off, then waited in front of a giant golem.

About five minutes after Mira summoned Fenrir, he and Eizenfald successfully destroyed all the laser cannons, so the battle changed dramatically. Now that they'd eliminated the Machina Guardian's flashiest attacks yet, the infantry could come back out from behind the castle wall. Eizenfald and Fenrir could also disperse their previously concentrated attacks, giving Mira more ways to take advantage of her two strongest allies.

Opportunities continued to flow in. Now that it had lost its cannons, the Machina Guardian's Rampage Mode began to subside.

Then, Christina signaled her charge was complete. "Ready anytime!"

All the stars had aligned, so Mira and Soul Howl decided to order their army to begin the final operation.

"Great. Now's the time to strike!"

"Yeah. Let's get 'em good."

Upon their signal, the whole army took the offensive.

"We must bring victory to Master!" Alfina and the Valkyries unleashed powerful attacks.

Alfina's slashes cut through the boss's plating, and Elezina's arrows became projectiles of light. The other sisters kept gouging into the Machina Guardian with their own favored weapons. The ashen knights charged and swung their holy swords too, dealing sure damage.

"Yes, Mother!" Eizenfald approached the Machina Guardian, neutralizing Diffused Ancient Rays with his dragon breath. Then he unleashed a point-blank dragon breath on the boss's leg joint before tearing the limb off entirely.

"I mustn't miss the action, either!" Fenrir's claws tore through the Ancient Ray cannon. The Machina Guardian's now-undirected energy exploded from inside, bursting into flames.

Once the boss lost its balance, Soul Howl's towers and castle wall fired all their cannons simultaneously. "Okay, now!"

Their powerful attacks continued endlessly until the Machina Guardian made a sound like an emergency buzzer, then proceeded to rumble with mechanical noises like none before.

Mira and Soul Howl knew of this phenomenon. It seemed their full-on attack had brought the Machina Guardian under 10 percent health, triggering it to change from Rampage Mode to its final phase—the far more dangerous Slaughter Mode.

If the boss completed this shift, they had no chance of winning. They had a victory rate of zero against it in-game. Even the generals of Atlantis, the game's largest player-led nation, could never defeat the transformed Machina Guardian. That proved just what a monster it became in Slaughter Mode.

They'd exhaust the mana they needed to maintain their forces before they polished the boss off. So, after much discussion, Mira and Soul Howl had planned to defeat the Machina Guardian before it finished transforming.

The Machina Guardian seemingly transformed by destroying and reassembling itself from the inside out. Faced with that, the mages' entire army retreated at once. However, one shadow flew above the boss: Garuda, carrying an enormous golem. Soaring directly overhead, it dropped the golem like a bomber plane dropping a bomb. The golem traced a gentle trajectory before landing directly on the Machina Guardian.

[Internment Arts: Light of Extinction]

There was a dazzling flash, followed by hellish red flames filling their fields of vision. Shortly after, a shock wave shook them to their cores, and a deafening explosion roared. It was even more powerful than Soul Howl's full-on bombardment.

This foolish task—having Garuda carry a golem too heavy to move on its own—was Death From Above, a combination of Mira's and Soul Howl's magic.

Even such an explosion wouldn't destroy the Machina Guardian. Now, though, it was finally time for the true protagonist to take the stage.

Another figure rushed into the battlefield, still cloudy from the explosion. Hidden by Wasranvel's power up to this point, Christina wielded a holy sword clad in a twenty-meter pillar of light.

When she unsheathed the holy sword—full of even more mana than when the Machina Guardian had designated her a threat—from the power of stealth, it unleashed strength like Eizenfald's dragon breath, shaking the air. From behind, Christina looked like a heroine of light.

"Whoa... This is a big responsibility..." The youngest sister faced the Machina Guardian, which continued to creak violently as it rebuilt itself, shuddering at the pressure it was building up. Still, Christina was confident that the holy sword, full of as much mana as she could gather, would finish off the foe before her.

After getting carried away in the battle with Chimera Clausen, Christina had honed her Christina Slash even more. Mana-focus training was a convenient excuse to slack on her usual training, but she had a talent for it. Solely in terms of a single-strike burst, Christina was probably the strongest Valkyrie.

If her holy sword full of mana struck a foe, the battle would be over.

Everyone watched with bated breath.

At that moment—with an even shriller metallic shriek—the Machina Guardian lurched, apparently dodging, although that wasn't enough to make Christina miss her mark.

However, it *wasn't* evading her. After even more mechanical whirring, the Machina Guardian fired something like a slender spear at Christina.

"Huh...?"

It was one of the boss's legs, flying so fast that she had no time to evade. Why could the Machina Guardian move before its transformation ended? Because it had transformed its leg first—another change from the game world.

The Machina Guardian's Slaughter Mode attacks were overwhelming. If they struck, they were sure to forcibly dismiss summons, and the mana condensed in Christina's sword would disappear. Mira and Soul Howl would lose their decisive blow, leading to their defeat.

Yet that problem had already been solved. Before Mira could tell the panicking Christina, the Machina Guardian's leg had stopped right in front of her.

"All is well. No problems."

"That scared me..." said Christina.

The Valkyrie saw Fenrir's many chains binding the Machina Guardian. Mira had Fenrir prepare Gleipnir ahead of time, just in case the raid boss did anything unexpected. Those sealing chains could bind even Fenrir himself. It would be impossible for the Machina Guardian to tear away quickly.

"Now, Christina. Strike the final blow!" Fenrir called.

"Okay!" Christina replied, readying her sword. After a moment of concentration, a vivid image of victory formed in her imagination. "True Christina Slaaaash!"

Bound by Gleipnir, the Machina Guardian was helpless as Christina swung the holy sword down with a mighty roar.

The slash seemed to sever sound itself, painting over everything with pure light. No doubt it destroyed the boss instantly. The light flashed brighter for just an instant before finally ceasing.

All that remained were the bisected remains of the Machina Guardian, Christina with the holy sword in hand, and Fenrir in the process of being dismissed as he timed out.

"We won!"

This final battle had taken hours and both Mira's and Soul Howl's maximum forces. The realization that she'd ended the struggle with her own hands took Christina aback, but what she saw finally convinced her, and she raised the holy sword out of sheer joy.

17

THE BATTLE with the Machina Guardian was over—or so everyone thought.

Suddenly, the wreckage collapsed, and something crawled out from within. Tension filled the chamber. Everyone, including Christina, readied themselves.

It looked to be some kind of machine. However, it was no Mechanized Wanderer or Protector. It was a simple doll, with no weapons nor armor. There was an even more striking difference: the doll had a moving face, though it was incomplete.

Its eyes widened, and it looked all around. After a moment, its mouth slowly opened. "THe BlAcK MOOn RIseS, anD DaRknEss encroAchEs. ThOSE wHo Have dEFeATEd my sUpREME GuaRdIAN and oVeRcOmE This tRiAl, You aRe wOrTHy oF iNhERITINg oUr PoWEr. TAke This anD mAKE REaDy FoR the bATTLE wITh thE cOMInG inVADER." Its voice sounded like it was coming out of a broken speaker.

Once the doll finished speaking, it held out a square plate of metal. Christina, who happened to be in front of it, hesitated and looked to Mira for help.

Alfina repeated the doll's words: "The black moon rises, and darkness encroaches. Those who have defeated my supreme Guardian and overcome this trial, you are worthy of inheriting our power. Take this and make ready for the battle with the coming invader."

While this never-before-seen event surprised Mira, her interest was largely piqued by the part about "inheriting our power." "Black moon," "darkness," "invader"—it was unclear what these words meant, but no doubt there would be hints on the metal plate in the doll's hand.

Suleiman could certainly figure it out, so Mira ordered Christina to accept the plate—cautiously, just in case. "If those words are true, then I presume the plate is safe."

Terrified, Christina slowly reached out her hand and accepted the metal plate from the doll. "Um, thaaanks..."

Its job done, the doll instantly collapsed into a heap of scraps. The accompanying sound of metal crashing on metal made Christina jump up and nearly drop the plate. "Whoa! That scared me *so* much!"

She managed to catch the plate and tried to play it off as if she *hadn't* been surprised. She couldn't let herself look pathetic while all eyes were on her.

Unfortunately, it was far too late. When Christina turned to deliver the plate to Mira, she spotted Alfina up ahead. "Ack!" she cried.

Alfina's eyes told her one thing: *If that was enough to surprise you, it's proof that you need more training.*

Sensing Alfina's anger, the other sisters gazed at Christina sympathetically. Christina had dealt the Machina Guardian a spectacular finisher, but no glory—only special training—awaited her upon their return.

After thanking everyone for their efforts and dismissing her army, Mira flipped the metal plate over several times with great interest. "Hrmm. I haven't the faintest idea what this could be."

Soul Howl peeked in from the side and surveyed the plate. "Those look more like figures than characters. I've never seen that either. Wonder what it all means."

The plate was black. It wasn't as heavy as it looked; rather, it was surprisingly light. The surface was covered entirely in symbols.

"It almost...looks like some kind of blueprint," Mira muttered to herself in realization.

According to the doll, this was the key to some power. When it said "*our* power," had it meant the people who'd built the Ancient Underground City?

"There are scholars back at the castle, yeah? Leave it all to them. Anyway, I've got work to do." Soul Howl had already lost interest. Or rather, he had something more important to focus on. He released his castle golem and quickly headed to the chamber beyond.

"Hrmm... Fair enough." The plate didn't make much sense at all to Mira, so worrying more over it wouldn't help her understand it. Deciding to simply leave it to Solomon, she focused on the most important matter at hand. Running over to the Machina Guardian's remains, she confirmed with Soul Howl, "By the way, you really mean to leave me all the loot, right? I won't have you telling me to hand it over later!" Hopefully, he would keep the promise he'd made yesterday.

"I won't, I won't. Take it all." Soul Howl chuckled at her desperation and walked right past, totally unbothered.

"Heh heh! I shall!" Mira muttered happily as she saw him off. Then she finally began rummaging for the Machina Guardian's drops. The boss was large, however, as were its remains—large and heavy.

Mira suddenly wished Eizenfald could pitch in. "I should've asked for help before dismissing him..." Since this was her first time digging through a pile of remains for drops, though, she chastised herself for forgetting and left it at that.

This pile wasn't something a single person could handle, so she summoned a team of workers.

[Evocation: Guardian Ash]

[Evocation: Garm]

[Evocation: Rotz Elephas]

Powerful beings appeared from magic circles and lined up in front of Mira: the gray bear, Guardian Ash; three-meter-long Garm; and the even more imposing white elephant, Rotz Elephas.

"Rotz, it's been a while. Happy to see you're well." Mira looked up at its giant figure, over seven meters high, and touched its long trunk. Rotz Elephas wrapped its trunk around her and made a soft sound in greeting.

The white elephant, Rotz Elephas, was a sacred beast that protected Paradise, a holy place for animals, deep in a forest on the Ark continent. Once upon a time, when Paradise had fallen into the hands of evil, Mira worked to restore it to its former glory. To repay her goodwill, Rotz Elephas had made a contract with her.

That was quite a long time ago, but Rotz Elephas seemed not to have forgotten that debt.

"Now, I'd like your help with these remains here..." Facing the defeated Machina Guardian, Mira asked the three to help sort the scraps.

"Thank you all for your work. Your strength never ceases to amaze. Ah, what a big help you are!"

The task was a little rough, but under twenty minutes later, they'd divided and sorted the giant Machina Guardian's remains. Going any further would risk damaging the drops Mira wanted, so she'd have to do this manually from this point on. Fortunately, the boss's plating had been removed, so human hands could pull the rest apart.

After thanking her summons profusely, Mira dismissed them and finally dove into the pile of treasure.

"Of course, I must begin with that one!" She decided on the first item to search for and fished through the remains of the boss's torso. Throwing useless scraps of metal and extraneous parts aside, she eventually found the shining red object. "Ooh... There it is. It's really there!" She raised the red jewel, as big as a human head, aloft.

That crystal was the core of the Machina Guardian's ultimate attack, Ancient Ray. It was called the Eye of Apollo. Neither Mira nor any of the other Nine Wise Men had ever seen it in person; it was extremely rare, even among legendary-class drops. Only three top players had ever obtained it: the King of Atlantis and two Nirvana Empire generals.

Mira now held the rare item in her own two hands. "Could it be? The legendary Eye of Apollo?! Hrmm... What shall I do with it?!"

The crystal was classified as a material. Atlantis's engineers had proposed many uses for it, including as gear, a magical item, or even a weapon. Of course, however it was used, it was sure to work tremendously well. Mira didn't possess a single item that incorporated a material better than the Eye of Apollo. It was sure to power her up like never before. How could she not be excited?

"We've only just started!" Mira gingerly placed the Eye of Apollo into her Item Box, then dug for the next material. Her greedy eyes wouldn't overlook a single treasure; she'd already stored all the information on the Machina Guardian's drops in her mind.

First, she found the Aegis Plate, a metal plate that protected the boss's power source. It was hard and moreover had overwhelming resistance to most attributes. Shields made with Aegis Plate counted among the most powerful paladin gear. Most paladins would die to have such a piece of equipment, but alas, Solomon had abandoned his own such shield entirely.

After that, Mira excavated the Anti-Material Crystal Engine that the Aegis Plate protected. Like a small black box, it couldn't be opened, giving no glimpse of what was inside.

In fact, it was very literally a black box—all people knew about it was that it used ancient crystal technology, so there was no way to employ it as a power source. Players instead combined it with explosives to use for attacks. It was a popular strategic weapon, its blast as powerful as the combined might of all Nine Wise Men.

Finding more and more loot, Mira now checked the head of the Machina Guardian, where the brain would have been. Removing the cranium cover and spotting the many spherical crystals packed inside, she squealed with joy. "Ooh! Goodness, look how many are in there!"

These were Neuron Crystals. On top of being usable materials for magical items, they worked extremely well with mage gear. Mira had even used them in equipment that she'd given Cleos for the sake of restoring summoning's reputation.

Neuron Crystals dropped often enough that players usually got at least one when they defeated the Machina Guardian, but now a *handful* lay before Mira.

"Goodness, *five*?! What a stroke of luck!"

She took all the Neuron Crystals before fidgeting with another part of the Machina Guardian's cranium. She then removed what might be considered one of the Guardian's "eyes." It was a plate of transparent glass, unscathed despite the fierce battle. About fifty centimeters in diameter and one centimeter thick, this was actually a metal item called Clear Materite Alloy Plate. It made a high-pitched metallic noise when Mira knocked on it.

"How mysterious it is..."

Amazed at how this fantasy setting allowed for transparent metal, Mira took both eyes, successfully recovering two Clear Materite Alloy Plates.

Next, she took the convex lens that served as the main part of the Guardian's eye. It was as big as her palm, and although players almost never used it as a lens, it reflected light extremely well. Its fantastic material, Ethemite, could be used in magical weapons and the like.

Mira took the other lens too. "Meh heh heh... Even today, these cost over a billion ducats. What a delicious trove of treasure!"

She still had four more unique drops to find, so she continued to search the remains for them. She gathered the New Link Magic Conduit, which was a conductive wire connecting the boss's head and torso, and the Carbonized Materite Plating used at the bottom of the torso. Those were followed by the High-Frequency Ignition Crystal used as the detonator for the explosion that followed Rampage, and the Reflective Prism from within the laser machine gun barrel.

CHAPTER 17

With that, Mira had a complete set of all ten unique Machina Guardian drops.

"I collected every single drop from a large-scale raid boss... Ha! It'll be hard to wipe this smug grin off my face." She snickered at the set.

Large-scale raid boss drops were extremely rare items sought by top players. People often fought over loot distribution, making the drops difficult and even dangerous to handle.

Considering the drop-rate mechanic that had existed back in the game, obtaining a drop wasn't as easy as simply defeating the raid boss. It was impossible—*unthinkable*!—in the old days for *all* the drops to be obtained at once. Of course, that had come with the risk of dying in the process.

Regardless, Mira had overcome that risk. She gazed at the Machina Guardian's scattered remains, wondering whether she'd left anything behind. She was a bit frugal when it came to this.

"The problem is processing them..."

The materials she'd obtained were exceedingly rare, beyond the skill of any but the most masterful artisans. Could Alcait's artisans handle them? Even if they could, could they bring out the materials' maximum potential? Some materials would need to go through several artisans' hands to draw out their true value. She couldn't take full advantage of this bountiful harvest without first finding several masters of their craft.

I see a long road ahead...

This would require much effort, but if she stuck to it, she would obtain valuables beyond her wildest dreams. Mira grinned as she fantasized about that moment, scanning for missed materials all the while.

"Hm...?" It was then that she diligently spotted something of a different color buried amid the wreckage. Wondering whether she'd missed it, she rushed over, uncovered the object, and picked it up. "A book...? No, some sort of diary?"

It was a booklet about the size of an average notebook. Or, more precisely, it was *like* a booklet.

It had deteriorated so much, it was hard to tell whether that was its original shape. Only a portion of its surface was left intact. Other parts were charred black. As Mira picked it up, it unsurprisingly crumbled; all that remained was the small unburned portion.

Why was this inside the Machina Guardian's remains...? Whoever did it belong to, anyway? Wondering if it was some new Machina Guardian item drop, Mira scrutinized the remains.

The first page alone, she realized, was still barely intact. The paper had deteriorated badly over the years, to the point that it seemed like just touching it might disintegrate it. Furthermore, parts were scratched off. Even in that state, however, some characters were readable.

Plan▪▪arth, Japan Branch▪▪▪▪▪year▪62 CE▪▪▪▪.

As planned▪▪▪▪▪sea coordinat▪▪▪▪at this point▪▪▪▪▪▪underground▪ ▪▪▪▪▪begun unified▪▪▪▪▪▪▪▪planned compl▪▪▪▪▪rth time▪▪▪▪.

However▪▪▪▪▪▪observed on surface▪▪▪▪▪▪▪▪req▪▪re more time.

After the facility is complete▪▪▪▪will begin. If all▪▪▪▪well▪▪▪▪▪ truly▪▪▪▪▪▪▪▪▪pray for▪▪▪▪▪prepare▪▪▪▪second.

At this ti▪▪▪▪▪no need to▪▪▪▪▪▪▪▪▪▪▪▪as such▪▪▪▪peers▪▪▪▪▪▪watch for developments▪▪▪▪▪▪.

As for▪▪▪▪▪▪plan to us▪▪▪▪same method▪▪▪▪▪▪recovered▪▪mp▪▪▪▪ shelter and protect the▪▪▪▪.

After reading that, Mira stood dumbfounded. There was a distant look in her eyes. She couldn't contain her surprise, not just at the contents but at the fact that they were written in Japanese.

Mira had studied this world's language so she could read and write in order to research spells. She occasionally ran into things that she couldn't read, but former players could also simply Inspect text to understand it.

All this world's writing, even in ancient ruins and documents, was in a common language. However, especially old materials used what was called "ancient writing." Nobody since had used it, and no amount of investigating it yielded meaning. Only some history nerds deciphered it as a hobby.

This world was full of history, and on this large a scale, Japanese was essentially a foreign language. Still, it existed here of all places, in sparse parts of the very end of the Ancient Underground City.

Could this sheet of paper be part of that mystery?

I feel as though I stumbled upon something incredible... What is this? A developer's diary? There must be meaning behind its existence... But there's simply too much that I don't understand.

Not only was the paper written in Japanese, it included the very word "Japan"—very evidently referring to modern Japan, at that. What did it mean for such a thing to be here? Mira repeated what she could read of it aloud, then asked the Spirit King and Martel if they understood.

"*What an interesting find,*" replied the Spirit King. "*Unfortunately, I have no idea what that is. This place existed long before I myself was born into this world. Even I don't know the details of what it was or why it was built. Delightful, isn't it?*"

Not even the Spirit King's wealth of knowledge broached this city's mysteries. That was why it so piqued his interest; he enjoyed finding things he knew nothing about.

Martel didn't know either. "*Sorry, honey. It's a mystery to me too. It might relate to something from before we were born.*" If the document had existed before then, exactly how old was this Ancient Underground City? Mysteries never ceased.

"Hrmm, I see," Mira replied. "Then I'll put this on hold and take it home to be investigated. But first..."

Perhaps Soul Howl would know something. He'd traveled all over the continent for the Holy Grail's sake, after all.

Mira realized it was taking him quite a while to return. "As I recall, he was searching for a Chalk Orb fragment here. Hrmm... maybe that takes time to retrieve."

Creating a Holy Grail required a piece from the Chalk Orb, an energy source that powered the entire Ancient Underground City. Soul Howl only needed a fragment... But, come to think of it, how did one obtain that?

Having finished collecting her spoils, Mira headed curiously toward the next chamber.

BEYOND THE BOSS CHAMBER was the Chalk Chamber, home to a crystal called the Chalk Orb. According to a lore-loving friend, that one item maintained all the Ancient Underground City's functions.

As Mira approached the chamber entrance, Soul Howl returned from inside.

"Oh ho!" exclaimed Mira. "You finally return. Took you an awfully long time just to recover a fragment."

When she greeted him that way, Soul Howl grimaced. He looked even more tired than he had after the battle. "You make it sound simple. I wish it were as easy as that."

He explained the process for obtaining a Chalk Orb fragment, sounding more like he was complaining than offering a genuine description. While it was straightforward, it required great concentration. First of all, Soul Howl explained, the Chalk Orb was made by scooping high-purity mana from ley lines and crystallizing it. That was essentially the very energy circulating through the world, so the Chalk Orb was harder than orichalcum.

When she heard "orichalcum," Mira was plainly surprised. "My word. It's that hard?" After all, orichalcum was an extremely rare item used in legendary-class gear. It was tough to find even on raid boss drop tables. Calling orichalcum "legendary" was no exaggeration.

"Human tools could probably never damage the thing." Soul Howl grinned at Mira, as if saying, *Get it now?*

One hot topic among players was just how hard orichalcum was. The fantasy setting didn't betray them. When they'd experimented by dropping a one-ton hunk of steel onto orichalcum wire from a high place, the wire won, cutting the steel clean in half. This game faithfully recreated the laws of physics, so the one-millimeter wire defeating an enormous, sturdy hunk of steel produced a legend worthy of the vaunted metal.

"So, how did you get the fragment?"

All players knew just how hard orichalcum was. If the Chalk Orb was even harder, getting even the smallest shaving would surely be impossible, let alone a fragment. Just how had Soul Howl obtained it?

"First, you need one of these." Soul Howl unsheathed a dagger hanging from his waist and showed it off.

Seeing the metal's reddish tint, Mira exclaimed, "And he whips out orichalcum!" Indeed, the dagger in Soul Howl's hand was made of the stuff. Its color—reminiscent of fire—was characteristic of simply forged orichalcum, though the metal's color varied based on how it was processed. "Okay. Then what?" she demanded. Based on the flow of the conversation, that couldn't have been all.

Complaining that this had been the hardest part, Soul Howl described the method for carving off a Chalk Orb fragment. It came down to mana. Since the Chalk Orb was solidified high-purity mana from ley lines, you could insert your own mana little by little, synchronize it, and temporarily decrease the orb's hardness. That alone didn't make it soft enough to carve, however, necessitating the orichalcum dagger.

"On top of releasing and adjusting mana, you're synchronizing simultaneously. That's what took longest." Soul Howl had been controlling his mana this whole time. The physical act of carving the fragment had only taken a second.

"I see. Sounds like a lot of work," Mira told him nonchalantly.

Soul Howl—who'd focused so hard, the fatigue was evident on his face—just shrugged to himself. Mira was always like this, after all.

"I'm surprised by how thorough you were, Elder," Soul Howl mused as he surveyed the scattered wreckage. When the necromancer left, the Machina Guardian had only been cut in half. Now it was so disassembled, its original shape was impossible to discern. Anyone could tell that Mira had put real care into salvaging its drops. "How was it? You made all this mess; did you find anything notable?"

He'd said he didn't want the loot, but he was still interested in the items. As a top player, that was natural, given the rarity of some of the raid boss's drops.

Mira knew exactly how he felt, so she answered smugly, "Anything? I found *everything*!" She showed off the most valuable drop of all—the Eye of Apollo.

"Wow. So that's the Eye of Apollo. It's bigger than I expected." Soul Howl approached, his fascination clear.

Mira hugged the crystal close protectively. "I don't care if you changed your mind," she insisted. "It's mine."

"I know, I know." Soul Howl lifted a piece of the wreckage and asked, "How much other stuff did you get? If I remember right, all this thing's drops were parts. That must mean you found them all, yeah?"

He'd picked up a mere piece of scrap metal, but the Machina Guardian was made of a metal superior to average iron or steel. If they took it all home, they could sell it for a nice sum. The fact that Mira had ignored all the scraps implied that she'd found things worth much more.

"Yes, a full set," Mira answered confidently.

"There was a Neuron Crystal in it? Can I have it?" Soul Howl asked.

"A Neuron Crystal? Why? Do you want to upgrade your equipment?" she demanded, looking him up and down again.

Soul Howl's outfit was more or less what one would expect—primarily focused on looking cool. Still, Mira knew what good gear looked like, so she could tell it was high-quality gear altered to suit Soul Howl's tastes. In fact, it was even stronger than the gear he'd worn back in Alcait. Neuron Crystals were powerful, yes—but surely not so much so as to justify an upgrade, so Mira was bemused.

Soul Howl's answer was a little surprising. "Upgrade... Yeah, I guess it'd be kind of like that. I didn't expect to unlock my advanced magic. Now that I have, I can update Irina's grave goods again. I planned to use the Neuron Crystal on her."

Irina was Soul Howl's trump card, summoned with [Necromantic Arts: Hadean Cycle]. The grave goods stored via Martyr's Coffin greatly bolstered her abilities. Unfortunately, Soul Howl had been forced to abandon updating the grave goods halfway, but the Neuron Crystal would help him complete them.

"I see. You want it for Irina." Mira certainly understood. Neuron Crystals were highly compatible with magic; one would surely bolster Irina's fighting power.

"Of course, it *is* yours. I'll pay you for it," Soul Howl said matter-of-factly. He began calculating. "How much are they these days? You don't see them on the market often, so I don't know the price. Back then, I think they were thirty million. So, given their rarity, supply, and demand..."

Even when top players had defeated the Machina Guardian weekly, Neuron Crystals had sold for thirty million ducats. The raid boss was now defeated far less often—perhaps this had even been the first time in the past thirty years. Since the crystals seldom made it onto the market, it was hard to gauge their modern price.

Soul Howl made a quick calculation based on the price he remembered. "Will three hundred million do? If the market price is higher, eh, I can pay the difference once I'm done with my work." He threw out the incredible sum casually, sounding like an aristocrat with no need of money. That reminded the frugal Mira of just how vastly different their wealth levels were.

"O-oh...three hundred million..." Her head spun. That would be a *massive* windfall. How much luxury could she enjoy with such a sum? She could stay in nice inns and eat as much delicious food as she liked. Feeling an odd déjà vu, she fantasized about what she'd do with the payment.

As she daydreamed, Soul Howl raised the offer further, taking her reaction as uncertainty. "If that's not enough, let's make it five hundred million. It'll be a few more months after I get back, though."

Mira's brain halted. Then the sheer ridiculousness of a two-hundred-million-ducat increase brought her back to reality. "Sure. Take it." She pulled a Neuron Crystal from her Item Box and shoved it violently at Soul Howl.

"Whoa. The deal's on? I can pay in cash or by check. Which do you want?" Soul Howl asked, still casually.

Mira puffed out her chest, resolving not to be bested. "I'm fine. You fought quite well in your own right, so consider it your cut of the loot." She didn't mention that she still had four more Neuron Crystals in her Item Box. Still, she'd hand over the loot he'd previously said he didn't want, offering it without expecting money in return.

"Man, you sure? Five hundred mil isn't a big deal for me. Don't you worry about my funds," Soul Howl said with overwhelming composure.

Mira held her ground. "I'm telling you, it's fine. Besides, bolstering your magic with the Neuron Crystal will help you finish your business faster, yeah? Come back sooner, and the peace of mind will be worth just as much to me."

It was true that the promise of five hundred million ducats had seduced Mira, but she was being genuine. Announcing the Nine Wise Men's return and building a military would be much easier if he returned sooner.

"...Yeah, you're right. If Irina can fight at full power, I can accelerate my plans. Two, three months at most, if all goes well," Soul Howl muttered to himself, then added, "In that case, I graciously accept." He placed the Neuron Crystal in his Item Box.

THE LOOT NEGOTIATIONS distracted Mira somewhat, but once she calmed down, she brought up something that had been on her mind.

"By the way, Soul Howl, this was among the loot. What do you make of it?" she asked, revealing the most incomprehensible item. She didn't know whether the page was from someone's diary or some kind of report, but its contents were very intriguing.

Soul Howl naturally knew that there were no paper drops on the Machina Guardian's loot table, so his interest was piqued. "Hm? What's that?" He pulled Mira's arm, reading over the page eagerly.

Plan▪▪arth, Japan Branch▪▪▪▪▪year▪62 CE▪▪▪▪.

As planned▪▪▪▪sea coordinat▪▪▪▪at this point▪▪▪▪▪▪underground▪ ▪▪▪▪▪begun unified▪▪▪▪▪▪▪▪planned compl▪▪▪▪▪▪rth time▪▪▪▪▪.

However▪▪▪▪▪▪observed on surface▪▪▪▪▪▪▪▪req▪▪re more time.

After the facility is complete▪▪▪▪will begin. If all▪▪▪▪well▪▪▪▪▪▪ truly▪▪▪▪▪▪▪▪▪▪pray for▪▪▪▪▪prepare▪▪▪▪second.

At this ti▪▪▪▪▪▪no need to▪▪▪▪▪▪▪▪▪▪as such▪▪▪▪peers▪▪▪▪▪▪watch for developments▪▪▪▪▪▪.

As for▪▪▪▪▪▪plan to us▪▪▪▪same method▪▪▪▪▪▪▪recovered▪▪mp▪▪▪▪ shelter and protect the▪▪▪▪.

He read over it once, then once more. After the third read, he finally let go of Mira's arm and thought deeply about the page.

"The first part looks like 'Planet Earth,' right? Planet Earth's 'Japan Branch.' If so, that has to mean something. I mean, why would you bother to put 'Planet Earth' if you already said something's in Japan? That has to imply that you can be somewhere *other* than Earth. Then there's a year and the abbreviation 'CE,' which implies a year measured in the Gregorian calendar. It's listing some date in a year we can't fully read. That's my limited analysis of it."

After a moment of thought, Soul Howl pointed out the first line to Mira again, now with some characters appended. Frankly, he couldn't be certain of those characters. If he was correct, though, a greater mystery emerged.

"I see..." said Mira. "That *is* one potential reading. Either way, the writer seemingly came from our old world."

"There's a lot of stuff we don't know yet, but it's clearly connected," Soul Howl agreed. It was unclear when, where, or why the page had been written, but as he'd said, the contents implied that the writer knew about Japan on the planet Earth. He and Mira agreed on that. "Did you ask the Spirit King and Martel?"

"I did, but they haven't the foggiest either. Apparently, this Ancient Underground City predates even them."

"*Whoa.* It's been here that long...?"

The history of spirits was incomprehensibly lengthy—humanity's paled in comparison. Yet the man-made Ancient Underground City was somehow older. An odd contradiction indeed.

"If it did exist then, there must have been a reason for that..."

"Right. There must've been." It was contradictory, but the Ancient Underground City's existence was proof that that was unquestionably true—even if they couldn't comprehend why yet.

Since they had no information to unravel the mystery of why the Ancient Underground City was older than the Spirit King, however, Soul Howl flatly declared, "Well, it's not worth thinking about now."

He turned his mind to the next line on the page—which might just get surprisingly close to the reason.

"Let's keep going. Based on the next sentence, it seems like this guy's researching something. 'After the facility is complete'— then we have 'begin,' 'prepare,' and 'second.' It seems like whoever wrote this was building a facility to research something underground. I think this might just be that facility. I mean, look at this seventh level; it's totally unlike the rest of the dungeon. It's not fantasy, it's sci-fi."

Soul Howl looked around. As he said, the place where they'd fought the Machina Guardian was covered in sturdy white metallic plates. And the passages leading here were more like those in a research facility than a dungeon or ruins.

"Sci-fi, hm? I suppose. The boss certainly fit that description. Mysteries never cease here, do they?"

This world had history. Since it was built for a video game, that history might be made-up; still, it supported the present so well, it seemed no different from reality. That was the odd part. If this was sci-fi mixed with fantasy, what *was* this Ancient Underground City that predated the Spirit King himself?

"See how it mentions '—rth time'? If you read that as 'Earth time,' it seems connected to the first sentence," Soul Howl noted.

"Hrmm. In that it suggests someplace *other* than Earth?"

If there was nothing relevant to compare "Earth time" to, one would just write "time." But if Soul Howl's reading was correct, the paper went out of its way to specify "Earth." In other words, it must've been possible to refer to some other time zone.

"As for the last sentence, you got me. It probably relates to the research, but I have no idea what they wrote. The end does make me curious, though. 'Shelter and protect.' What were they sheltering and protecting, exactly?" The part toward the end was halfway readable, but not particularly specific, so Soul Howl had given up. However, the last few words stuck in his mind.

"That does make me wonder too," Mira agreed. "If it meant a group of people, I'd assume it was residents of the city's first to sixth levels."

If the Ancient Underground City had originally been built starting from the seventh level, it could be considered a playground constructed by the builder of the facility. They might've been protecting those people, although it wasn't yet clear why.

"Yeah, that's possible too. But what were they planning, and why? It feels like the answer is getting closer and farther at the same time."

They'd tried deciphering the page, but they didn't know the most important part: the writer's motive. In the end, it was only one page, and even that was missing too many words.

"Well, I suppose it's a mistake to try to derive truth from such limited information." Mira shrugged. Deciding that further thought would just be a tiring waste of time, she deposited the scrap of paper in her Item Box and said her usual line: "I'll have to leave it with Solomon." Her style was simple: when she didn't understand something, she just left it with him.

"True. I hear the Hinomoto Committee is trying to figure out the truth of the world under his leadership. Get that page to them, and I bet they'll love you." Already losing interest in the scrap of paper, Soul Howl agreed with Mira's assessment. He wasn't entirely like her; rather than being lazy, he just believed in giving jobs to the right people.

"Ah, yes. I believe I heard something like that. In that case, that paper would be perfect for them."

There were several departments under the Hinomoto Committee's jurisdiction. One was the World History Research Institute, which had formed to uncover the history of this world. Mira had a faint recollection of hearing about that from Solomon once. This slip of paper seemed like an important historical item. She grinned slightly; she couldn't wait to see what a shock it gave him.

"I'm surprised you know about the Hinomoto Committee," she added. "Wasn't it so secret that only heads of state know about it? Where did a wanderer like you come into such knowledge?"

Despite how openly the pair discussed the committee, it was a secret organization, created by former players who'd risen to heads of state. Information on the committee was top secret, and even former players shouldn't have been able to learn about it easily.

Luminaria had told Mira about it, but the main reason she was allowed to know was probably because she was close to Solomon, a committee member. Where would Soul Howl have heard about it when he was busy working toward a Holy Grail? Mira had asked out of pure curiosity.

"Oh, Smithy told me."

When Mira heard the name come out of Soul Howl's mouth, she piped up in surprise, piling on questions. "Smithy? You mean the blacksmith? You two knew each other?"

Smithy was a top player who spent their time as a blacksmith. They mainly produced metal weapons and gear. Any warrior would drool over a Smithy-forged weapon.

However, as a mage who fought without a weapon and was uninterested in metal armor, Mira had only exchanged a few words with Smithy when the latter happened to be with Solomon. Moreover, most of the Nine Wise Men presumably had nothing to do with Smithy, beyond knowing the blacksmith as Solomon's friend. Yet it seemed Soul Howl had met them here in this world.

"Yep, that's the one. We weren't well acquainted back then, but we got to know each other while I was figuring out Irina's grave goods. That's when I heard about the Hinomoto Committee," Soul Howl explained.

Perhaps because this related to his beloved Irina, he suddenly became a lot more talkative. Once upon a time, back before he'd ever considered making a Holy Grail, he had a phase when he was obsessed with upgrading Irina's grave goods. Thanks to his tireless efforts, that process went well, and he was able to start giving her high-quality equipment as a result. However, as he repeated the process, he began running out of weapons worthy of her rank. He'd ranked her up to the point that gear made by a reasonably famous blacksmith and with reasonably rare materials wouldn't be enough, so he was forced to search for a greater smith.

He sought out Smithy, the *greatest* blacksmith, despite not knowing whether Smithy was in this world—let alone *when* they'd been brought to it. However, Soul Howl's search was surprisingly short. Since he knew which country Smithy had allegiance to, it was easy to find them. At that point, he learned Smithy had retired from making weapons, so it was especially difficult to convince them to create some.

"Smithy retired from blacksmithing and now directs the Hinomoto Committee's Modern Technology Research Institute. That's how I learned a little about the committee."

"I see. That's the connection." Mira was finally aware of Soul Howl's source.

Smithy might not have been a head of state, but as a top player, they naturally had a high status.

Adequately convinced, Mira transferred her interest to the laboratory. "By the way, what does this 'Modern Technology Research Institute' look into?" It made sense for her to be curious; after all, the institute was led by a player whose name was known to all other players.

Soul Howl simply answered that the Modern Technology Research Institute researched whether they could replicate Earth's modern technology in this world.

"They lump it all under the umbrella term 'modern technology,' but they research things like engineering, shipbuilding, architecture, medicine, agriculture, even space travel—dozens of fields. They're the largest-scale operation under the Hinomoto Committee. The continent-spanning railroads and airships up in the sky are the results of their research. They've got great personnel too. Around half the players known for production are in their ranks."

Soul Howl wrapped up the explanation by adding that he'd visit the institute soon to have the game's best jeweler, Tiphanus, craft something using his Neuron Crystal. Under the Hinomoto Committee, he noted, the Modern Technology Research Institute had countless top-class crafter players at its disposal.

Hearing that, Mira exclaimed happily, "Oh ho! What a delightful place it must be!" Her reason for rejoicing was the same as Soul Howl's: having the Machina Guardian's drops was great and all, but those were essentially top-tier materials, so the number of crafters who could handle them was very limited. Although she had the ingredients, she hadn't known what to do with them until now. With this revelation, she had her answer.

"So? Where can I find them? I happen to have just come across a few materials, so I'd love to know!" The laboratory was now her holy land; she begged Soul Howl to tell her just where it was.

Quick on the uptake, Soul Howl replied, "You know, now that you mention it, the average crafter couldn't hope to handle a Neuron Crystal, Clear Materite Alloy, or Ethemite—let alone that Eye of Apollo you got. Everyone tells me the institute's location is secret, though." After a moment, he finally added, "Well, I'm sure they'd make an exception for you, Elder."

First, he explained that most of the Hinomoto Committee's research facilities were located in player-governed territory; the rest were generally hidden carefully all over the continent. The former were mostly for academic research, while the latter were mostly for technological research.

The Modern Technology Research Institute fit among the latter. It was well hidden on an island between the Ark and Earth continents and north of Cadiasmight Isle, surrounded by steep mountains.

"They certainly built it in a...precarious location," Mira chuckled.

North of Cadiasmight Isle was a mountainous region reaching up to eight thousand meters, with a number of peaks exceeding six thousand meters. Building a laboratory there was hardly convenient.

SHE PROFESSED HERSELF PUPIL OF THE WISE MAN

When Mira commented to this effect, Soul Howl answered that they had no choice. "They still have a lot of things in the prototype and research stages, but they're all way too advanced compared to this world's level of technology. More advanced technology and greater power just lead to war. What they want isn't war, but a better life. They'd be happy to help fight monsters, but everyone knows what else that could lead to. Smithy says that's why they built the institute in a natural fortress."

Technology made to fight monsters could be turned against people, depending on the user. Even things not made for battle could be misused to hurt others. These pacifists at heart feared that, and hid themselves from human eyes, but continued to conduct research to improve the world. A laudable stance indeed.

"Hrmm. I see. Then it's a suitable location after all."

In a mountainous area surrounded by steep slopes, nigh impossible to simply wander into, the laboratory wouldn't be found by mere chance. However, that made it difficult to visit. Anxiety found its way onto Mira's face.

"I heard Smithy got tired of invitations from warmongering nations and fled to the laboratory. When I went there, Smithy was obstinate about never forging tools for war again. That made things hard for me..." Soul Howl recalled it with a sigh. Then, with an exasperated grin, he added, "I get it, though. That's what happens when something you love is used to hurt others."

He added that many others had gone to the institute for much the same reason.

"The crafter's life is a difficult one," Mira agreed. She only seemed to half understand, and quickly brought the conversation back on track. "So, what is the laboratory's precise location? I'd rather not spend my life searching the whole area."

Having once seen the island with her own eyes, she pulled out the big map of the continent she'd recently bought and looked for it.

Listening to Soul Howl's directions, she drew right on the map with a pen. She listened especially intently to the landmarks he mentioned to make her search easier. "Oh ho ho! I see..."

"...You'd better not show anyone that map, got it?" Soul Howl reminded her as he gazed at the map, which was open with what were essentially national secrets written brazenly on it.

"I know, I know!" Mira replied, as if it were a given. Then, apparently just in case, she wrote *Top secret!* on the top-right of the map.

"Oh, Elder..." Soul Howl muttered, sighing.

She
Professed
Herself
Pupil of the
Wise Man

20

"**Y**OU KNOW, they're laudable people. This is a world full of fantasy and wonder, and they stay inside to work for the betterment of society," Mira murmured in admiration as she stared at the laboratory's location on the map. This world contained quite a few hazards, but its wonders far outweighed them. As someone who'd learned that through many adventures, Mira had to admire the goodwill of those who would miss those wonders for the sake of the greater good.

Fortunately, her sympathy on their behalf turned out to be unneeded.

"I don't think it's that deep," Soul Howl replied. "They just prefer research to adventure. I mean, that's why they ended up famous top-class crafters, right? They might enjoy it even more than you do adventuring."

If you saw the laboratory workers as people who'd gone into hiding to avoid being used for war, you might pity them. But according to someone who'd actually visited them, it was hardly that tragic.

"Some did it just because they wanted to live in their old environment," Soul Howl continued. "They made a prototype AC powered by magic stones. Some are researching TVs and video cameras, just because they want to see what TV shows made in a fantasy world would be like."

Modern Japan had myriad accommodations and environments, and according to Soul Howl, an awful lot of people lived to see those again in this world.

"AC and TV, hm? The two essentials for daily life," Mira replied, laughing that those were fine goals. She'd always wondered how a certain favorite TV show of hers would end.

"By the way, Elder, are you sure you don't want to pick this up?"

"Hm? Pick what up?"

Soul Howl pointed at the Machina Guardian's wreckage, but Mira had already stripped its main drops. She cocked her head in confusion.

"Oh, I get it," Soul Howl muttered. "I meant the corpse itself. That metal's way harder than average, and the only thing lighter is mithril. Look how much there is. I figure it's a waste to leave all that. Seems useful as material to me." He picked up a piece of scrap metal at his feet, examined it, and tossed it at Mira.

She caught the debris scrap and gazed at it for a moment. "You know, I think you're right!" she exclaimed, as if the scales had fallen from her eyes, and surveyed the wreckage. "Silly me. I was too distracted by the Eye of Apollo..."

Perhaps because her instincts from long ago remained, or perhaps because she'd obtained the Eye of Apollo for the first time, Mira had totally excluded things *not* on the Machina Guardian's drop list from her search. Metal couldn't be taken as material way back when, but now, it was possible to recycle all the metal composing the Machina Guardian's body.

"This might make a good souvenir for Solomon!"

When it came to military goods and the like, no country could possibly suffer from having too much metal. It even had uses beyond simple weapons and armor, such as in the Accord Cannon and other technomancy-powered arms Solomon had shown off.

One after another, Mira stuffed the Machina Guardian's plating, parts, and more into her Item Box. Some items were too large to place inside, so she had a dark knight wielding Sanctia cut larger scraps of metal into the perfect size. The metal wasn't included in the drop table, so they still didn't know what kind it was. Identifying it would be the first step toward using it.

Although they couldn't use it right away, it was still a lot of metal. No doubt Solomon would find a good use for it, Mira thought, gathering every last bit. Running a country required lots of metal.

Soul Howl must've thought it would be a good gift for Solomon too. "Guess I'll help you sort it out."

He began helping her pick it all up, but his legs didn't take him toward the Machina Guardian's remains; instead, he headed to the Mechanized Protectors' carcasses. Those were fine hunks of metal as well.

"Seems useable to me," he muttered after checking their condition, then made golems to haul the Protectors to Mira. There were dozens, but Soul Howl's golems made quick work of them.

"Goodness, this is a lot..." Gazing at the growing pile of Protector corpses, Mira worked even harder to recover the metal.

After some time, they finished collecting the corpses, including that of the Mechanized Wanderer they'd defeated along the way.

"Thanks, Soul Howl. I can just imagine Solomon's shock!"

Collecting many tons of metal had been backbreaking work, but when it was all done, Mira was delighted. Frugal as she was, she was happy to recover the metal she'd almost wasted.

"Took longer than I thought..." said poor Soul Howl, who'd naively offered to help. An hour had passed before they knew it. "That's another item checked off the list... Elder, you said you had something else to do?"

Their surprisingly difficult labor had ended, and Soul Howl had obtained a Chalk Orb fragment. Mira gazed at him. They had both accomplished their goals in the Ancient Underground City, but she'd found a new goal along the way.

"Indeed. I plan to find a way to go deeper."

Mira hadn't told Soul Howl many details about Fenrir during the strategy meeting before their big battle, instead focusing on the coming fight. Now that things had settled, she divulged more: the reason Fenrir was in this Ancient Underground City, why he was sealed by Martel's power, and the mystery held deep within. After explaining those details one after another, Mira told Soul Howl that her next goal was to find what had corrupted Fenrir and driven him to insanity—and, if possible, deal with it once and for all.

"Close to the power of gods, huh?" Soul Howl said as he gazed at the ground below him searchingly. "I don't know anything about it." He shrugged, smirking. "Sounds interesting. I'll help you find it."

He'd offered to help simply because it interested him. In truth, the prospect of greater mysteries sleeping beneath the already mysterious underground city fascinated him.

But Mira felt he'd offered half out of worry for Fenrir. Soul Howl was the kind of person who couldn't let something go once he was involved. After all, he'd gone so far for a woman he hated.

She feigned ignorance. "Ooh, really? Much appreciated. I gladly accept your help, then."

This far-too-vast dungeon indeed hid even more secrets below. To investigate the secrets revealed during Mira's meeting with Fenrir, she and Soul Howl set about a renewed search of the seventh level.

Finding a mysterious area previously unknown to them proved difficult in such a large zone. After searching the whole seventh level for a day, Mira summoned the mansion spirit, in which they made plans for the next day's search.

"If only we knew what the entrance was like..."

"For real. Going without any hints is rough."

The seventh level was noticeably unlike the rest of the dungeon. The corridors were all metal, and the walls and ceiling were painted white, with embedded lights that illuminated them to this day. You also needed a key card for many of the doors, which opened and closed automatically.

It was a total science fiction aesthetic. The only fantasy aspect was the skeletons that spawned—which weren't a threat at all now that the apex necromancer Soul Howl was with Mira.

The duo spent the next day scouring the environment as well. Since a day had passed, new skeletons spawned here and there, but Soul Howl kept them away without issue. That second day ended without them finding any particular clues, but on the third morning, they realized something.

Once they'd finished morning preparations and left the mansion to begin the day's search, Soul Howl said, "Now that I think about it, this chamber is weird. Why is this the only place skeletons don't spawn?"

Skeleton spawn points were all over this level, even in the Machina Guardian's boss chamber. The entire seventh floor was essentially a skeleton spawn spot. The only place they didn't appear was the Great Temple. Yet skeletons didn't spawn in this otherwise normal chamber. That was rather strange when one thought about it.

"Hrmm... Now that you mention it, it is odd."

At a glance, the chamber was the same as anywhere else in the level. Knowing the circumstances, one had to be suspicious. Could it contain secrets?

Now in agreement, Mira and Soul Howl quickly split up and began searching the chamber. However, it was the second-biggest room on this floor after the Machina Guardian's boss chamber. Seeking an entrance they didn't know the form of was arduous labor.

The room contained white walls, a white ceiling, a gray floor, and nothing else. It would be easy to tell if there were discrepancies, but after an hour of searching, they found nothing of the sort. The whole room's construction was uniform, with not so much as an opening or a keyhole.

That caused one possibility to cross Mira's mind. She'd just recently encountered something quite similar, in fact.

"Could it be...? What if it's here too?" Mira examined the room's walls again, this time making sure to feel them with her hands.

Twenty minutes after she began her renewed investigation, she heard the Spirit King's excited voice. *"Miss Mira, there!"*

The possibility she had hit upon was a divine mineral wall—like what she'd found when searching for Martel—and her hypothesis was right on the mark.

Quickly finding the difference in the wall, the Spirit King added, *"Now, let's investigate it."*

While he analyzed the wall, Mira called, "Soul Howl, this way! This wall over here!"

"Huh? You find something?" Soul Howl looked up from his concentrated wall-poking, ran over, and looked at the wall Mira was touching. "Uh, what about it? I don't see anything special."

His confusion was obvious. The color and texture were the same as the other walls, and he didn't see hidden switches or anything.

"Go on, Spirit King," Mira said, smugly watching for Soul Howl's reaction. He was sure to be surprised if the wall suddenly disappeared.

However, things didn't go as planned. Rather than seeing the divine mineral wall open up, Mira next heard the Spirit King's surprised voice. *"This is surprising. The composition differs from the mineral on the way to Martel's home."*

According to him, the wall Mira was touching was different from the last one—in other words, from the divine mineral made by the Trinity's power.

"What...?"

Something other than the Trinity had created this wall. Last time, Mira had been surprised by the Trinity's involvement, but she was even more amazed now that something else was involved. The city's mysteries grew ever deeper.

While Mira stood there stunned, Soul Howl stared at the wall and sighed, "Uh... So, what do we do, Elder? Just wait?"

According to the Spirit King, though the Trinity hadn't created this divine mineral wall, its foundation was the same. Once he analyzed it, he'd get through it just fine.

"Hrmm... Well, you see..." Mira had missed the ideal timing for surprising her friend. Now they *did* have to wait, since it would take the Spirit King five or six minutes to analyze the divine mineral. That forced Mira to spill the beans.

Before long, the Spirit King finished his analysis, and the divine mineral door opened.

Seeing that, Soul Howl muttered in admiration, "Ooh, that's how they hide it? Incredible. Now, what's behind the door?"

He stepped inside, and Mira silently followed. Behind the door, a long, long staircase extended far below. It occasionally turned 180 degrees, but always continued downward.

It was all black, with only white handrails, and was plainly no ordinary staircase. It even had perfectly divided upstairs and downstairs paths. It almost looked like it'd turn into an escalator if someone just found the button to turn it on.

The now-motionless stairs continued down one, no, two hundred meters, until Mira and Soul Howl finally reached the bottom.

"It's...a door," Mira said.

"Yeah. Looks high-tech. But it's a door, no doubt."

The airtight door in the metal wall looked like it might have been used in a nuclear bomb shelter. It was made of thick, heavy metal, and was closed tight to keep inside and outside well separated.

"Okay. How do we open it?" Soul Howl asked.

Though dusty and old, the door still did its job well. No amount of pushing or pulling budged it.

"Another difficult riddle even now, hm?" Mira mused.

She and Soul Howl started brushing away the dust. When they did, they saw a few phrases:

CURRENTLY IN LOCKDOWN.

RESEARCH BUILDING MANAGER AND DIRECTOR:

ISURUGI TOUKO

SECURITY LEVEL: 5

Moreover, all the text was in Japanese again.

"Hrmm. 'Isurugi Touko'... This place seems connected to the real world, doesn't it?"

"Yeah. It felt like that before we came here too."

Beyond the door, there might be more to help the diary tie this world to modern Japan. They felt especially sure of that when they saw the director's Japanese name.

The existence of Japanese in this world had been a mystery since the beginning, but now wasn't the time to focus on that. The pair kept their attention on the security level the door displayed. That was something they'd seen on the seventh level.

"Anyway, what do you make of this?" Mira asked her companion.

"Let's try it and find out," he replied, wasting no time.

He took out a single card—one of the authentication keys you could obtain on the seventh level. They were necessary to get through secure areas, so Mira naturally had one as well, though getting one took time and effort.

Soul Howl put the authentication key on the panel as a test. In no time, there was a response. After a beep, the panel glowed slightly, and the color changed from red to green.

Instantly, the door made a loud noise. A few more seconds later...

"Ooh...it opened!"

"You never know if you don't try."

Seemingly an extension of the seventh level, this door used the same security as those above. Fully unlocked, the door slowly yet surely began to open.

"Now...what hides within?" Soul Howl immediately stepped forth. Air they'd never felt before flowed behind the door. It was as crisp as a forest in winter, but also stale and artificial, like someone's home.

"You ought to be a little more cautious," Mira warned the necromancer, who'd stepped in without hesitation despite not knowing what was within. But curiosity spurred her to follow anyway.

Behind the door, yet another staircase led downward. How far down did it go, exactly? They continued to descend, still wishing they could find a button to turn the stairs into an escalator.

The walls were metal until now, but eventually, a different scene unfolded.

"Goodness, this is... Well, it fits the description 'secret research facility,'" Mira murmured.

The seventh level and the path leading here had already been science fiction chic, but the research building itself went so far beyond those that they seemed primitive. The walls and ceiling ahead were made of a transparent material, giving them a view of the space beyond. It was like a research institute right out of a sci-fi flick.

A cylindrical hole went straight down, seemingly hundreds of meters—perhaps even a kilometer—deep. Everything within its circumference was some kind of facility. All the inner walls were transparent, and the lighting still worked, making the view from the stairs spectacular.

The stairs extended to a pillar in the center of the cylindrical hole. As Soul Howl and Mira reached the floor above it, they gave their frank impressions.

"Man...it looks like our tower ten thousand years in the future."

"I...see the similarity."

It was constructed just like the Linked Silver Towers. Mira and Soul Howl knew what the modern world was like, so they quickly understood what the central pillar was—an elevator. The place they'd reached was an elevator bay.

The space inside the pillar seemed about fifty meters in diameter. They could see remnants of rest areas and even shops here and there. Passages also extended from the elevator bay to the circle around it. From the top floor, they saw countless passages below. It seemed people had used this elevator to traverse the facility long ago.

"Still, it's bigger than I expected. Searching this facility seems like backbreaking work..." They'd come to ascertain the mysterious force that had corrupted Fenrir, but the area's size made Mira hesitate.

"Agreed. It looks harder to search than the whole seventh level. I guess that goes to show how much they were researching." A quick look confirmed that this research building's total area *was* greater than the seventh level's. Their first order of business, Soul Howl added, was to figure out *what* had been researched here.

"Indeed. Even if we found that a research project here caused Fenrir's corruption, that'll mean nothing until we know exactly which project." They still didn't know whether there was a causal relationship between those things, but based on what they saw here, that seemed likely.

"Ridiculous..."

"Ridiculous, indeed..."

Surveying the facility from the elevator bay, Soul Howl and Mira shuddered at the difficulty of the task before them.

But if they never started, they would never be done. What was hidden in this research building? What research had been performed there? They decided to split up and investigate the facility in halves: one the top half, and one the bottom half.

Mira, in charge of the latter, tried pressing the button to summon the elevator. When it began to move, she was delighted. "Ooh, this still works too. How useful."

Meanwhile, Soul Howl looked uneasy. "Are you sure that's safe? There's no way it's been maintained." His caution was realistic and reasonable. The elevator hadn't undergone maintenance in hundreds, perhaps thousands of years. Common sense dictated that it shouldn't even work anymore.

"Oh, I'm sure it's fine. The stuff on the seventh level worked adequately. One or two elevators can't be that bad." Though it shouldn't have worked, it had, so Mira optimistically assumed things would be okay.

The elevator arrived, and the door opened. After Soul Howl checked inside it, his unease turned to relief. "Ooh, it's the electromagnetic-rail kind. Yeah, I guess this should be fine," he said. "See you in three hours, then." He turned to the passage that led to the encircling research building.

"Worrywart," said Mira. Soul Howl hadn't changed in that regard.

Watching him as he left, she entered the elevator and pushed the B100F button. The elevator interior was so clean, one had to wonder if it had *really* been sealed for hundreds to thousands of years.

"Hrmm... Yes, I think this will work just fine."

The electromagnetic-rail elevator descended quietly, without making any concerning noises. It used linear motor technology, so no wire was attached to the ceiling for it to hang from. Therefore, even if the elevator broke and began to fall along the way, Mira could simply use Air Step to escape danger. Soul Howl had seen that, which was exactly why he finally let her use it.

After a quiet, minute-long elevator ride, Mira arrived at the one hundredth underground floor.

She
Professed
Herself
Pupil of the
Wise Man

SURPRISINGLY, the hundredth floor—the facility's bottom level—wasn't dark and dreary; it was pretty much the same as the floors above. All the fixtures and equipment still worked fine, and it was full of artificial light.

However, there were differences. Perhaps because this was the very bottom floor, it wasn't just a cylinder; the space was part of the facility. There was a floor around the elevator, as well as a transparent ceiling.

"Goodness. Just looking up gives you a totally different impression." Doing so, Mira saw the cylindrical space with facilities lining the outer walls. Compared to looking down from above, it had a very different impact that added to the sci-fi vibe.

How many researchers had worked here? Looking around the elevator bay, Mira imagined seeing it bustling with activity. The remnants of shops and rest areas remained here too. As she gazed up at them, she wondered how to begin her investigation. Then, what she was looking for happened to catch her eye.

"Ooh. I thought there might be one of these, and there is!" It was a facility map. In such a huge space, researchers were sure to get lost at points, necessitating these maps in the central elevator bays. "Oh ho ho! And what a simple structure."

Despite its size, the hundredth underground floor had a simple design split neatly into zones. There were even details like FIRST LAB, DIRECTOR'S OFFICE, and STORAGE written on the map, giving Mira clear goals regarding where to investigate.

Hrmm... This place must *be connected to modern Earth.* As she gazed at the map, Mira became even more certain of that, for the words written on it were all in Japanese. Traces of Japanese influence existed all over the research facility hidden beneath the Ancient Underground City.

What was this place? Why had it been built, and why had it been abandoned? Most of all, what kind of people had lived here?

Wondering about those questions, Mira surveyed her surroundings again. It was clear that research of some kind had gone on here. Soul Howl was probably right that the Ancient Underground City above was some type of playground created in the course of that research. That sounded very sci-fi indeed.

"This place might have greater implications than we ever imagined..."

Though Mira sensed that she was approaching a mystery of this world, she did her best to shake the thought out of her mind. This wasn't her field of expertise; moreover, her priority was to find the cause of Fenrir's corruption so he could leave again.

"All right. This way, then." She could simply report this find to Solomon and leave the world's mysteries to the experts. Checking the map once more, Mira began walking toward the room labeled DIRECTOR'S OFFICE.

"It's...inexplicably eerie..."

The state of this research facility was suspicious, including the fact that the elevator still worked. One would expect it to be quite old, but it was still perfectly intact.

There wasn't much damage to be seen, although the transparent ceiling had gathered some dust, making the glass look foggy. But nothing was broken, and there was suspiciously little degradation.

There was also something indescribable about the corridors. They had little to no dust, but odd black, fist-sized blobs were stuck to the walls and the ceiling here and there. Chairs, flowerpots, carts, and the like also lay on the ground, broken or otherwise damaged.

Furthermore, there were claw marks on the walls, ceilings, handrails, and lights, seemingly caused by a stray animal. In some places, there was greater damage, but the facility lights shone brightly on all that. The place was ruined and decrepit, yet still functioning.

Mira proceeded carefully, worried that security systems might still be running, as they had been on the seventh level. Without much incident, she arrived at a door labeled DIRECTOR'S OFFICE.

A nameplate beside the door read ISURUGI TOUKO. That same name had been on the airtight door leading in here. In other words, this was the office of the most important person in the research facility.

"What information lies in here?"

There was a reason Mira came here first: a big shot's office was sure to have materials on the research being conducted here. Locating that would be faster than searching haphazardly. Mira complimented herself on her quick thinking and put her authentication key on the door scanner.

It beeped, but shortly after, the scanner light turned red and buzzed.

"What...?" Mira tried again—after all, it had worked above—but that led to the same result. No matter what she tried, the door wouldn't unlock. "How dare you...?! I never..."

On closer inspection, there were words on the scanner. When Mira read them, the reason the key wasn't working became clear. To her shock, she needed a security-level-*eight* key to open the door. Her and Soul Howl's keys were only level five. At this rate, she'd never get into the director's office.

This had cruelly dashed Mira's plan to easily obtain the information she desired.

"I wonder if it's just lying around somewhere unexpected..."

She couldn't simply destroy the door when she didn't know whether there was a security system, so she abandoned it and searched the places she could. She hoped that, if all went well, she'd find a high-level key lying somewhere.

After an hour of walking around the hundredth floor, it became clear how secure it was. She wasn't sure whether it was just this floor or the whole facility, but every laboratory she tried required at least security level seven.

Therefore, Mira had yet to find useful information. There *were* rooms she could enter with her current key, but they were all places like break rooms, rec rooms, and showers.

"Hrmm... If only some lazy fool left out their notes or something..."

So Mira hoped, but she found nothing of the sort in any location she was able to search; the personnel had seemingly handled research-related information quite diligently. Anything she found was simply a note unrelated to research. The notes' contents were varied indeed. One mentioned borrowing a book called *Good Morning Sunshine*; another asked where someone put the prism analyzer.

Others were typical messages:

Meeting @ 8:00 today.

Make sure you clean up after Love goes potty, please...

Celebrate! Curry tonight!

You need to shower more.

The notes had been left in different rooms, on the floor, and so on. Mira read them all and realized something.

"This was surprisingly...analog communication."

From the equipment used in the labs, it was clear their society had developed Internet-like technology. They could've sent such messages easily using handheld devices, surely. Instead, they'd left real paper notes.

Although Mira wondered why, she felt an odd warmth in the notes left here and there. They were all simply personal messages. They didn't lead to the information she needed, but they gave glimpses of daily life on a human scale, which made them fun to read.

As she continued to look at the vestiges of these past lives, she noticed a difference between the men's and women's messages.

"Hrmm. A woman wrote this one."

The specific difference was the use of envelopes. The notes seemingly written by women were in varied envelopes. They were worn out from age but had probably been much cuter long ago. There was a wealth of shapes and designs. Among them were extremely uninteresting notes no doubt sent just for the sake of using those envelopes.

The staff had sent a few business communications through notes as well. Mira thought they *really* ought just to have emailed such things, but she found a note in a locker room that very gently informed someone that they owed a fine.

It was a simple document, but it bore the signature of Director Isurugi Touko. Apparently, the fine was for a lost item. What in the world had the recipient lost? Mira couldn't help being a little curious about this person named Fuwa Mariko.

Glimpsing life in the past through the notes, Mira continued down the corridor in search of another room she could enter.

As she continued through the undistinguishable hallway, she heard a distinct noise. "Hm? What's that? There shouldn't be anyone here but me and him..."

Confused, Mira hurriedly used Biometric Scan to search her surroundings. No response.

One might assume the security system had gone off for some reason, but if it was the same system as above, an alarm would still be sounding. Yet the place was silent, apart from the previous sound.

Undead monsters were another possibility, but it was hard to imagine them here. This place didn't have the atmosphere of one where monsters appeared. Those places had a particular aura that Mira had learned to sense after much training.

Shuddering at the eeriness of the noise, she sought its source. "Hrmm...here, perhaps? I feel like it came from this direction." Returning to the entrance of a lab she'd passed about ten steps back, she approached the door warily. She couldn't open it; it had high security. However, it also had a small window that let her peek through.

The lab lights seemed to be broken. It was dim inside, with only a small emergency lamp on.

"I can't see well..." She strained her eyes but only saw dark silhouettes with no detail.

The mysterious sound in the lab had piqued the Spirit King's interest; he could no longer just be a spectator. Pointing out a suspicious figure, he urged Mira to look. *"Miss Mira, what's that to the left?"* However, she only saw a bunch of tools for experiments lying around—hardly worth his excitement.

Martel was fascinated as well. *"There! There, Mira. That's suspicious!"* she squealed at the machinery in the dim room. In fact, there *was* what looked like a medical table with a monster lying on it.

However, it only looked like that. It was just equipment, rather than a monster.

"I'm not seeing anything special..." The size of the window limited Mira's range of vision. By changing her angle, she got a decent view, but still saw nothing notable.

Perhaps they just imagined it? she wondered. "Hm?!"

"Oh!"

"Goodness me!"

It looked as if something had moved behind the table in the middle of the dim room. Mira had jumped in surprise; it happened right when she let her guard down. She feigned calm and focused on the movement's location.

As far as she could see, there wasn't movement anymore. She double-checked with Biometric Scan; yet again, there was no response.

"Well, you know how it is," she mused. "I suppose a Wanderer or two is left down here."

The seventh level did contain robotic foes, including things like the Machina Guardian and Mechanized Wanderer. Perhaps some still operated down here. In that case, it would make sense that Mira's Biometric Scan got no response.

"That's possible too."

"You might just be right!"

Traces of technology more advanced than the seventh level's were visible in this facility. The laboratory in front of them was one of the most secure rooms, so it wouldn't be odd if it contained a security robot. Mira, the Spirit King, and Martel decided to leave it at that.

Immediately, though, there was a loud noise unlike the odd one before. A banging followed as something with bloodshot eyes filled Mira's view through the window.

"Ngrah!"

"Whoa!"

"Eek!"

The three screamed in unison. Mira fell backward, hit her head on the wall behind her, and curled up in fear. She couldn't stay that way forever, so she tearfully looked at the window again.

It was no longer there.

It hadn't been alive, but it had a real physical presence—it was no machine nor hologram. The only other option was that an undead monster was locked inside, despite the fact that they couldn't spawn here. Mira was confused; she hadn't seen a monster with such eyes before.

There was no sign of the door having opened. The window hadn't cracked either; it must've been sturdy.

"Well, doesn't look like it'll come out..." Relieved by that fact, but still leery, Mira decided to get away from that lab.

"Goodness, that was shocking..."

Sitting a safe distance from the lab where the unidentified thing had startled her, Mira racked her brain over what it might've been.

"It blindsided me. How many thousands of years has it been since something got me that good?" The Spirit King had witnessed the creature through Mira's eyes, and tension was audible in his voice.

It had rattled Martel too. *"I can't take jump scares..."* She sounded ready to cry.

It was natural for them to be terrified, confronted with that thing. Mira mentally praised her pelvic floor muscles for keeping her from wetting herself.

"What do you think it was, though?" Mira asked her spirit companions once they had settled down, hoping they might have some idea.

She'd only seen the creature for a split second, but she wondered if it was something simple, like a security robot. If it wasn't a living thing, monster, *or* robot, she really had no idea what it could be, beyond some evil spirit.

"Hmmm. It was an odd being." The Spirit King sank into thought for a while before revealing that he didn't know. *"I don't think I've seen anything like that before."* Despite his vast and deep wealth of knowledge, he had no idea what it was.

"Same here. It clearly wasn't normal, though. Jeez!" Martel's shock had turned into anger, but she couldn't identify the creature either.

One look at its creepy eyes, and they'd never forget them. If even the wise spirits weren't familiar with it, it was possible the thing was a new breed. If so, no amount of thinking would provide a clear answer as to what it was.

Either way, it was obviously wisest to steer clear. After coming to that unanimous agreement with her companions, Mira resumed her search—detouring around that lab, of course. It was best to let sleeping dogs lie.

A while after she'd encountered the unknown new breed, Mira searched the remaining rooms with an ashen knight guard, just in case. There didn't seem to be anything like that creature in the other rooms. As for the facility's research, she ultimately made no discoveries about that.

Instead, she got a sense of why the researchers had left so many notes behind. That was related to the reason this facility had been locked down. After they'd decided to close it, and most of the researchers left, ten had secretly remained until its total closure a year later.

What had they done in this facility during that period? From the notes they left, it seemed like they'd been cleaning up after some kind of research.

Said cleanup was against orders, so they had to work in secret to avoid being noticed. They didn't send any electronic communications that would leave records, instead using work notebooks for work matters and notes for personal matters.

"Oops. It's getting to be that time."

Although it was interesting to learn about the historical researchers and goings-on, it was no help in accomplishing her goal. Only the locked laboratories would contain such useful information.

"I need to do something about the security..."

I'll have to search with that in mind next, Mira thought as she returned to the arranged meeting spot.

At the top floor elevator bay, Soul Howl returned one minute ahead of schedule. The pair sat down and told each other the results of their searches.

Soul Howl took his turn first. "I looked all over the place, but I didn't find any clues at all." According to him, he hadn't gotten so much as a crumb of information on the research.

His investigation of the upper floors had revealed that most of the facilities up there were the foundation of the researchers' everyday lives. All the chambers were gyms, shower rooms, training rooms, and the like. The researchers here must've enjoyed quite a bit of luxury, Soul Howl added.

"One place I found was pretty interesting," he added. "Wanna guess what it was?" Despite his smirk, he looked serious.

Mira pretended to think for a moment, but quickly gave up. "I don't know. What was it?"

Soul Howl wasn't perturbed. When Mira gave up, his smirk widened, and he revealed the answer. "Get this...they have a theater!"

A theater optimized to view movies and other visual creations logically meant that they *had* things to view. Mira hypothesized they might've left behind research-related videos she could view, but Soul Howl's continued explanation dashed that hope. He'd tried everything he could think of, but all the machines in the theater were broken and inoperable. Even if they found videos remaining, viewing them would be impossible.

"That was a real shame. I'm dying to see *Zombie Island Ages* again," he murmured and let out a genuinely disappointed sigh.

"Hm?" Mira had some memory of the series he'd mentioned. "Wait, didn't that one just have an anime?"

Soul Howl confirmed that, nimbly snatching a DVD out of his Item Box. In fact, it was titled *Zombie Island Ages*; somehow, he had retrieved a modern anime DVD from the theater. He couldn't watch it, since the devices were broken. Still, he'd brought it anyway, for the sake of the distant future. It was an odd anime, in which zombie girls within the military aimed to be idols in space, but it was one of Soul Howl's favorites.

"That...certainly is *Zombie Island Ages*..." Mira acknowledged.

Familiar characters were illustrated on the packaging, which also showed staff names, a barcode, and the like. Those made it clear that it was the very same DVD sold in modern Japan.

The anime had been broadcast about ten years before they were brought into this world. This was such a modern research facility, yet in a place connected to a former video game. What did it mean for a modern item to be in the facility? The ever-deepening mystery confused Mira.

"Well, they must've had a way to bring it here," Soul Howl said matter-of-factly. "Based on that scrap of the diary we saw, this isn't just a normal video game world. And it's not like racking our brains over it will change anything." He added with a chuckle that he'd bring the broken machines he'd recovered to the Hinomoto Committee, to see if they could do anything with them.

One committee department was investigating this world's biggest mystery: why players had been sucked in. Soul Howl's plan was to let them figure the objects out.

"Well, you're not wrong. There's a limit to our knowledge, no matter how we try." Mira agreed to simply report this to Solomon and leave the hard work to him. Then she asked whether Soul Howl had found DVDs of *Lyrical Survive*—a hot-blooded magical-girl survival anime she, Solomon, and Luminaria were all fond of.

"Yeah. Pretty sure they had the whole series."

"My word... I must salvage them!"

After Soul Howl finished his report, Mira made him take her to the theater, where she prioritized retrieving the entire *Lyrical Survive* series.

They'd leave the remaining DVDs for the Hinomoto Committee, which would come to investigate. Mira claimed the ones she liked and left the theater, reporting her investigation's results as they returned to the elevator bay.

She'd found many laboratory-like rooms, but all of those were locked; she'd only gotten into rooms unrelated to research. The research subject was still unclear.

Mira's statement surprised Soul Howl. "There are doors you can't open?"

"Oh, right. The section you investigated had nothing to do with research," she recalled.

Looking back, Soul Howl's floors had been full of rooms related to daily life. Those kinds of rooms unlocked without issue even on Mira's floors, but the laboratories were set to a high security level that their authentication keys couldn't handle. Mira explained that to the best of her ability as well.

"I see... There are higher security levels than our keys can access, huh? That's an annoying problem," Soul Howl muttered to himself in thought.

Mira grumbled in agreement. What was corrupting Fenrir? They'd likely find out if they investigated the research here, but the information was so carefully protected, it was hard to get a foothold.

They still had yet to search many rooms, but it was unlikely they'd find anything on the research—let alone anything that might help save Fenrir—with the keys they had. Unfortunately, for now, all they could do was bet on that small chance. Their only other hope would be finding a higher-level key or a way to raise their authority and search the other rooms. Either way, it would all come down to luck.

"Shall we scour the next floor as well now?" Mira pressed the elevator button, ready to investigate the other levels for useful information.

When the door opened, Soul Howl—who'd been deep in thought—seemed to remember something. "Hey, wait..." After thinking for another moment, he finally said, "I know. We can use that thing."

When Mira asked what he meant, he answered that he'd found notes on security-related matters during his investigation.

As it turned out, notes were scattered all over the higher floors too. Most were similar to those Mira had seen—minor work-related and everyday exchanges. Among them, however, Soul Howl had found a single helpful message about a key card that could reset the security system.

"Along with a few notes, I found a researcher's diary. It was tattered, but I learned a few things about those days. I'd say the researchers here were pretty close friends." They must've trusted each other a lot, he added with a sarcastic chuckle, then told Mira about the security situation he'd learned of in the diary.

According to him, things back during that research period had been the opposite of today. Many rooms were never even locked. However, when the facility and its subpar security were abandoned, a higher security level was initialized—that is, the security system was reset and rebooted. After all, they couldn't just leave the security like that.

"That probably leads us to now. Anyway, I remembered that the diary had info that might help us get out of this bind—which would be the key card."

When it was time for the researchers to reset and reboot the security, Soul Howl went on, one issue had come up. They'd lost the key card the director had issued—the one needed to initialize higher security. They'd given the person who lost it a lot of crap in the notes, he added, which surely proved what good friends all the researchers were.

Ultimately, that lost key card was never found, and they were forced to issue a new one. That new key card reset the system successfully, and that was the end of it.

After Soul Howl explained all this in detail, Mira smirked. She'd caught on to what he was implying. "Hrmm, I see. In other words, the key card they lost could very well still be lying around somewhere."

They might just be able to use it to reset the security system. If all went well, they'd be able to enter previously locked rooms.

"Exactly." Soul Howl nodded in satisfaction. With a dry grin, he added, "Either way, unless we can magically find out how they lost it, we still have to comb the whole place."

"Well, I'd say things look more hopeful than before, and that it's worth betting on," Mira replied as she boarded the elevator.

Soul Howl boarded as well, though a little timidly, and pressed the button.

22

BELIEVING THAT the key card to reset the building's security system might lie somewhere within the facility, Mira and Soul Howl split up once more. Soul Howl would again search the higher floors while Mira searched the bottom ones.

At this point, Mira pressed her advantage as a summoner to the fullest. She called First Pupil and Woofson; they were masters of investigation, so they were useful helpers at times like this. They reported back to her in their own unique ways.

"I didn't find nyathin'!"

"Nothing here either, Ms. Owner."

"Hmm. Very well, then I presume it isn't on this floor. Okay, on to the next!"

The trio searched rooms one by one before moving to the next level. They also searched the hallways from top to bottom. But since they couldn't get into the laboratories, there were few places they could raid, so their pace from the ninety-ninth to ninety-fifth floors was surprisingly fast.

After searching that way for a while, they reached a floor near the middle.

"Now, let's see..." With practiced steps, Mira headed to the elevator-bay map and checked the floor's room assignments. "Hrmm. This one does seem worth investigating."

This floor was seemingly reserved for researchers' personal rooms; the map had a list of people's names. As long as those rooms weren't labs, there was a good chance Mira's current authentication key would open them just fine.

First Pupil balanced his sign, then claimed they should head in the direction it fell. "What matters is instinct! When you get a hunch, you gotta follow it."

"That's hardly proper investigation, woof. We should analyze the situation, form a solid hypothesis, and then act!" Notebook in hand, Woofson laughed derisively, then suggested finding out who dropped the notebook and investigating their lifestyle.

First Pupil slapped the notebook out of Woofson's hand, shrugging, and sneered back, "This stuff is ancient hiss-tory! How are we supposed to know?"

"We've found enough information to make decisions already, woof. If you can't tell when that's right before your eyes, you must be stupid!" Woofson sighed in utter exasperation. Taking his pen, he wrote on First Pupil's sign. *Checkmate, stupid cat.*

"Stubborn dog!"

"Better than being a hotheaded cat."

Angry sparks flew between the pair as they glared at each other.

"That's enough, you two. We have plenty of places to search now. Time to get serious." Mira picked up the two slackers—or rivals, as they fancied themselves. Comforting both of them, she walked down the corridor toward the living quarters.

Though her companions were at odds, they shifted into work mode quickly.

As expected, her current authentication key opened the doors, so there were many places they could search. Despite how competitive they were, First Pupil and Woofson were also efficient, splitting up and investigating different areas to finish searching each room one by one.

While they searched the tenth room, Mira found a notebook inside a drawer. "Ooh, a journal! What diligent researchers these must've been."

There were characters seemingly meant to form names on the cover, but they were scratched and unreadable. Still, Mira could at least tell there were multiple names. On top of that, she saw different handwriting on different pages. In other words, multiple people had maintained this journal.

"Will there be any useful information in here...?"

Could the journal possibly contain clues regarding the facility's research or the lost key card? Betting on that ray of hope, Mira flipped through the pages.

My application was a success. I finally get to see season eight of The Running Dead*!*

Don't just skip season seven...

When's the next purchase day? Someone lend me body soap, please...

Sure, if you're fine with men's soap.

Volume 3 of Beginning of the End Credits *has been on loan forever!*

Sorry, I've got that. Wait a little longer, please.

You're still making me wait? LOL

Hey, are Maejima and Yumesaki going out, or what?

Huh? What the heck? Give us the deets!

Has spring finally come for Maejima?!

Edit: Apparently, he was just helping her buy a gift for Imai.

Whoa... Rest in peace to him.

RIP

RIP

RIP

However many entries she read, she saw only boring everyday conversations, and it seemed like the journal would continue in that vein. There was nothing noteworthy to find.

Yet as Mira kept skimming the book, ready to give up and deposit it back in the drawer, a line caught her eye.

I lost the security key card. I'm screwed! What do I do now?!

Apparently, one of the very writers of this journal was the blunderer. Following that line were endless excuses, comments on how the director would get mad at them, pleas to people to help find it, and so on. The other writers' reactions were exasperation, laughter, laughter, and more laughter. It became clear what kind of person the blunderer was.

From the journal's entry order and handwriting, along with the names that came up here and there, Mira pinpointed the blunderer: a woman called "Mariko" had lost the key card.

"Hrmm...it seems this 'Mariko' character dropped the ball," she muttered. "Okay. Time to go search this Mariko's room."

This was genuinely useful information. If Mariko lost the key card in her own room, it was very possibly still within. Thus, Mira had decided on her first destination to search.

With First Pupil and Woofson in tow, she returned to the elevator bay and sought Mariko's name on the map.

"Mariko, Mariko, Mariko..." About a minute and a half after she started searching from one side, she found the name FUWA MARIKO. "Ooh, it must be this one!"

The name was familiar too—no doubt that had been the name of the person fined for misplacing something, presumably the key card itself. That confirmed that Fuwa Mariko was the "Mariko" from the journal.

Now certain, Mira carefully noted the room's location and returned to the living quarters area. Though she got a little lost amid the undistinguishable hallways and rooms, she managed to find Mariko's quarters and opened the door without issue.

"Listen, now. Don't overlook a single speck of dust!" Mira ordered her summoned companions.

"No, ma'am!"

"Leave it to me!"

The trio put their backs into searching the room. There were still shelves, a desk, and other furniture inside. They searched thoroughly, paying special care to checking under and between things. They left no stone unturned, even when it meant brushing away accumulated dust or dealing with scattered trash.

About thirty minutes later...

"I can't find it!"

"Nothing here, Ringmeowstress!"

"Woof! Not a single card in sight!"

Their search ended fruitlessly, and they sat down in exhaustion. Sighing, Mira stared at Mariko's desk. Its drawer was bursting with endless notes and a few shared journals. Since there was no key card in this room, Mira decided to search everything in the drawer for clues.

As far as she could tell, the notes were the same as the others—simple messages and the like. Next, she looked at the shared journals. There were three in the drawer, each full from start to end. In other words, Mariko had stored finished journals here.

If they figured out her daily habits well enough, they might narrow down the places where she could've lost the card. Mira read the journals' contents aloud to let First Pupil and Woofson handle the deductions. The journals were mainly about daily life in the facility. They never discussed research, instead just describing hobbies, entertainment, and other trivial things. It was all so lax, Mira had to wonder whether the researchers had actually been doing their jobs. Yet occasional technical jargon that went back and forth at least proved they were real researchers with knowledge of their field.

After reading all the journals, Mira put them back. "Hrmm..." she muttered. "The library was the only place that jumped out to me."

She'd learned one major fact from the journals: Mariko had been obsessed with a certain author's work at one point, and she'd seemingly frequented the library on the tenth floor. Other researchers had left her many warnings in the journal, such as *Stop leaving envelopes in books to mark that you finished them!*

Another notable message was *Don't borrow so many books at once if finishing just one will take you ages!*

Perhaps as a result of such complaints, some of Mariko's books had been forcibly confiscated, since she'd kept them so long past their due dates. Mariko had objected *I was still reading those!*, but almost everyone else agreed that she'd deserved it.

"Meow! If you want a book, there's one right around here!" First Pupil opened a cupboard on the side of the room. Inside were surprisingly well-maintained silverware and about ten books.

"Why are they in the cupboard, of all places...?"

Was it just Mariko's sloppy side showing again, or was that where she kept the books hidden from would-be confiscators? It wasn't clear. That said, the books in the cupboard were stamped as library property. Despite the many warnings Mariko had received, she'd never stopped monopolizing books.

"Hrmm... All these books are by the same author," Mira noted. The volumes were so weathered, they were hard to read, but they all bore the author name "Hanesaka Iori." That, as the journals indicated, was the author Mariko had been obsessed with. "Still, knowing that doesn't help much..."

"We still lack necessary information," Woofson agreed.

They'd gleaned some personal information on Mariko, but the element that mattered most—the key card—remained lost.

"For now, the library—" As Mira began to pursue the possibility of Mariko having dropped the key card at the library she frequented, she noticed something had been left between two pages of a book. "That's...!"

Could it be the key card? Mira took the book and opened it. She was immediately let down, for it was just an envelope—one of the ones with cute illustrations used for the female researchers' note exchanges. No doubt Mariko had used it as a bookmark.

The envelope contained details about something called "Job A," with a date, time, and supervisor listed. At the end was Isurugi Touko's signature. It appeared to be an important work document, but it didn't seem like a useful lead to the facility's research topic or the key card's location.

"Little scamp, getting my hopes up," she grumbled.

"For real!" First Pupil closed the cupboard, shrugging in disappointment at the useless find.

"That's it, woof!" Woofson piped up in a flash of inspiration. He reopened the cupboard, took the book back out, and placed it gently on the floor. "The key card we're searching for might just be in the same kind of place!"

Woofson opened the book, pointed at the envelope, and explained his deduction. In addition to the work document they'd just found, they'd already discovered other minor professional communications conducted via notes. Based on the most recent one, Director Isurugi Touko was one such lover of cute envelopes.

As for the key card itself, the director had likely given it to Mariko directly due to its importance. What if it were enclosed in an envelope, like some other professional correspondence?

"If Mariko took the key card out immediately, this deduction is meaningless, woof. But if she didn't..." Woofson began analyzing her personality based on what they knew from the journals and notes. "As we've seen, she's the type of person to use a nearby envelope as a bookmark. A journal revealed that she returned books with envelopes stuck in them too." Having explained that, Woofson paused and turned to First Pupil. "Surely even a cat can understand at this point."

It took First Pupil a moment of holding his head and groaning, but he finally arranged all the information in his mind and reached the answer. He puffed out his chest smugly, replying, "Of course! Basically, like... Yeah! Uh... Ooh! You think it might be in an envelope, right?!"

"What say you, Ms. Owner? This is my ultimate deduction based on the information we have so far, woof." Ignoring his feline rival's pretend smarts, Woofson ran to Mira proudly. Perhaps he was confident that he'd made the perfect deduction; his tail wagged, and his eyes sparkled. No doubt he was awaiting praise.

"Indeed, that does seem possible. Fantastic deduction. Good job, friend." Mira picked Woofson up and petted him, just like he wanted. While he smiled blissfully and basked in his reward, First Pupil watched hatefully with gritted teeth.

"All right. On to the library!"

"Yeah!" the cat and dog answered in unison.

After a thorough investigation of the room, they'd found no key card, but they *had* established that it could be in an envelope left in a library book. They left Mariko's room and headed straight for the elevator bay, taking the elevator to the tenth floor. There, Mira ran straight to the floor map.

"Hrmm...this looks tricky too."

As far as she could tell, the library comprised the entire tenth floor. Despite being underground, each floor of the facility boasted enormous square footage, and this was no exception. Although Mira knew which author Mariko favored, this still seemed a daunting task.

On the other hand, First Pupil and Woofson were more than excited to have their chance to shine. They boasted about their abilities while holding each other back.

"Witness the power of a cat's instincts!"

"Woof! My deductions will pinpoint it right away!"

"Good. First, find an author named Hanesaka Iori!" On Mira's signal, the pair split up and plunged into the library. "Now, where to begin...?"

A look at the map showed Mira that the shelves were arranged by publisher. Why had they been sorted that way if this wasn't a bookstore? Was it an investor demand? Such pointless questions filled Mira's mind as she headed to a familiar publisher's shelf.

While First Pupil and Woofson competed to investigate the rest of the library, Mira rejoiced, "Ooh, they have every single volume!"

She'd found books from her past life here, just like the DVDs from before: paper books, printed in small quantities for the limited number of customers in a rapidly digitalizing world. As one of those few customers, the sight of so many books on one shelf was moving and nostalgic to Mira. She picked up a book and flipped through the pages. When she saw the *suggestive* insert illustrations, she grinned creepily to herself.

One major difference between digital and physical versions was the degree of *expression*. With the changing of the times, restrictions had been placed on digital works, while the law was lax with physical ones. Truly, paper books were superb.

While she savored the sights and scents, Mira continued her search. Eventually, she noticed a sheet of paper attached to a clipboard on the circulation desk. "Now, what could this be?"

It was obviously tattered, but on very close inspection, she discerned that it was a loan list. Beyond borrowers' names, it contained the dates books were lent, the return dates, and each book's title and ISBN. The lines of the table were uneven and distorted, proving that the loan list was handwritten—likely for the same reason that kept the researchers from using communication devices.

"Ooh, this is just perfect!"

Reviewing the table, Mira saw Mariko's name several times. She also found the location of the shelves where Mariko's favorite books were.

Hanesaka Iori had evidently written for multiple publishers. There were five different publisher names on the list, and Mariko had borrowed three books from each.

"With this, I ought to be able to check them all with ease," Mira murmured. It was essentially a list of books that might contain the key card, so if all went well, she might just find it. What a useful clue.

Just as Mira became certain of that, she heard First Pupil scream, "Anyather dud!"

What was he doing? Curious, Mira made her way to him— with the loan list in hand, of course. "What? Is something wrong?"

It seemed First Pupil had found some Hanesaka Iori books already. Six lay next to him when Mira ran over. Just as the complaint in the journal had mentioned, there were envelopes in the books. There was a problem, though.

"They're all empty!" First Pupil lamented. None of the envelopes contained *anything*, let alone the key card.

"Hrmm, I see..."

The empty envelopes made her a little uneasy, but she had no choice but to check each and every one. Calling Woofson over, Mira gave her companions the loan list and her next command: use the list to collect all the books ever borrowed by Mariko.

"Roger that, Ringmeowstress!"

"Yes, ma'am!"

They replied promptly, then began reading through the list—competing to do so, of course—and raced off to the shelves.

Since the list was in Japanese, neither could read it. But they recognized the characters in the book titles, as well as Mariko and Hanesaka Iori's names, so they could at least search for them on the shelves.

Their constant competition was childish, but they had the skill of real professionals.

"Hrmm... Well, I think that's all."

Thanks to First Pupil and Woofson's rushed efforts, plus Mira's slow-and-steady looking, they'd assembled every book in Mariko's lending history. In addition to the ten in Mariko's room and the six First Pupil had already pulled, there were twenty-five candidates in the library.

"It must be in this one!" Woofson picked up a book and confidently opened it. Inside was an envelope, proof that Mariko had read the volume. "Awwoooo... Empty..." His tail drooped sadly.

Meanwhile, First Pupil laughed gleefully. "Too bad for mew! I say it's this one!" He snatched a book from the lineup.

The two were apparently competing over which of them could find the book with the key card first.

"C'mooon! Fingers crossed!" First Pupil flung open the book, plucked the envelope from inside, and gently opened it. "Noooo!" he cried, throwing the envelope aside.

"The battle's only just begun, woof!"

"This cat's gonna win!"

Neither had won the first round, but they eagerly moved to the second. First Pupil reached his paw out, as if trying to sense the key card's location. The sign on his back read LET ME HEAR YOUR CRY!

Woofson focused more on the list than the books themselves. "If we consider when she borrowed and returned them, along with when the key card was lost, the answer should arise on its own..." He planned to identify the book based on timing. His eyes were truly those of a great detective, but given his adorable shih tzu appearance, he could never look more serious than cute.

I suppose...I should just watch them...? Mira wanted to simply rip all the envelopes open herself, but she hesitated to interfere with the extremely serious battle of wits.

The second round began.

"Agaaain?!" First Pupil cried.

"Not so much as an envelope?!" Woofson howled sadly.

"I can't believe they were all duds..." Mira sighed.

The guessing contest had shockingly ended with neither First Pupil nor Woofson as the victor. Indeed, none of the books in Mariko's loaning history contained the key card. They'd checked between all the pages, not just in the envelopes, so they were certain the card wasn't here.

"What a purr-fect waste of energy that was..." Sighing at the scattered envelopes, First Pupil glared at Woofson, as if demanding, *What happened to all your confidence that it was in here, huh?*

"It can't be..." Woofson was enormously daunted by this revelation. A deduction he'd been certain of had proven false, and his immense confidence translated directly to immense pain. The pup hung his head in utter shock, but the light hadn't left his eyes. "I'm not done yet... It must be in here..." he muttered, staring at the books.

To be fair, his deduction had been both persuasive and plausible. Yet the envelopes were empty, left with not so much as a note inside.

Mira realized something was wrong. *Now that I think about it, there were things inside the envelopes back in Mariko's room. Yet the ones here are empty. Doesn't that mean she picked different envelopes specifically upon returning them?* Had Mariko intentionally left *empty* envelope markers in finished books?

Guessing as much, Mira picked up the one book that was an exception. Its title was *Good Morning Sunshine*. It was the second book Woofson had tried, and was the only one that lacked an envelope. Had the envelope fallen out somewhere? Or had someone taken it out?

"Hm? Now that I look at it, this title..." The memory of seeing that title elsewhere flashed into Mira's mind. But where was that?

Tracing her memory back a few hours, she finally remembered the moment. "Of course. This is...!"

It was when she'd searched the hundredth floor. This title had been mentioned among the many notes left there.

"What did the note say again...?"

What had the researcher written? Casting her mind back, Mira managed to remember it. The gist was that the writer had planned to borrow that same book, *Good Morning Sunshine*. "Aha! That's this one!"

Upon this revelation, a hypothesis formed inside Mira's brain.

The book from Mariko's lending history. The note someone had left saying they'd borrow it. The information Mira and her companions gleaned about Mariko from the shared journal. All those pieces of information melded together.

A slow reader who borrowed multiple books at once and used envelopes as bookmarks. And, most of all, Mariko's claim in the journal that she had still been reading a book when it was confiscated.

What if that book was the one Mira was looking upon now? If Mariko had been using the envelope within as a bookmark, rather than to mark a finished title, the envelope's contents were likely still inside. And of course, if she had been in the middle of reading the book, the bookmark would still be in there.

If the key card was in the envelope when the book was confiscated, wouldn't that connect directly with her losing the key card afterward?

There was no envelope inside *Good Morning Sunshine* now. In other words, whoever left that note must've taken the envelope out.

Had they reused the envelope as a bookmark afterward or discarded it? That detail was unclear, but if the key card was inside, it likely went unnoticed, given the hubbub about the lost card that followed immediately.

Finding the person who borrowed it next will be the fastest way to get closer to the truth, Mira decided. "Say, you two. What do you think of this?" With that, she passed her deduction on to her companions.

23

"**W**ow! What an incredible deduction!" Woofson instantly recovered from wallowing in a sea of regret, declaring that Mira had to be right.

First Pupil cocked his head in slight confusion for a moment, but eventually caught up with the others. "That's paw-esome, Ringmeowstress!"

"I say we look at that lending list from before," Woofson suggested. "The book came from this library, so if someone borrowed it after Mariko, there must be a paper trail."

Mariko had kept the book so long after its due date, it was confiscated and presumably loaned out again. If it had been, Woofson believed the person who next borrowed it must've obtained the envelope holding the key card.

"Mm-hmm. You must be right," Mira agreed and immediately gazed at the list.

First, she found Mariko among the many past borrowers. She found the next person to borrow the volume about a month after Mariko; they were named Shidou.

Shidou seemed to have been a more varied reader; instead of reading Hanesaka Iori single-mindedly, like Mariko, they borrowed books from various genres. In fact, Shidou occupied one-third of the loan list.

"First things first—we should search this Shidou person's room." Certain they'd find *something* there, Mira and her companions picked up the scattered books and left the library.

At the elevator bay on the floor full of researchers' quarters, she looked for the name "Shidou" and found one name that matched: SHIDOU TOSHIOMI. They headed straight for that room, unlocked the door without issue using Mira's authentication key, and entered.

"Goodness, this is...a room..."

The floor plan was no surprise, since it was similar to the others, but the rooms' furniture apparently depended on the resident. In Shidou's case, bookshelves covered every square inch of the walls. Their powerful love of books was more than obvious. Shidou must've taken all the books with them; the shelves were empty.

"If we find nothing in this room, we're back where we started. Let's search it top to bottom!"

"Okay, Ringmeowstress!"

"Woof! Yes, ma'am!"

This room was the likeliest yet to contain the key card, but that also meant they'd need to give up if their search came up short.

Thus, the trio eagerly and thoroughly scoured every inch of the room—every tier of every bookshelf; in and under every drawer; even up above, in spots where the envelope couldn't possibly be.

In the process, First Pupil reported, "Meow meow! There're tons of things stuffed in here!"

What was stuffed where? "Hm? What's the matter?" Mira ran over to check.

In front of First Pupil was a desk that looked like a typical work area. He was gazing at the drawer. "This." First Pupil pulled out the top drawer. Inside were piles and piles of bundled papers. "There's a whole lot in here!"

"Ooh! This might just be the jackpot!"

The papers were neatly collected notes. It seemed this Shidou person was methodical. They'd taken notes they received, bound them together, and stored the papers in their desk. Those notes included not just minor work communications and directions but casual conversations as well. Shidou either couldn't be bothered to weed those out or liked them enough to keep them. The researcher's methodical nature was evident; at the bottom of the drawer was a bundle of brightly colored papers.

"It might just be among these..." Mira quickly put the bundles on the desk and picked up the colorful one. As she expected, it was a bunch of cute envelopes.

The one Mariko had used as a bookmark might be mixed in; in fact, that was absolutely possible.

"I'm going to check them one by one now." Mira picked up an envelope and looked inside as if checking a lottery card.

Her companions watched with bated breath.

"My little heart's beatin' out of my chest..."

"It has to be in there. It has to be!"

There were still notes in the envelopes. Upon inspecting them, it became clear that Shidou was a trusted figure among the researchers.

The notes included work handoff requests, people asking for advice, and even requests like *Tomorrow is May 22, the director's birthday. Keep her in one place for us!* Many asked Shidou for help with love. There were other notes about birthdays, implying that everyone celebrated those together.

"Hrmm... Shidou was more sociable than I expected."

Based on the state of their room and their apparently serious personality, Mira had expected them to be less appealing. It seemed they'd been a central pillar of this community.

Shidou had seemingly been generous too. One note from Mariko read *Thanks for helping me search. I still couldn't find it, though!* Based on that message, the note was surely about the key card.

A few envelopes later, Mira found one still sealed.

"Ooh... There it is! It's there!"

Mira had finally found it: the key card she'd been searching for. The card in the envelope was about half the size of her palm—smaller than she'd expected. With it was a memo: *This is the security-blanking key card. Don't you lose it!* — *Isurugi Touko.* The note also included instructions on using the card.

They now at least had the key card. Setting aside the question of whether it still worked, First Pupil and Woofson piped up with glee. Despite their rivalry, the pair always rejoiced together in the end.

"We did iiit!"

"Spectacularly done!"

While the other two celebrated, Mira gazed at the envelope containing the key card. "Still, what an uncanny chain of coincidences led to this," she murmured.

Neither Mariko nor Shidou would've imagined that the card was in here. Still, that was *why* Mira was able to find it. Part of her had to feel grateful that they'd delivered it to her through time.

After mulling that over for a while, Mira dismissed First Pupil and Woofson and left Shidou's room to meet up with Soul Howl.

When Mira proudly told Soul Howl the story of how she discovered the key card, his first reaction was surprise. "I can't believe you actually found it..."

It seemed he hadn't had much faith that they'd locate such an ancient relic and had focused on investigating a way to issue a new key card. He'd found that issuing a new one wasn't especially difficult, although the process had several steps. It would take about a week to do so; the method was time-consuming, but certain.

"If this key card has an expiration date, we'll want to look into your method next. Of course, mine comes first." Mira chuckled, then pointed out the next problem: having obtained the necessary key card, they needed to figure out how to use it. Their work would affect the entire facility's security. Surely they couldn't just go and use it anywhere.

While Mira began to think about that, Soul Howl found an opportunity to be smug. "Oh, no problem there. While I was looking into how to issue a new card, I read a few things about how to use them. Just leave that to me." Soul Howl claimed he'd found a room that security personnel had used. The materials remaining there, though fragmented, had been enough for him to work out the method from. According to him, they could use a terminal hidden at the facility's entrance. "Ready to go?"

"Very well. Let's get this done quickly."

Once they knew how to do something, they wanted to do it right away. Mira and Soul Howl followed their usual policy and headed straight to the elevator. They took it back to the airtight door at the entrance of the hidden facility.

The wall initially seemed to consist of featureless metal, but the documents Soul Howl had found claimed there was a security panel there.

Gazing at the wall, Soul Howl took a step sideways, and then another. "According to the text, it should be around here..." he mumbled. Mira simply watched him. He'd said to leave this to him, and he hadn't offered any details. Apparently, explaining the process was too big a hassle. "Oh, there it is. Nice! Now, we just do this, and..."

Soul Howl pressed a few points on the wall. They began to glow red; after that, points of blue light appeared on the opposite wall.

"All right. Elder, I need you to touch the top-right light and the light third from the left, second from the bottom."

"Mm. Very well." Mira followed Soul Howl's orders and touched those points on the wall. They glowed white and faded. With a mechanical whirring, part of the wall changed, and a touch panel and monitor-like screen appeared. This seemed to have been a success.

"Ooh, this must be it!"

Words appeared on-screen.

Security Control System
Loading...

This *was* the security terminal, if nothing else.

"Now we just need to operate it," Soul Howl said. "The details were on that memo you found, so good luck."

SHE PROFESSED HERSELF PUPIL OF THE WISE MAN

"All right. I'll do it."

The key card envelope had included a memo with instructions on resetting the security system. Mira took the memo out and stood in front of the terminal. Using the instructions, she brought up the Menu screen and finally reached a screen that directed her to insert the key card.

"Well...I'm counting on you..." *Please work now. Don't have a time limit,* Mira prayed as she fed the terminal the key card.

Loading...

She and Soul Howl watched with bated breath, hoping the card would work without a hitch. Immediately, the screen changed and revealed their fate.

Resetting time specs.

Scanning facility.

Repairing corrupted sectors.

ERROR.

Initializing settings.

Restoring default values.

The terminal displayed one message after another. There were sounds all around, as if things were beginning to move. The key card evidently worked, even now.

The screen changed at a dizzying pace until it finally stopped and displayed the words *Preparing security settings.*

Then a problem came up. Under that line, the screen read *Enter security code: XXXX.* Judging from that, they needed to input four digits, but Soul Howl's investigation had yielded no such code.

"A password, huh...? Is that in the memo?" he asked Mira.

"No. It only says to input things based on the instructions."
Rather than providing such a code, all Mira's memo included was
the post-input process, which was an unexpected hurdle.

"Well, this sucks..."

The fact that neither of them had come upon the four numbers thus far was proof that secret codes were safeguarded at this
facility. However, there was still one ray of hope: the facility's
security situation back when it was active. The location might be
locked tight now, but the notes left behind gave the impression
that security back then had been lax at best.

It was probably lax because, on top of the fact that the research
team was made up of trusted members, they ran no risk of someone
intruding upon this location. In light of that, it was very possible
that the secret code was simple.

Soul Howl tried putting in sequences like "0000" and "AAAA"
at random, but they all returned authentication errors. "Hmm...
nope. Not that one either." His actions led another problem to
pop up. "Oh. This has limited retries..."

On closer inspection, there were dots on the top-right of the
screen. Each mistake decreased the number of dots; now, only
three were left. Seeing this, Soul Howl hurriedly backed away
from the touch panel.

"Look at you, wasting our retries. Good grief..." *Thoughtlessly
trying things out right away is one of his bad habits.* Mira sighed,
absolving herself of any wrongdoing as she thought over what
the code could possibly be. *Well, I suppose the only option is just
to try something.*

They didn't have hacking technology on hand, so if they had no hints regarding the code, all they could do was guess. If that didn't work, they'd have to think harder. Mira steeled herself and entered the first number that came to mind. Upon doing so...

Authentication complete.

Incredibly, the terminal indicated the entry was successful and moved to the next step of the process.

"Huh?!" Mira was the first to be shocked by this. At the same time, she chuckled to herself; truly, the researchers' security was *bad*.

"Oh, you got it? Good guess," Soul Howl said, impressed. "What'd you put in?"

"'0522.' I just gave it a try, and would you look at that?! It worked," Mira answered proudly. When Soul Howl asked what that number meant, she smirked and said, "It was the director's birthday."

"Birthday, huh? How'd you know that?"

"Ha, please. But a small feat for me."

Since that birth date was the code, a casual note in Shidou's room had helped them in an unexpected way. Grateful toward the lax researchers, Mira and Soul Howl continued the security process.

When they reached the final step listed on the memo, they'd already succeeded in shutting down the research building's security system.

All room locks disengaged.

Please reestablish settings.

So the screen said, but that had been the last of their work. Now that they'd nullified the building's security, they could finally explore the places that had been locked before.

"Shall we go uncover some secrets now?" Mira pressed the *Cancel* button onscreen to finish the operation, then made her way straight to the elevator bay.

"They guarded their research info a lot better than the rest of the place," Soul Howl mused. "I'm getting a little excited."

By now, they'd gotten an idea of the researchers' lives and attitudes from multiple angles, but the research itself was still opaque. What had the researchers protected so cautiously? Fenrir was an important part of that question, but pure curiosity drove Mira and Soul Howl onward as well.

They took the elevator down to the bottommost floor.

Security had been disabled, and no alarms or strobe lights went off on the hundredth floor, but that was more or less the same as when Mira first went down there. If there was one difference, it would be the laboratory doors.

"Ooh! They're really unlocked!"

The doors that had refused to budge so far now opened with ease. Their strategy was a great success; it had given them exactly the results they wanted.

Although the doors had opened, the lab lights were still broken. Soul Howl used illumination magic to create a ball of light that lit his surroundings. After looking around a bit, he turned to Mira and asked, "We're free to investigate all we want now. Want to start with this room?"

She shook her head and pointed down the hallway with a smug grin. "No, I'd like to start down there. The director's office is that way. Don't you think it would have the most information?"

If they wanted to know what research had been done here, surely rummaging in the director's room would be the most efficient way to find out.

When Mira noted that she already knew where that room was, Soul Howl replied, "Sure, sounds good to me. Let's go there first, then." He extinguished his light and backed out of the lab. After closing the door to the eerily dark laboratory again, he looked down the hallway and asked, "How far is it from here?"

The instant she was confronted with the dim room again, though, Mira realized something odd.

"Oh, right. I forgot to mention, but..." When she'd investigated this floor a few hours ago, she and the spirits observing through her had found something *unusual* in a locked room. A scene right out of a horror movie flashed through her mind again. She shuddered and told Soul Howl about what had happened.

"Basically, that unidentified *thing* may have left the laboratory. We should probably be careful." After explaining as much, Mira summoned a holy knight just in case.

"Man, tell me that before we come down..."

The mysterious being in the laboratory hadn't seemed to be a monster, but it didn't seem to be a living thing either, since it didn't produce a signal on Biometric Scan.

What was it, then? Some sort of abomination the researchers here had made? Imagining that, Soul Howl rolled his eyes in exasperation before summoning his own golem to protect himself.

"Don't blame me," Mira complained. "I only just remembered." To brush off the subject, she headed away at a brisk walk.

As Soul Howl followed her, curiosity crept into his eyes. In his mind, if the thing in the laboratory was neither monstrous nor living, then surely it must be robotic—or really undead.

She
Professed
Herself
Pupil of the
Wise Man

THEY PROCEEDED down the hall for a while, ready to respond to any situation. Fortunately, they reached the director's office without encountering the abomination.

"Perfect. This one's unlocked too!"

The security reset had also applied to the director's office, so the door opened with ease. This had required many detours, but now they could finally investigate the room. They rushed inside and split up, ready to scrutinize everything they got their hands on.

"Let's see what information we can find here..." Soul Howl looked around the room with an orb of light at hand, then started turning over things close to him.

Accompanied by her own orb of light, Mira rushed to the back of the room. "Good, good. I was worried at first, but they left behind some paper documents."

They positioned both their orbs of light to illuminate the entire office. In the middle was a large desk. Shelves surrounded it, and metal boxes were piled by the wall. Mira and Soul Howl didn't know what was inside, but the boxes ranged from small to large. There was also a bookshelf in the corner, but with documents stuffing the shelves rather than books.

Given this facility's cutting-edge technology, Mira had worried the office wouldn't contain paper artifacts, but the researchers had seemingly understood the reliability of analog documents.

That said, paper documents only illustrated part of the story here. Investigating the cases on the shelf, Mira found that they were full of a cutting-edge recording medium called "crystal cubes." The plates labeling the cubes revealed that they contained video and audio from experiments.

"Hrmm... If only we could play these..."

Crystal cubes had been used in modern Japan. Since Mira hailed from there, she'd held them before and even knew how to use them. The lack of a device to read them was the problem. Mira had pinned her hopes on the computer at the director's desk, but naturally, it was broken. However many times she pressed the power button, the computer didn't respond, leaving her no way to read the data within. She had to entrust her hopes to the paper documents.

"This is about meetings... And this one... Hm, this one too."

The books on the shelf were actually all meeting notes. Research topics, methods, budgeting, priorities, and the like had all been discussed, according to those records. It was difficult to glean details of the research, experimental processes, progress, or results. However, the minutes at least revealed information on what kind of research they had performed here...or tried to reveal that. *Understanding* any of the records was tough in its own right.

"Hrmm... 'Adjusting the atmosphere's composition'... 'Analyzing changes in the ether element'... 'Observing unified thought density'... 'Correcting interference of the'... Goodness, I don't understand a word of this." Mira had tried reading the documents from the left side of the shelf onward, but all the words were too difficult for laypeople. She understood that the research was complex, at least, but how did any of it relate to Fenrir?

Many more documents remained; surely there was something Mira could understand. Hoping that would be true, she checked the other materials. They seemed to be sorted into chronological order. As she proceeded from left to right, the dates gradually became more recent.

"Oh ho... 'Conditions to change the properties of mana,' 'stabilization of the environment'... 'On the existence of "monsters"'... What a range of research they conducted."

As Mira reached the latter half, she found more and more research she understood based purely on the wording. Some were similar to the Linked Silver Towers' experiments, piquing her interest further.

After inspecting the volumes one at a time for a while, she eventually reached the final one. What was the last round of research performed here? Expectant and excited, she looked down upon the book—and her face contorted in shock.

"What...? Were they saying such a thing is possible?!"

The topic of the document she was holding was the creation of an artificial god. If one took those words at face value, they meant making a deity using human hands.

Could such a drastic thing be possible? What *made* a god in the first place? Most of all, what had the results of this research been? So many questions, so much curiosity, and so much unease welled up at once.

"How did they research such a thing?" Mira was taken aback by the *grandiosity* of the facility's final moments. At the same time, she hit upon a possibility.

Fenrir had claimed he came to the depths of the Ancient Underground City because he felt power akin to his siblings'. Meanwhile, Mira was here to do something about the power that had corrupted him. Its cause was something that could affect Fenrir—a being able to devour even gods. The research here was varied, yes, but Mira felt that a few experiments couldn't possibly enable someone to stand up to Fenrir.

That is, until she found this supposed "artificial god" experiment. Whatever its contents, it was related to gods. That alone connected it to Fenrir, a god himself.

"If there's a chance, surely this must be it."

Of the research topics she'd found so far, this was by far the most suspicious. Upon discovering it, Mira ran over to Soul Howl—who was searching the other side of the room—and smirked at him.

Soul Howl hadn't expected this either. When he saw the document Mira found, he muttered in astonishment, "Creation of an artificial god, huh...? They did some crazy stuff in here."

The Spirit King and Martel were shocked as well. Despite their silence to this point, they were forced to speak up now.

"To think, a god created by human hands... And they attempted it so long before I was brought into this world..."

"People from the past had big ideas, didn't they?"

The team's apparently relaxed natures hardly led one to imagine such grand research, so the disparity alone took them aback.

Mira agreed. "I was surprised as well. I never expected them to be doing such research here..." She had to wonder to herself—were all researchers mad scientists, or was this facility's team the exception? "Now, how do we investigate this?" she asked Soul Howl.

"How *do* we, huh? I think it'd speed things up if we could play these crystal cubes, but..."

The many crystal cubes sitting on the shelves could store vast quantities of data for an indefinite duration. Based on the number of them here, and the words written on the boxes, it seemed as though all the research carried out in the facility had been preserved in this very room.

The inception of an artificial god, the process, the data the experiment yielded, the results, how they tested it, *why* they did it, and most of all, whether they'd succeeded... The existence of this world's gods was a great mystery. Information was so close at hand, yet so far away due to its unreadability.

"Well, there isn't much point hanging around here, is there? Shall we go to the B3 laboratory this document mentioned? They conducted all the experiments there, so they may just have left more artifacts."

Mira was curious about the experiment's results, but as things stood, she wasn't about to learn those. Thus, she had to prioritize uncovering and resolving the cause of Fenrir's corruption. She quickly realigned her focus and departed the director's office, though she left much curiosity behind.

"Fair enough," said Soul Howl.

However many interesting tidbits they found, they couldn't forget their original goal. If they could create a god, harnessing even some of that power would surely help save that religious woman faster. But Soul Howl shook off that thought and followed Mira for now.

The two couldn't head straight to the laboratory at that point, since "B3" meant nothing to them. They had to go back to the elevator bay first.

"Oh, here it is. Hmm... 'Cultivation room.'"

The map didn't just include rooms and their numbers; it also included information on what each room was for. There were sterile rooms, organic and inorganic chemistry labs, a microbial biochemistry lab, a genetic biology lab, a paranormal science lab, and more. The team had seemingly used different rooms, depending on the research they were doing.

The document Mira and Soul Howl had obtained said that creating the artificial god was tested in the cultivation room labeled B3. Such a grand undertaking must surely have required a wide range of experiments, yet the documents described no work in other rooms.

An artificial god's cultivation—the madness of these researchers was only growing more pronounced.

"Cultivation room... I feel nervous about this..." Mira noted
the location and began to walk, frowning at what they might find.

"Oh, yeah. Same here," Soul Howl agreed, but his steps were
oddly jovial. He was surely imagining the same horrors as
Mira, but apparently found them worthy of excitement rather
than fear.

Carefully proceeding down the hallway, they arrived at the
cultivation room—a place Mira remembered well. "Urk... This
just had to be it, didn't it...?"

This was indeed the very room where the unidentifiable abomination had been. Mira timidly approached the door, setting her
sights on its window.

The Spirit King's and Martel's voices echoed in her mind.

"Slowly, Miss Mira. Slowly."

"Take it slow, Mira!"

They were just as wary of that horror-movie monster as
Mira was.

"I know, I know," Mira replied and carefully peered into the
window.

The room was as dark as ever, but knowing it was the cultivation room where they'd researched artificial gods made it even

creepier. In order to focus on looking into the room, Mira had a holy knight stand next to her to protect her in case of attack.

Was there anything lurking in the corners? Anything moving? Where was that abomination? She carefully sought the answers. Just then, the door abruptly opened.

"Whoa!" *Is it attacking?!* Mira hurriedly jumped back, but someone looked at her in exasperation.

It was Soul Howl. He'd gotten tired of watching her fool around in front of their objective and opened the door himself. "What are you doing? Let's get in there and investigate."

"I just told you, didn't I?! I saw some kind of abomination, and I swear to you, it was in this room!" Mira warned, flustered, and hid behind her holy knight. "So? Is it safe?" she demanded.

"Man, you could've told me that before we got here, instead of just messing around..." Soul Howl grumbled, creating a wall-like golem and sending it into the room. He followed up by making a knee-high golem to scout. When it found living things or objects that moved, that golem would send signals only its master could detect. In a way, it was like a motion sensor. "Hmm... I'm not getting any response. Either it's staying still, or it's gone. I'm guessing it escaped and started roaming, like you said. Or you just thought you saw it when nothing was there to begin with."

Confirming that his search hadn't found any hostiles, Soul Howl released his wall golem and entered the cultivation room.

"No, that can't be. I saw it with my own two eyes!" Mira wouldn't mistake something like that. Her Biometric Scan hadn't reacted to the creature, and it didn't seem to be a normal monster, but she knew it was there.

When she protested, the Spirit King and Martel piped up as well, though Soul Howl couldn't hear them.

"That's right. I saw it too!"

"Yeah! It was clear as day!"

"The most likely conclusion is that it's out in a hallway, huh?" Soul Howl muttered.

It was very possible that the unidentified being had already escaped the unlocked door and was wandering the halls or hiding somewhere. Reaching that conclusion, Soul Howl created an orb of light, as he had earlier, and looked around the cultivation room. Just in case, he checked desk drawers and other areas his golem couldn't search.

"That must be it. It couldn't have been an illusion," Mira insisted. There were three witnesses; it had to be real. She bolstered her defenses with more holy knights before entering to search the cultivation room.

They used their orbs of light to illuminate the room. Apart from the many tables, they spotted things like microscopes, devices typical of chemistry labs, vials of mysterious substances, and sturdy metal containers scattered around. After their thorough search of the room, nothing stood out as a potential cause of Fenrir's corruption. All they found were crystal cubes, trivial notes, and a door to another room.

"Well, I guess that room is all that's left," Soul Howl said.

"I suppose so."

Although they hadn't turned anything up in the cultivation room, the door in the back seemed unusual. It wasn't the kind of high-tech door installed everywhere else in the facility; it was a common household door, knob and all.

On either side of the door, shelves extended all the way to the sides of the room. The metal boxes stacked atop them reached the ceiling. It was clearly suspicious.

"It seems like they split a room in half, doesn't it?" Mira muttered, looking around the cultivation room again.

The room had seemed cramped at first glance, and there was far too much equipment for such a small chamber. She and Soul Howl had even had trouble walking through some spots, making it feel even more cramped.

It was then that they'd noticed the door and shelves. What if the researchers put those in the middle of a larger room to halve it? In other words, this side might be cramped because everything from the other side had been moved here.

What remained on the other side, then? What had been worth going to all that effort to put over there?

"Okay. Here we go."

"Right. Be careful, now."

This door's presence meant that the abomination might be behind it. Going through it was fine for a human, but it was hard to get their tanks—the larger golem and holy knights—to fit, so Soul Howl first sent the motion-detector golem through the slightly open door.

"No reactions in there..." It seemed that nothing lurked in the room beyond, so Soul Howl threw open the door and charged in. "Oooh...!" he gasped, seemingly more amazed than aghast.

"What? What'd you find?" Wondering what he had seen, Mira rushed in behind him. She simultaneously saw both Soul Howl's elation and what he was looking at. "Could this be...a *gravesite*?"

"Yeah, I think so."

In this space, which the researchers had intentionally split the cultivation room to build, was a pile of what appeared to be coffins. It wasn't yet clear whether anything was inside them, but there were quite a few.

What influenced the pair's impression of the room most strongly were the things placed in front: a seemingly handmade shrine, a carved wooden Buddha statue, and a tombstone constructed from metal plates and the like.

Given the materials and surrounding environment, this gravesite had evidently been slapped together with things on hand. Still, any Japanese person facing the sight would immediately recognize it as a place to mourn the dead. As such, the room's atmosphere was tranquil.

Mira gently put her hands together in prayer, then walked toward the tombstone standing in the center. Letters were etched on it, surely related to the people resting in the space. "Something's written here. This seems to say...'unworthy gods,' I believe."

The rudimentary tombstone, handmade from various materials, was labeled A GRAVE FOR UNWORTHY GODS.

"Unworthy gods, huh? I think that tells us everything about what's in here." Soul Howl's head poked out from behind Mira. When he saw the text, he gazed at the gravesite with a look that couldn't be described as either joy or sadness.

"You may be right..."

Unworthy gods... Falling short of godhood... Considering the research and experiments performed here, the meaning of that quickly became clear—for what purpose those beings had been born, and for what purpose they had died. Mira put her hands together in remembrance of their unfruitful suffering.

"This is...a whole lot more than I expected," Soul Howl said while Mira was steeped in sentimentality.

When she looked over at him, he'd already begun opening the coffins. "I can't believe you, opening those without blinking at a time like this..."

Where had his melancholy expression from before gone? Now, he dug through the coffins like he was searching for buried treasure.

Soul Howl probably had misgivings himself, but as a necromancer, corpses were a direct power source for him. Plus, he had a thing for undead girls, so nobody could keep him from his equally outrageous and productive deed.

25

THE MAKESHIFT GRAVESITE behind the cultivation room was full of so-called unworthy gods' corpses.

Mira looked sidelong at Soul Howl, who opened coffin after coffin to appraise the contents. She frowned at those contents. "All these are their unworthy gods... What awful sins the researchers here committed."

Inside the coffins were capsules of various sizes. They were transparent, giving a view of what lay within. The beings in the smaller coffins hadn't taken shape yet, but the bigger coffins—about the size of human babies—contained abominations too painful to look upon. The beings in the large coffins also had large silver collars fitted around their necks.

All those capsule-bound beings had been created through experiments and died, failing to become gods.

While Mira looked on, horrified by just how many corpses there were, the Spirit King's voice echoed in her mind. *"Miss Mira, would you please touch that vessel for me?"* He seemed to want to inspect something through the blessing.

"Very well," Mira replied. When her right hand touched the biggest capsule, the mark of the Spirit King's blessing appeared on her body and glowed.

Curious about what Mira was doing, Soul Howl stopped rummaging around. "Hm? What's up?"

At the same time, the glow brightened until, after a while, it faded.

"I'm certain this was the cause of all that happened," the Spirit King declared, then offered his analysis of the situation. The corpses here contained lingering regrets due to their inability to become gods. With so many gathered in one place, they'd melded into a single will that remained in this location. *"The wooden statue provides them some comfort. Still, the arrival of a godly being—Fenrir—awakened both jealousy and longing in them. That longing was overwhelming."*

Thus, the failed gods' single spirit had caused Fenrir's corruption.

"I see..." As they'd expected, the research into artificial gods was affecting Fenrir. Understanding that, Mira realized that numerous lingering regrets blending into one greater will was something she'd encountered quite recently. *"It reminds me of that Oni Princess. Is this also something we can dispel with the holy sword and your powers combined?"*

The Oni Princess was a collective of the hatred harbored by onikind, and a key figure in the creation of Chimera Clausen. Remembering that, Mira asked if they could cleanse this spirit in a similar way. The Spirit King's answer didn't come quickly.

After a while, he finally replied, *"This one... I believe so. However, it will differ from the last. It requires not purification but something closer to calming the soul."*

The different emotions swirling within this entity gave rise to that difference. It wasn't feeling hatred but a mixture of simple admiration, envy, regret, and despair.

"Hrmm, I see... That does make sense."

The unworthy gods had probably perished in this facility long before any hatred could possibly arise. Their single will had sprouted from beings who'd only been able to cling to life and knew nothing of hatred. Nonetheless, their purity and immaturity had disrupted Fenrir's godly powers and sent him on a rampage, according to the Spirit King.

"By the way, I've been thinking. Was the thing I saw back there similar to the angel that possessed the Oni Princess?" Could the abomination Mira had spotted actually have been something possessed by this hive mind?

Although she wondered that, the Spirit King refuted her train of thought. *"No. I sensed no such emotions through your hands."* After confirming outright that the hive mind wouldn't have tried to possess something, he added, *"All that I felt was a longing for Fenrir."*

Perhaps Fenrir's power had made him something akin to a parental figure to the failed gods.

"A parent... That's sad indeed," Mira murmured, gazing at the capsules.

A certain someone poked his head from behind her again. "So, what'd you figure out? You were talking to the Spirit King, right?" It was Soul Howl, of course. Having seen Mira touch a capsule while glowing with the blessing, fall silent, and finally speak cryptic words, he urged her to share what she'd discussed.

"Yes, yes, just a moment." With a hint of melancholy, Mira briefly summarized what she'd heard from the Spirit King and what she was to do next.

"Gotcha. We were right to think this was the cause." They'd found the source of the power corrupting Fenrir, and a solution as well. Learning this, Soul Howl added, "I've helped you enough already. Don't think I owe you, okay?" He closed the coffins again.

"Fair enough," agreed Mira. She never would've arrived at the answer this quickly on her own. Then she asked, "So? You don't need to pick a favorite?" Clearly, she was referring to a favorite corpse for Soul Howl to use in his necromancy.

"No. They're all empty and useless now. I guess everything got sucked into that hive mind thing or whatever." He shrugged.

Though they were failures, the beings in the chamber had been created in hopes of making gods. No doubt they could've been fantastic vessels for necromancers, but unfortunately, Soul Howl's investigation found them unfit for such a purpose.

"Let's have our little memorial service so we can go home." Soul Howl couldn't possibly have checked all the coffins yet, but he seemed ready to give up the search. He sat down in a corner. "So, will you dance like a shrine maiden or something?" he joked, apparently planning to wait patiently until the pitiful single will calmed.

"Please. All I have to do is swing a sword." Mira chuckled at his exaggerated inquisitiveness while she prepared. First, she summoned the necessary conduit, the holy sword Sanctia. "Shall we begin now?" She focused, holding the sword as it glowed with divine yet gentle light. The Spirit King's blessing covered her body once more. Through her hands, his prayers poured into Sanctia.

In contrast to the purification of the Oni Princess, warm and peaceful light flowed from the sword. Mira swung it powerfully, pity and compassion in her heart.

Light swelled forth and rained upon their surroundings. It gently engulfed the handmade shrine, wooden statue, numerous coffins, and the single spirit will. The scene was both mystical and melancholy. Before long, that light subsided quietly, and Mira heard the Spirit King's voice in her head again.

"Their lingering regret is stronger than I thought. One more time, Miss Mira."

They had performed the ritual with their strongest prayers, but these were the lingering regrets of those who'd wished to be gods. One or two swings of Sanctia wouldn't soothe them fully.

"Understood." Mira swung the sword a couple more times, wishing peace to the unworthy gods.

After thirteen swings, the air in the room turned palpably lighter.

The Spirit King declared that the job was finished. *"Well done, Miss Mira. That one seemed to quiet them."*

"I-It's over... Finally..." Mira collapsed, exhausted from having focused, prayed, and performed the ritual with all her might. Most of the power was the Spirit King's, but her mana had been necessary to release that power from the holy sword, so it had fallen to below a quarter of its maximum amount.

With this, they'd managed to cut off the source of the power corrupting Fenrir. The Spirit King claimed that, after a month passed, all the power that had spread would be gone. The matter was definitely settled.

While Mira lay down in exhaustion, Martel's voice rang through her mind: *"Thank you, Mira. Now Fenrir can be free. Oh, and I have a message from him!"*

After thanking Mira for fulfilling her promise, Martel passed on the message from Fenrir. It seemed Martel had been narrating things for the pup, so he knew everything about what was going on in the research facility. His message thanked Soul Howl, First Pupil, and Woofson alike.

When Mira seemed like she was finally recovering, Soul Howl stood and declared, "Welp, job's done. Time to get going."

"Mm, right. It's already late at night." She'd rather rest her head at an inn than rough it here. "Here goes..." She groaned like an old man as she stood. Still a little lethargic, she opened the door and left the unworthy gods' gravesite behind.

Immediately after reentering the cultivation room, Mira let out a weird scream from sheer surprise. "Whaaagh?!"

"What's wrong?!" Soul Howl asked. He rushed over and peeked out.

Before them was something...humanoid that looked almost like a woman.

Near the cluttered cultivation room's entrance, the woman appeared dark gray, as if in shadow, although the orbs of light illuminated her brightly. The eyes that occasionally peeked through her long black hair were terrifyingly bloodshot.

"It's her... That's the one I saw—" Seeing those eyes made Mira certain that this woman was the unidentified being she'd glimpsed before. As she realized that, the creature groaned creepily and abruptly attacked. "Nwhaaa—?!"

Though panicked, Mira managed to summon a holy knight precisely between herself and the foe, blocking the assault. Shockingly, the gray woman clung to the holy knight. Then, with ridiculous strength, she overwhelmed it despite the difference in size.

"Goodness... She's that strong?" Although they were lesser summons, Mira's trained holy knights couldn't be pushed back easily. Yet now, just hugging the knight was enough for the woman to stop its movements and even dent its armor. Quickly judging that she needed greater firepower, Mira began setting summoning points.

Soul Howl stepped forth to stop her. "Wow. So this is that abomination you mentioned." He gazed calmly at the gray

woman. Then, as the holy knight creaked and shattered to bits, he instantly summoned a golem to wrestle her down. While the gray woman screamed and struggled, Soul Howl had a second golem help hold her back as he surveyed her. "Oh, wow... Very interesting."

Mira timidly approached to see her true identity too.

What was this woman? If she didn't come up on Biometric Scan, she couldn't be a living being. It was starting to seem likely that she was a surviving unworthy god. Did that make her an undead monster? If this was a spawn point, there should've been other monsters as well. It would be unnatural for there to be just one.

Then what? Mira and Soul Howl arrived at one possible answer.

"Do you think she underwent fiend transformation?" Mira suggested.

"Yeah..." replied Soul Howl. "With an unworthy god's corpse as a base, at that."

That answer came from direct observation and a few assumptions. They suspected she was an undead fiend, and only one thing could've served as the base. Most significantly of all, there was a familiar silver collar on the woman's neck.

At this point, the mechanism behind fiend transformations was unclear. All they knew was that it could happen anywhere. The pair believed some criteria had been met that turned the sleeping unworthy god's corpse into a fiend. There was no precedent for a human turning into a fiend, so although they had humanoid forms, the unworthy gods weren't human.

What tugged at the duo, though, was the creature's appearance. The capsules in the coffins were only the size of babies. But the being in front of them was as large as an adult woman. Had she begun as an adult, or, even stranger, had she grown over all this time? The reason for her size was unclear, but that itself made sense, for the unworthy gods were unknown beings.

After they'd observed her for a moment, the gray woman struggled even more violently and shook off the golems' restraints.

"Whoa...!"

"Mgh!"

She began to leap around more spryly than before, jumping forth to attack.

"She's a lively one... Oh, yes, very nice. *Very* nice." Soul Howl grinned creepily as he fended off her assault with golems.

"Ugh. Out comes the freak side again..." Mira grinned caustically.

Her first impression of the gray woman had been poor, but now that Mira got a better look, it was clear she'd once been beautiful. Yet her eyes were vacant, lifeless, and bloodshot, all at once. When she stood still, she slumped. Still, her nude figure was oddly enticing, which easily explained Soul Howl's attitude.

Mira quickly stepped back; she didn't want to get between the two. She watched the battle from behind a holy knight to avoid stray attacks. In front of her, a fierce battle unfolded.

Even when they originated from small animals, fiends could be more dangerous than B-rank monsters. With an unworthy god as her base, the gray woman was surely beyond A-rank.

Supernatural events occurred before Mira's eyes, like a poltergeist's attacks taken to an extreme. Desks and machines floated and shot like bullets toward the golems and Soul Howl. The gray woman herself flew freely in midair, too, attacking with blackened hands.

It seemed hers were not normal hands; every time they touched the golems, the latter eroded and even collapsed. From this angle, Soul Howl was clearly losing. He created golems continuously, only to see them barely fend off attacks before collapsing. It was as if the creature was toying with him.

Mira didn't move. No matter how the gray woman struggled, her fate had been sealed the moment Soul Howl laid eyes on her. Undead girls couldn't escape his clutches.

"Oh, wonderful. How powerful, how beautiful. Come, dear. Be mine!"

The "poltergeist" turned even more violent, but its storm of objects became meaningless instantly after.

Soul Howl's [Necromantic Arts: Dust Golem] gathered everything in the room and turned it all into one golem. The dust golem held out its limbs, withstanding the poltergeist-like power. With this, Soul Howl had canceled out one of the gray woman's methods of attack.

But she didn't stop there. This time, she reached her blackened hands directly for Soul Howl. This was, unfortunately, a poor move.

"Oh no. She's done for," Mira chuckled.

The agile gray woman flew through the air and struck deftly. Her hand was mere inches from Soul Howl, but just before it hit, it sank into mud that appeared out of nowhere. This was [Necromantic Arts: Mud Golem], whose mud stopped and engulfed all in its tracks.

The woman's blackened hand destroyed the mud golem from the inside, but she would need more instantaneous firepower to deal with the continuous stream of golems Soul Howl was generating.

In the end, his endless mud golems won out, swallowing the woman whole. After a while, the mud golem finally backed off. The gray woman remained, pinned to the floor with rocky restraints.

If she hadn't been up against Soul Howl—or rather, mages like him and Mira—the woman might've been a ferocious threat that took many victims. Unfortunately for her, the poltergeist-like attacks and her blackened hands had been easy for the two to deal with.

Wise Man Flonne's Ethereal Arts could control hundreds of giant rocks at once. To someone who'd seen Flonne fight, these attacks were just inferior copies. Likewise, Wise Man Meilin could easily destroy anything her Immortal Arts touched. She even had the ability to grasp a target from a distance, making her much more difficult to battle.

Since they knew those two Wise Men, it was easy to fight off the gray woman. She was undead to boot, so Soul Howl's victory was overwhelming.

While the gray woman struggled against her restraints, Soul Howl approached gleefully. "Now, be a good girl for me."

If they weren't dealing with a fiend right now, this would look awfully criminal. He turned to Mira with a big smile. "Oh, Elder. Sorry, I hope you don't mind waiting a minute."

"Yes, yes, I know," Mira replied. She pulled a chair out of the pile that was once the dust golem, then patiently watched as Soul Howl worked his magic.

He pinned down the restrained gray woman and used a special necromancer spell that would turn her back into a normal corpse. Although it depended on the state of the corpse, that spell could heal moderate damage and decay. In a way, it was like healing magic for undead targets. And it came with one special use: cast on undead fiends, it could bring them back to their senses.

However, it wasn't perfect. It couldn't *undo* a fiend transformation, due to the crystal within the body that caused that transformation. When the spell was cast on it, the crystal actively worked to maintain the fiend form.

"Okay. There it is." Seeing the crystal's reaction, Soul Howl stabbed the corpse with his knife—minimizing damage to the gray woman herself, of course.

She immediately shrieked like never before. It was a bone-chilling scream, accompanied by a wave of black miasma.

Her restraints shattered the instant the miasma touched them. She didn't stop there, but screamed again, shaking the room itself violently. The desks, chairs, and other furniture went flying.

Soul Howl's grin only deepened. "Whoa! Guess that's what happens when you're locked in a place like this so long. All that history hasn't gone to waste, has it?"

"What was that? Resurrected's Dying Cry? Goodness, that was intense." Mira rolled her eyes in irritation and backed off farther. Then something surprising happened: perhaps as a result of the quaking, the shelves dividing the room collapsed spectacularly. "Oh, now look what you've done..."

When Mira turned, the unworthy gods' gravesite was visible. Fortunately, only the nearby walls had sustained damage; the shrine and coffins were intact.

Mira and Soul Howl knew what the gray woman did to cause that. It was the final, enraged attack of undead fiends with a particularly long history behind them: Resurrected's Dying Cry.

Resurrected's Dying Cry used that black miasma to bolster the user's abilities and nullify some attacks. It also materialized wandering souls. More than just *materialized* them—as a bonus, it amplified the negative emotions within them.

Materialized souls would go berserk to vent those emotions. If a dragon's or beast's spirit happened to wander by when Resurrected's Dying Cry was used, it could potentially turn a battle's tide all on its own.

The opposite was true as well, however. Faced with the souls the cry had materialized, Mira furrowed her brow. Only the souls of the unworthy gods were wandering that area, and only juvenile emotions were left within them. They were innocent souls, lost before they developed complex emotions—let alone knew good and evil.

Therefore, though dozens had materialized, none fought for the gray woman. They didn't even seem to understand the situation.

"Is this a message, my dear? You're telling me you want to have lots of children! Oh, you're so sweet!" Soul Howl was feeling better than ever.

Though the wandering spirits hadn't bolstered the gray woman, the miasma had powered her up. Restraining her would be harder, and her poltergeist attacks would grow more frequent and intense.

But Soul Howl was ready to overcome all that—to make the gray woman his and dote on her freely with his own hands.

She Professed Herself Pupil of the Wise Man

26

THE BATTLE was fierce, though perhaps as a result of Soul Howl's perverted love, it didn't appear as violent as one might expect. Soul Howl simply used mud golems reinforced with the power of Resistance to slowly adapt to and nullify the miasma.

Things ended up the same way they had been before the gray woman used Resurrected's Dying Cry.

"I'll be done in no time," Soul Howl said as he bound her to the floor once more. Even as she struggled, he gently put a hand on her cheek and again stabbed at the crystal inside her, then skillfully carved it out. "Take care of this for me, Elder."

As soon as he retrieved it, he lobbed the crystal at Mira. It was a mass of magical energy that could change not just animals but even holy beasts and spiritual beasts into fiends. It was pure poison to humans.

"Don't throw these things, fool," Mira complained, then ordered her holy knight to crush it to pieces.

After that, Soul Howl buried a Soulstone—a fake soul created through necromancy—in the gray woman's body. "There, there.

Good girl." What followed was his specialty. His magic slowly but surely turned the ashen fiend back into a normal corpse.

According to Soul Howl, fiend transformation caused problematic mutations that took time to undo, so they needed to wait. To Mira, though, there was something more pressing.

"Say, is there anything you can do about…those?" Mira asked, looking toward the unworthy gods' souls, which the woman's dying screams had manifested. One began to cry, triggering the others to cry in unison.

"All yours," Soul Howl replied shortly. He was focused purely on the woman whose cheek he currently caressed; his words contained absolute conviction that he couldn't bear to waste even a moment on anything else.

"Mrgh… And what do you want *me* to do with them?"

Souls manifested by Resurrected's Dying Cry didn't disappear when the fiend itself was defeated. The pair were aware of that, and they had disposed of similar souls many times. Normally, they just fought them off without hesitation. After all, they were hostile spirits that attacked if left alone.

This time was different, though. The location was simply too special, and Mira was unsure what to do. She couldn't bear to use force against such innocent children—but that didn't mean she could abandon them either.

Mira racked her brain for a more peaceful way to put them to rest, and once she couldn't bear the crying any longer, she snatched up one of the babies.

"Theeere, there. Good baby. Good baby." She tried consoling it like a normal infant. Then she sat down in the midst of the spirits, putting a few more in her lap as she tried to console them. "Aww, what's wrong? What are you crying about?"

Clinging to a ray of hope that the babies themselves might actually answer, she tried to think up any method she could. How could she stop them from crying? How could she calm them?

One baby leaned close to her breast as if demanding something. Had its instincts remained in its soul?

"Hm? What? Milk? Sorry, I can't exactly give you *that*." Mira quickly realized what they wanted, but she had to confess that she couldn't provide it.

A flash of inspiration passed through her mind, though— what if she used the effects of Resurrected's Dying Cry to her advantage?

Manifested souls rampaged because their negative emotions were amplified. When they did, the emotions dispersed, which returned them to normal. But the babies' innocence meant that there were no negative emotions to amplify. The fact that they were crying, though, must've meant *some* related agitation was involved. If Mira could resolve that agitation, wouldn't they return to normal spirits?

She couldn't provide breast milk, so she looked for a substitute in her Item Box. She found different flavors of fruit au lait. All were delicious drinks—a perfect combination of fruit and milk. A memory resurfaced then, however—one from when her younger sister was born. At the time, she'd been proactive about caring for the new family member.

"Oh, right... Cow's milk isn't good for babies, is it?"

Having learned that from her mother, Mira put the beverages back in her Item Box and thought again.

Caring for creatures who couldn't express their needs was very difficult. Recognizing how it would feel to be a parent, Mira continued to try to soothe the crying babies and happened to notice something unusual about their behavior. It seemed like the one that had faced her chest before only did so instinctively because she'd hugged it. The others, meanwhile, were all looking upward.

What did the babies truly seek? Mira knew one way to find out. When she'd touched the capsules, the Spirit King was able to unravel the emotions within. Couldn't he do the same with the babies' spirits?

"Spirit King, do you have any way to read these babies' emotions?" Mira asked.

He replied gently, *"I think so. Let's give it a try."*

The mark of his blessing reappeared on her body. Through her hands, he touched the baby's soul.

"These are remnants of the fiend's power... A quick detour, and..." The situation made things tricky, but the Spirit King was no slouch. Before long, he reached the infant's heart. *"I've figured it out, Miss Mira."* After that confirmation, he declared that the powerful emotion in the baby's heart was longing.

"Hrmm... Longing, you say? In that case, they're looking up for..."

If the emotion amplified in these beings who'd died before attaining godhood was longing, then Mira might return their souls to normal if she relieved that yearning. She wondered how she could do that, though.

At least it was clear who the unworthy gods admired. The object of their yearning was far, far above—indeed, it was Fenrir. The babies were crying over their longing for that god.

If they meet Fenrir, maybe that'll do it... But they also caused his erosion...

The ritual should've solved that problem, but Mira worried there might be no turning back if the unworthy gods met Fenrir in person.

Just then, Martel's voice came through. *"Mira, Fenrir would like you to summon him there. He wants to meet them, talk to them, and pray for them in person."* No doubt she'd explained this situation to Fenrir as well, and the pup resolved to step into the place that had driven him mad.

"Very well. If that's what he wants, I'll trust him."

Mira couldn't shake her worry, but she respected Fenrir's wishes, quickly preparing a summoning circle. With the Bound Arcana positioned in a four-corner formation, she sublimated them into the Mark of the Rosary and began incanting her spell.

Mana overflowing with power energized the summoning circle, creating a guiding gate to link spaces. A current of power rushed through the cultivation room, causing a rumble, until the power finally condensed in one place and became a key that opened the large gate.

"Thanks, Miss Mira," Fenrir said after appearing from the magic circle.

"I should be the one to thank you. I was just hoping to ask for your aid," Mira replied.

Immediately, she witnessed the results of his presence. Seeing the object of their yearning had an enormous effect on the babies. As Fenrir approached, they suddenly stopped crying. More than that, they started *smiling*.

"You're a hit, friend," Mira chuckled.

One baby started crawling toward Fenrir. Once it was close enough, it hugged him tight—but it was so clumsy it fell over.

"Whoops. Careful, now." Fenrir didn't miss the opportunity; he got under the baby to catch it, sitting down on the spot, which left the baby straddling him. Apparently comfortable there, the baby sank into Fenrir's fur and fell asleep. Its face was blissful, eliciting warm smiles from those who watched.

I'm certain this was for the best, Mira thought.

The babies' souls would normally have returned to where they belonged—the Celestial Shrine of Nirvana—but everything that had happened finally gave them the chance to meet Fenrir, their idol. No doubt that was what truly soothed their lingering regrets.

Leaving aside the question of whether this would restore them, Mira was certain it was the right thing to do. While she watched emotionally, an unexpected sound reached her ears: babies crying.

"What?! What happened?!" She whipped around to see. The source of the sobs was clear at a glance; they came from the babies still too young to crawl. "This is where I step in." Mira entrusted the baby in her arms to Fenrir, then diligently picked up the others to bring to him.

Once she'd brought them all to Fenrir's side, the crying finally ceased. Cheerful laughter gradually replaced it.

Though Fenrir was subjected to the full range of baby behaviors—hugging, plunging, playing, petting, hitting, putting things in their mouths—he laughed as he played with the failed gods. "Babies are curious little things, huh?"

The sight of Fenrir—basically a giant puppy—playing with children was so heartwarming, it would fit right into a picture book. One couldn't help smiling at it.

Perhaps Mira's feelings got through to the babies too, or perhaps they felt motherly warmth from her, for some of them took a liking to her as well.

"Indeed they are. I can't take my eyes off them," Mira agreed, cradling a baby and remembering her little sister. Though she'd been a handful, her growth was wonderful to witness.

After lots of playing with Mira and Fenrir, the babies got tired and relaxed, falling asleep contentedly one by one. Their sleeping faces were innocent, adorable, and peaceful.

Fenrir caught the sleeping infants and said, as if praying, "Rest well, children."

"May you all have sweet dreams," Mira wished, hugging the babies falling asleep in her arms. Had the failed gods let go of their longing? Had their dream come true?

Eventually, the babies turned into faint light and returned to their original existence as souls. The shimmering particles they left behind gently enveloped Mira and Fenrir before dispersing.

All that remained were soft warmth and the sense of accomplishment that came with a good deed.

27

THEY'D FINALLY FREED the babies' souls from Resurrected's Dying Cry. Having successfully restored those spirits to the world without violence, Mira thanked and dismissed Fenrir, then checked on Soul Howl.

Despite the previous fuss, his work was going well. His obsession and concentration were equally terrifying. His spell had proven effective; the traces of the gray woman's fiend transformation were all but gone. She'd returned to her original form, and beauty had taken the place of her horror-movie-monster visage.

That made the current situation look *more* concerning. Since the gray woman was still bound to the floor, this appeared even more criminal than before. Fortunately, no normal people were around to be scarred by the sight.

"Well, isn't she a beauty?" Mira grinned lasciviously at the gray woman.

"Yeah. I don't know what you can call this other than fate." Now acting completely depraved, Soul Howl pulled out a bunch of women's clothes, excitedly picking out garments for the gray woman to wear.

Martel misunderstood once again. *"Poor man... This is how he copes with being unable to save his true love."*

The Spirit King alone calmly tried to analyze things. *"Becoming fiends... I wonder what manner of beings those unworthy gods truly were."* Unfortunately, nobody was listening.

After Soul Howl had obtained a new wife, things proceeded without incident. They left the cultivation room, went to the elevator bay, rode to the top floor, and headed all the way to the facility's entrance.

"This place seems to hold a lot more secrets, but we should leave such things to the experts."

"Yeah. I already got what really matters—let them do what they want."

When they turned around on the stairs leading up, they saw the expansive facility behind them through the glass. It seemed certain that this place was related to modern Japan, but that didn't mean they would learn anything by investigating on their own.

Thus, Mira and Soul Howl were in full agreement: they would just need to pass this on to the Hinomoto Committee. Of course, part of their reasoning was that they didn't want to put in any more effort.

When they reached the exit, having left no regrets behind, Mira gazed at the location where the security terminal was hidden.

"The security... Is it okay just to leave it?" she asked.

"Seems fine to me, but...I don't know. Want to set it up again?"

Since all the security was currently disabled, anybody could trash the facility as completely as they wanted. Then again, it *was* deep below a dungeon that already took ages to clear. And you needed at least a security-level-five authentication key to enter; to get that, you had to enter the Machina Guardian's boss chamber. Reaching it wasn't exactly easy, so it made sense that leaving things as they were would be fine.

Mira and Soul Howl didn't know whether the key card was reusable either. If it had limited uses, then reactivating the facility's security might temporarily keep the Hinomoto Committee from investigating. That would require the committee to fall back on the authentication-key update process Soul Howl had found, which would take a week at minimum.

Since they knew an investigation team would come soon, this was a dilemma. But despite all appearances, Soul Howl was prudent; he suggested setting up the security again.

His main reason was the absence of the Machina Guardian. In a way, that raid boss had created even more robust security than the facility system's former settings. Now that the Machina Guardian would be gone for a while, anyone could easily obtain an authentication key of a high-enough level to enter.

"Hrmm... Well, it's not as if *we'll* have to wait. Besides, I'm curious whether it will work." Mira agreed, ran over to the security terminal, and fed it the key card. It again displayed this text:

All room locks disengaged.

Please reestablish settings.

She pressed the *Settings* button, followed by the *Reset* option.

Even when the monitor displayed *Resetting...*, they could do little but wait and watch.

After a while, the words *Lock Complete* appeared. With that, things returned to the state they'd been in before Mira and Soul Howl arrived.

Mira tried feeding the terminal the key card again as a test. It displayed *No permission. Please issue new key card.* "Hrmm... The key card *was* limited."

"Then I'll have to tell the committee how to update it too," Soul Howl replied.

In other words, when the Hinomoto Committee inevitably visited someday, waiting for a new authentication key would delay them by a week.

Soul Howl would report to them; he'd have to stop by anyway, since—thanks to the Machina Guardian's loot—he could now upgrade Irina's grave goods.

"Finally! We're back!"

"Back on the seventh level, sure."

Mira and Soul Howl left the room with the hidden terminal behind and, after a long trudge up even longer-seeming stairs, headed to the boss-chamber door. It had no handle—no protrusions at all, in fact, save for one single slit near the edge.

Soul Howl took his authentication key out of his Item Box and pushed it into the slit. Rays of light spread over the door, and after a moment, it opened without a sound. When Soul Howl went through, it quickly shut again. This door was designed so that only one person could go through at a time.

"You know, I guess it's very sci-fi in that regard." More intrigued, Mira gazed at the door and inserted her own authentication key.

Beyond the door was a small room enclosed by metal walls. Various devices lined the chamber. In the center, a tube went through the ceiling, continuing all the way to the surface. Inside, a capsule stood by as if waiting for a passenger; it could fit one person.

Soul Howl entered the capsule. "All right, see you in five minutes," he said sarcastically.

The capsule in the tube was essentially an escape pod. When its lid closed, it shot through the tube as if being sucked upward. Since the facility was so deep underground, it took a full five minutes to exit.

Another capsule quickly appeared in the tube. Mira likewise entered, joking, "Well, I suppose this counts as high-tech..."

The lid closed, and the capsule moved. It looked awfully fast from the outside, but the environment inside was surprisingly peaceful. One would expect serious g-force, but the user felt nothing. Assuming that was the result of sci-fi technology, Mira calmly waited the five minutes the capsule took to reach the surface.

About five minutes later, the capsule stopped—as it did so, one didn't even feel the inertia—and reopened. "High-tech indeed..." Mira muttered to herself as she alighted.

"Seriously. But how come only one exit is like that?" Soul Howl said, gazing past the capsule. His tone indicated that he was complaining.

"Feels like hostile design to me," Mira agreed.

The escape capsule had brought them to a corner of a large stone chamber. Looking toward the center, they could see six small, altar-like objects placed from end to end. Each altar was surrounded by four stone pillars and had a stone tablet engraved with a magic circle embedded in its center.

While Mira and Soul Howl glared at the altars in irritation, the second magic circle from the back glowed. Instantly, five people resembling adventurers appeared.

The five headed to the chamber's exit, discussing how they'd divide their loot. Along the way, they locked eyes with Mira and Soul Howl in front of the tube.

"Hey, you two there. That's only an exit. It's not gonna open, no matter how long you wait," a balding man laughed before leaving. He was in an awfully good mood—no doubt he'd earned a lot of money. The four following him bowed apologetically to Mira and Soul Howl.

"We know, you fool," Mira muttered to herself as the adventurers left.

As the balding man said, the tube *was* only for leaving. This chamber, for its part, contained all the Ancient Underground City's exits. All *except* the seventh-level exit used teleportation magic, so there was no need to wait five minutes to exit the other levels. That was why Mira and Soul Howl had complained.

"I guess nobody expects someone to be returning from the seventh level in this day and age," mused Soul Howl. "I'd say you'll make a pretty penny off that loot you grabbed."

To use the escape pod, one needed to reach the seventh level and obtain an authentication key. Given the adventurer's misunderstanding, Soul Howl was probably right that accomplishing such a thing was extremely rare in this era, which would mean the price of seventh-level loot had risen to match.

Mira smirked broadly at his words.

The stone exit chamber was beneath the oldest chapel in Grandrings. Mira and Soul Howl exited the chamber, climbed a long staircase, and entered the chapel through a door at the top.

Though the chapel was old, it was well maintained and had a dignity that outweighed its years. Sculptures and wall murals told the story of its history, and the candlelight gave them an even more enigmatic sheen. All in all, the divinity of this space could give even an atheist pause.

Many worshippers were lined up in the chapel, and a priest wearing vestments that indicated his high rank was preaching something to them. Mira and Soul Howl's arrival in such a solemn location was rather startling, but nobody paid them any mind.

On the pillar nearest the door they'd entered through was a single large sign labeled TO ADVENTURERS RETURNING FROM THE ANCIENT UNDERGROUND CITY. It read as follows:

IF YOU REQUIRE TREATMENT FOR INJURY OR ILLNESS, THE FIRST ROOM ON THE LEFT IS AN INFIRMARY. YOU MAY USE IT FREELY; ONE OF OUR BEST PRIESTS WILL ALWAYS AWAIT YOU THERE.

WEEKDAY PRAYERS ARE FROM 2:00 P.M. TO 4:00 P.M. PLEASE BE QUIET DURING THIS PERIOD.

ON WEEKENDS, WE DELIVER SERMONS ON FABLES OF THE TRINITY FROM 6:00 P.M. TO 7:00 P.M. IF YOU ARE INTERESTED, FEEL FREE TO ATTEND. IF YOU'RE IN A HURRY, PLEASE EXIT IN A QUIET, ORDERLY MANNER.

DEPENDING ON THE DAY AND TIME, WE MAY HOLD EVENTS SUCH AS WORSHIP AND SERMONS. IF YOU RETURN DURING SUCH AN EVENT, WE APOLOGIZE FOR THE INCONVENIENCE, BUT ASK THAT YOU NOT USE THE MAIN DOOR. PLEASE FOLLOW THE ARROWS ON YOUR RIGHT AND, KEEPING QUIET, EXIT THROUGH THE SIDE DOOR.

After skimming the long message, Mira looked around. "Interesting..." she murmured.

Long ago, that sign hadn't existed. After all, there'd been no such thing as adventurers. This was another symbol that time was passing.

When the Adventurers' Guild Union formed, it had led to the explosive growth of the adventuring profession. Many more people had visited the Ancient Underground City and, plainly, had to return at some point.

The Ancient Underground City took time to explore, but it contained instant-teleportation magic circles as dedicated exits. Everybody used those, naturally, and the chapel's sign was a result of that trend. No doubt many adventurers had come through making too much ruckus to ignore.

"That's politely written. I bet they can't stand adventurers." Chuckling at the repeated use of the word "quiet," Soul Howl peered around the chapel.

Just then, another group of adventurers came into the chapel. They whispered to each other as they scurried along the arrows to the right.

"Oh, they're mid-sermon."

"Ack! That's the iron-fisted priest!"

"Don't make a peep!"

"I'll pass on another of *his* diatribes."

Hearing their whispers, Mira wondered what had them quaking in their boots. "They're awfully scared of something."

She looked toward the priest giving the passionate sermon. He appeared to be in his midfifties, and his expression was calm and peaceful. At a glance, one hardly expected a nickname like "the iron-fisted priest" to refer to him.

Soul Howl also looked at the man, then snickered to himself. "Want to know why? Inspect him. You might learn something fun."

Mira followed Soul Howl's example and Inspected the priest. "Aha. This is a rather delightful little development, isn't it?"

The priest's physical stats were higher than the average veteran adventurer's. That wasn't what she and Soul Howl were focused on, though; it was his name.

"That's what you get in the city that gathers the best adventurers on the continent," Soul Howl mused. "Even the priests are jacked."

"Adventurer" was a mere catchall; the term described people as diverse as could be. There were polite ones, and there were ruffians. In a city like Grandrings, problems involving adventurers popped up daily, so citizens needed the power to overwhelm adventurers when necessary.

The church that served as the underground city's exit saw the second-most adventurer foot traffic in all Grandrings, after the Adventurers' Guild Union.

What priest had taken a position at a chapel with such a high rate of adventurer-related problems? That would be Zatzbald Bloodycrimson Kingsblade, the strongest champion in the history of Ozstein's underground arena, boasting a win-loss record of a thousand-to-zero.

Zatzbald bloodycrimson kingsblade had been the champion of the underground arena. Mira and Soul Howl had been involved in various events with him, which added to their surprise when they saw how he carried himself now. They were very curious about how such a change had occurred.

Once upon a time, fighting was Zatzbald's supreme joy. His life's mission had been to make a shower of his enemies' blood. He'd been up-front about constantly raring to fight, glaring daggers and baring his fangs at challengers. How did he become a calm, compassionate priest delivering a sermon about the gods?

Anyone who'd known him back then would think this was a different person, yet here he was.

"From champion to priest... Wonder what happened."

"Beats me. That's the most random combo I can think of."

As the mystery piqued Soul Howl's and Mira's interest, another adventurer group who'd just arrived spotted the priest, hid their presence as if they were in mortal danger, and tiptoed toward the exit.

Seeing this, Soul Howl urged Mira to go ask them about the priest. Getting information out of people was easier for a cute girl than a suspicious-looking guy, after all.

"Fine, I guess," Mira grumbled. She stopped an adventurer, whispering to the young man, "Excuse me! I have a question for you."

He looked back and forth between the priest and Mira before finally looking back to her, making his mind up, and replying, "What is it? Ask me anything."

Evade the priest's tongue-lashing, or talk to a cute girl? The adventurer had seemingly picked the latter, though he kept his voice low.

"That priest is no ordinary man, is he?" With her eyes, Mira indicated the priest. Then she whispered even lower, leaning closer to the adventurer as if they were sharing secrets. "If you know anything about him, would you share it with me?"

When she leaned toward him, he blushed, yet casually tried to draw personal information out of her. "Uh, you mean Father Kingsblade? You haven't been in town long, have you?"

"No. I just got here. I've heard people call him 'the iron-fisted priest.' For a priest, iron fists are an odd trait, aren't they?"

"Yeah, I guess. If your first impression is that he's not a normal priest, you've got a good eye. Everybody else knows that, though. Once upon a time, that priest was apparently the underground arena champion." The man showed off his knowledge proudly, but Mira had already known that. What mattered to her was why Zatzbald had changed careers.

"Oh ho! That is impressive." She feigned surprise, then asked her most pressing question. "Why did that champion give his title up for priesthood?"

The man glanced around quickly. Then, even more quietly, he whispered, "I've only heard rumors about this, but..."

Zatzbald Bloodycrimson Kingsblade's legacy as the strongest fighter in Ozstein's underground arena had kept him famous to that day. He'd once lived a turbulent life, believing in nothing but his own strength. He'd fought out of the belief that victory was the only way to leave your mark on the world, and that defeat meant losing your identity.

You might've called him an utterly idiotic meathead. Still, those precepts had given him strength, pushed away defeat, and became a firm part of his identity. After years upon years of fighting, everyone acknowledged his strength, and he'd become a living legend.

However, seven years ago, his legend had come to an end. The undefeated fighter suddenly met defeat at the hands of a girl training to be a warrior. He'd lamented losing his identity, but the girl had told him something: that power was only one way to prove himself. Although he had been defeated, as long as he still lived, his story wasn't over.

He'd struggled to accept her words; they refuted his very life prior to that point. While he struggled, the girl told him something else: if someone stronger than him said that, it must be true. Odd words, for someone who'd just claimed power wasn't everything.

Still, the girl's words reached him. Her spirit—her belief that strength wasn't everything, despite her own overwhelming strength—set his firm new ideology into motion. Awakened from his indifference to all but power, he asked how he should live his life from now on.

She answered that he should try a life that was the exact opposite of the one he'd lived thus far.

"So he got baptized, trained, and became a priest. Crazy, right?" The adventurer wrapped up Father Kingsblade's history with a look of admiration.

The priest had found a new place and established a new identity for himself, without relying on his power as a living legend. It seemed he was revered just as much as he was feared. Furthermore, Kingsblade didn't normally use his legendary strength—but he made an exception for adventurers, the man added with a shudder.

At one point, when a group of A-rank adventurers made a ruckus during a service, Kingsblade balled them up and threw them out like rags. From that point on, he was known as "iron-fisted."

The explanation was both moving and stupid, but Mira had an inkling of how sincerely *Zatzbald*-like it all was. She smiled gently at the priest, who had yet to finish his sermon. "I see. What an interesting background..."

"By the way...do you like strong men?" the adventurer suddenly asked, noticing how Mira's eyes were drawn to Zatzbald.

Mira imagined her ideal chivalrous form. "Hrmm... It's good to be strong, but I believe gentlemanliness is the true path to manhood," she declared. These days, that was a faraway aspiration for her.

"Gentlemanliness, huh...? Makes sense," the adventurer murmured in response. Giving an utterly awkward performance as a "gentleman," he made his pass. "Miss, if you don't mind, I'd love to take you out to dinner—"

"What are you doing here, dude? The priest's gonna notice you—damn, he's already got his eye on you!" One of the adventurer's party members had returned warily and peered toward the back of the chapel. As soon as he checked back there, he grabbed his friend's collar and ran off with him in tow.

The young man tried to say something to Mira as he was dragged away, but he didn't dare yell during a sermon, so his words didn't reach her. Neither did she care enough to find them out.

Still, the adventurer had clarified the history of this champion-turned-priest. Ignoring the man being forcefully towed out, Mira turned to Soul Howl, who'd listened next to her. "Well, there you go."

"Everyone's got their own story, huh? That's a crazy reason to become a priest," Soul Howl said, equally amazed and amused.

Mira fully agreed. "No kidding. I'll never understand people who speak with their fists," she replied, revealing her amazement at Zatzbald's dynamic lifestyle.

"You're more like them than you think, Elder."

Soul Howl's casual remark didn't seem to reach her ears. "Hm? What was that?"

"Nothing."

"A life that was the exact opposite of the one he'd lived thus far." Those cheap words were easier said than done. Soul Howl was impressed that Zatzbald had embodied them, but he focused most of his attention on the girl who'd told the fighter to do that.

"Hey, you know that girl from the story? Gotta wonder..."

Mira felt that suspicion as well. "Maybe..." she murmured.

They were thinking of the same person: Wise Man Meilin.

Warrior training had essentially been an everyday routine for Meilin. Maybe another girl trained like she did, but when one restricted the pool to close-range fighters, not many girls out there could've defeated Zatzbald. Hell, there might not be *any* others who could; among the other players, Zatzbald was rumored to be inferior only to the Three Great Kingdoms' generals.

"If it *was* Meilin, do you think the priest knows where she is?"

"Doubt it," Soul Howl said. "That was seven years ago, right? Master Meilin never fights rematches, and she's not the type to stay in one place long."

"Hrmm. Fair..."

Soul Howl was right. Back in their gaming days, Meilin spent her time wandering around, calling it "warrior training." That became so habitual that when she *did* return to her tower, it meant a big siege was about to happen. As such, the likelihood that Zatzbald knew her whereabouts was nearly zero.

"Anyway, we'd better get out of here too..." Soul Howl looked around the chapel and grimaced.

When Mira glanced around the interior as well, she made eye contact with Father Kingsblade. "Right..."

Kingsblade hadn't once paused his sermon, but one thing *was* different now. Instead of looking around his congregation cheerfully, he was glaring daggers at the duo. He'd apparently noticed them huddled in the corner, whispering to each other. He'd clearly mellowed out since becoming a priest, but his eyes were just as sharp as they used to be.

"Let's hurry up and escape!"

"Yeah, let's!"

At this rate, they might end up subjected to Father Kingsblade's legendary iron fists, so Mira and Soul Howl decided quietly to retreat. They followed the arrows out of the chapel. Even along the way, they heard the sermon. Today, Kingsblade seemed to be lecturing the congregation about gods and prophecies.

"Long ago, darkness engulfed the world, but it was dispelled by the combined efforts of the Trinity, spirits, and mankind. Only by clasping hands can we overcome all darkness. Our gods also watch over us hand in hand, after all. That is the greatest proof."

The Church of the Trinity was the most influential religion on this continent and had the most worshipers. Adherents believed the three pillars of the Trinity advocated working hand in hand as the only way to overcome hardships and weaknesses. The continent's three largest nations—Grimdart, Ozstein, and

Alisfarius—each protected and worshipped one of those three gods. The nations obeyed the Trinity's teachings and cooperated, never quarreling, while leading the continent as absolute rulers.

As Mira recalled lore she'd been fed at the start of the game, the chapel exit came into view, and the sermon continued. "The Trinity told us to work together to prepare for the coming future, in which the same darkness that once engulfed the world will appear once more in the form of an abyss. There is no need for us to fear. As long as we continue to work together, the light will surely come—"

When she and Soul Howl exited and closed the door, the priest's loud, clear voice suddenly cut off. In its place were the murmuring night breeze and city commotion.

The chapel's side exit led to a quiet back alley. A large building towered ahead, while the alley extended to either side. The area was illuminated, perhaps out of consideration for adventurers returning at night.

When they left the alley and circled to the front of the church, the light was even brighter. Ahead of the chapel was a large plaza. Countless candles surrounded its central fountain, warmly illuminating the surrounding area.

"Already that time, hm?"

Stars shone in the darkness of the night sky. When they checked, it was already past 7:00 p.m. It had taken a long time to investigate and resolve Fenrir's corruption; half a day had already passed since they'd awoken. Still, from a gaming perspective, they'd cleared an enormous facility extremely quickly.

"Ah, finally outside again... It's been so long," Soul Howl murmured emotionally as he looked up at the sky. Being underground for ages tended to make you miss the endless sky.

"Ah, fresh air," Mira sighed in response, looking up as well. The fragrant aroma of food wafted over. Thinking back, she realized she hadn't eaten since breakfast. "Now what are you planning to do?" she asked Soul Howl. "Surely all the affordable accommodations nearby are long booked."

"I'm about to leave, so I don't care," he replied, looking from the night sky to the fountain in front of them. "I'd like to get as close to my next objective as possible."

Relaxing rooms, clean beds—Soul Howl paid no heed to those luxuries or the peace of mind that came with them. Instead, he was opting to rush to his next destination.

"What, leaving already? How impatient. Here I was willing to let you stay another night in my lovely mansion." In other words, Mira's mansion spirit was open to Soul Howl again if he couldn't find an inexpensive place.

Soul Howl looked at her suspiciously and sighed. "Get real. You just want me to cook for you."

"Ngh..." Though he'd seen through Mira's plan, the sore loser retorted, "Well, still—if you leave now, you'll surely have to camp."

Heading out at this point, it would be difficult to reach another city that same day, which *would* mean camping. However, Soul Howl smirked as if that wasn't a problem at all.

"I've had to do that ever since I started my travels," he replied. "It doesn't bother me now. Besides, I've got ways to fend off wind and rain, although they might not be as comfortable as your mansion."

Since Soul Howl started his journey, he'd consistently prioritized speedy travel. Even if he reached a city at night, he pressed on if he had no business there. And if he wasn't in a city when it was time to rest his head, he camped. Each time, he explained, he used a small fortress golem to keep rain and wind at bay.

"Oh ho! A fortress golem..."

"Yeah. You'd be surprised how useful necromancy is."

That application of golems hadn't existed in-game, but it apparently created a fortress as small as a normal home, plenty sturdy enough to withstand wind. Even when his journey got difficult, Soul Howl added nostalgically, that allowed him to get some rest and keep going. Humans always slept best in a room put together just for them.

"That said, a fortress golem doesn't have a shower, toilet, or kitchen like your mansion. You're basically cheating." The perfection of Mira's mansion spirit had apparently surprised him.

"Bonds with spirits win again," Mira replied proudly.

"Anyway, it's about time I head out," Soul Howl said, then cast a spell.

Next to him, the Bicorn skeleton with the broken horn appeared. Its eerie, sinister aura caused a clamor around them, but Soul Howl didn't seem to care. That was normal for him.

"Get your business done and come home to us," Mira reminded him. "I'll tell Solomon I said as much."

Her mission was to bring the Nine Wise Men back to Alcait, but she couldn't strong-arm Soul Howl into that; he had work he absolutely needed to do. Instead, she had him promise he'd come back once he finished, adding that he should prepare a means of contact in case of an emergency.

"Yeah, I know. I've been thinking of settling down for a while now, so I swear, I'll be there as soon as I'm done. Now that I can use advanced magic again, I should wrap up much faster. As for a means of emergency contact—eh, I'll see about that after I visit the Hinomoto Committee. Might as well discuss it with Solomon." It was only a verbal promise, but Soul Howl answered as sincerely as ever.

"Good. I'll be waiting." To Mira, a verbal promise was enough. When Solomon and the Nine Wise Men swore, they *always* meant it. Their word was their bond.

Soul Howl climbed onto the Bicorn, turned around, and added, "Oh, speaking of: tell the Spirit King and Martel I said thanks again. Things are about to be a lot easier thanks to them." There was rare emotion on his face. No doubt he was *very* happy to be able to use advanced magic again.

"I shall," Mira agreed, then telepathically passed on the words Soul Howl had just told her. "Rather, I already have. They say 'We did it because we wanted to' and 'Good luck!'"

The Spirit King and Martel were still observing and offering support through Mira. They seemed to like Soul Howl so much that they hated to see him leave.

Soul Howl smiled a little at their words. "That so? Well, see you. You were a big help, Elder." After a quick, sheepish thanks to Mira, he rode his Bicorn onto a nearby building's roof.

"Right. Get your job done, and get it done right!" Mira encouraged him.

She watched him leap from roof to roof and disappear into the darkness of the night, then walked in the opposite direction.

29

AFTER PARTING with Soul Howl, Mira walked toward the city. When she passed the front door of the chapel, it suddenly opened, and Father Kingsblade appeared. Up close, he looked even taller than his two-meter stature and was impressively intimidating. Such a giant appearing seemingly out of nowhere made Mira twitch and look up at him.

Seeing her, the priest recalled what had happened inside a few minutes ago. "You were in the chapel before..."

She and Soul Howl had left the Ancient Underground City and loitered in the church, whispering about something. He remembered them well.

Kingsblade approached Mira quietly, stooped as if speaking to a child, and asked gently, "Miss, I received word that a man was using suspicious necromancy out here. Do you know anything about that?" His eyes weren't those of a gentle priest; they had the glint seen in Kingsblade's old days.

Mira didn't know the details of this world's religions, but it would make sense if there were rules against necromancy—magic closely tied to the dead—on church grounds. She feigned ignorance, hoping to skip the trouble.

"No..." she replied. "Doesn't ring a bell to me!"

The glint in the priest's stare sharpened. He looked her right in the eye and questioned her further. "I heard that a cute little girl like you was close to that suspicious man. Are you *sure* you don't know?"

This "report" was beginning to sound awfully detailed. Kingsblade seemed to know the whole situation already. At this point, he probably realized exactly who the necromancer was. It'd be difficult for Mira to evade the question.

"Er...did this necromancer you're speaking of do something rude?" What crimes had he committed? Mira decided to get a feel for the severity of Soul Howl's deeds.

But things apparently weren't what she'd expected. The report Father Kingsblade had received was that the necromancer was abducting a cute little girl. When the priest came outside to confirm this, he'd only spotted a little girl matching the description, while the necromancer was nowhere to be seen.

"Tell me, are you absolutely certain you don't know?"

Now understanding that she wouldn't get wrapped up in any annoying trouble, Mira finally told the truth. "Oh, right, of course—him. Yes, I know him; he's a friend of mine. Goodness, I'm so familiar with his necromancy that it hardly registers as suspicious. I certainly understand thinking that at first glance, though."

"I see. He was a friend of yours? Good to hear. Apologies for taking up your time, Miss."

The priest emphasized the "friend of yours" part, then turned and spoke to a woman waiting by the chapel door. "Everything seems fine here." That woman had seemingly made the report.

Father Kingsblade had seen Mira and Soul Howl together at the exit of the Ancient Underground City, so he could've gathered that they were friends. He'd only pursued the matter to convince the woman, and to be absolutely sure.

"Oh, really? Thank goodness." Relief was clear on the woman's face. She thanked the priest and disappeared into the church.

Being accused of such a thing would've felt bad, but since Mira was the one being protected, she watched the woman with mixed emotions. Then she chuckled to herself, now knowing that people saw Soul Howl as a suspicious man going after a young girl. This would make for a fun story the next time she met him.

The priest turned back to Mira and said cheerfully, "One more thing. Next time you see your friend, please inform him that using magic on church grounds can be a criminal act."

That was apparently only the case sometimes, but it seemed the restriction applied to *all* magic, not just necromancy.

Faced with the intimidation lurking behind the priest's cheerful look, Mira meekly replied, "Yes, sir."

"Now I'd best be going. Thank you for your cooperation." After Father Kingsblade said what he wanted to, his imposing aura all but faded away. At that point, he began returning to the church.

"Say, can I ask you something?" Mira called out to the priest.

He turned. "Yes?" he responded genuinely kindly. "What can I do for you, Miss?"

"I heard earlier that, back when you were a champion in the underground arena, a girl training as a warrior sent you along this path in life. Did she tell you her name? Also, if you have any idea where she is now, I'd like to know."

She and Soul Howl had agreed that girl was very likely Wise Man Meilin. They'd concluded that the priest probably wouldn't have any clue as to her whereabouts, given that he'd encountered her seven years ago. Still, there was still a chance. Since the priest had approached Mira, she figured she might as well ask.

"...I see. That's what you were whispering about earlier, isn't it? Why do you ask about her?" The priest's ferocious aura reappeared, perhaps proving that his violent temper long ago hadn't been easily fixed.

"Oh, I didn't... Uh... She just sounded like a friend of mine," Mira stammered, trying desperately to avoid eye contact.

The priest's demeanor changed entirely. "Wait. You mean to say you're acquainted with her?!" he pressed Mira, as if he'd just met a goddess.

Kingsblade's sudden enthusiasm took her aback, but she managed to reply that the girl's actions just sounded like something a friend of hers would do—she wasn't certain they were the same person.

"I see... To answer your question, I didn't get her name. In battle, she called herself 'Taiyaki Kuri-Youkan.' I only learned later that those are apparently the names of confections." The priest was clearly disappointed, but he offered that name in case it provided clues.

As soon as Mira heard the pseudonym, she became certain. "Ah... Yes, that's almost certainly my friend. Those are two of her favorite foods."

Meilin enjoyed both taiyaki and kuri-youkan. She'd once overeaten them to the point of weight gain, which forced Kagura to diet alongside her in real life. Mira remembered it rather nostalgically.

The priest didn't leave her to her nostalgia for long, however. "Wonderful! Finally, I get to meet a friend of hers... How long has it been since I had such a fantastic day?!" Despite his status as a priest, he was virtually worshipping Mira instead of his god. It seemed Meilin was equal to a deity in his mind, and now he saw her through a false idol, Mira.

"It's a bit of a silly errand, but I'm searching for her. Do you have any idea where she is?" Mira asked the enthralled priest.

"No, unfortunately..." he replied. Based on his reaction, Mira had already known the answer. "However, I've heard she went on to fight in even greater arenas. She led me to this path in life. All I want is to meet her again and express my gratitude." He seemed to be praying. If he only knew where Meilin was, he'd probably dash off right away.

All in all, Mira could be certain that the girl who'd caused Zatzbald Bloodycrimson Kingsblade's career change was none other than Meilin. But all this really told her was that Meilin hadn't changed in seven years. Mira already knew that much.

Just about two months ago, Garrett and his companions had gone to the Fools' Wunderkammer to collect an important item, and a powerful monster attacked them. However, a girl appeared out of nowhere and trounced that monster with ease.

The description of the girl in that report had matched Meilin. The more Mira heard about Meilin, the clearer it was the girl was still adhering to her "wandering-warrior training" shtick.

"Even greater arenas," hm? It seems like she's still out there training. Maybe investigating from that angle would be faster.

Mira now had a goal in mind in her search for Meilin. "If I ever find her, I'll let her know you're grateful to her," she told the priest, then left.

Father Kingsblade thanked Mira profusely as she went, while gathered onlookers looked upon her with curious eyes. Who was this little girl, and why did the iron-fisted priest revere her so?

Days later, rumors of an angel's descent into the church spread, but didn't reach Mira's or Kingsblade's ears.

Shortly before 8:00 p.m., Mira reached the biggest hotel street in Grandrings. After walking around for a while to find lodgings for the night, she stopped in front of a building that could've been a small castle. This spot appeared to be the most expensive of the classy inns in this part of town.

"Hrmm... I'm leaning toward this one."

Folkspeak, the fairly expensive inn she'd stayed at the other day, had been comfortable for its price. How would an even more expensive inn serve her?

It was hard to let go of luxury now that she'd tasted it. Anticipating greater opulence, Mira gazed up at the inn before her. It stood regally, like a castle, lit from top to bottom in defiance of the dark night. Although it wasn't really intended for royalty, it was bigger than the surrounding lodgings and exuded an altogether different aura.

A whole hoard of magic stones... Loot from the Mechanized Wanderer and Machina Guardian... My treasure pile should easily be worth a hundred million. I don't have to worry about finances anymore. I say it's my responsibility to splurge!

Classy inns were, of course, distinguished by their indulgent meals and rooms. Their employees were also cut from a different cloth. Such inns employed specialists in various fields to offer a wide range of services.

That said, Mira had already experienced top-class service along those lines. After all, she'd stayed at the Palace of Alcait, which was far more luxurious than any inn could aspire to be.

It was a literal palace, so it was inherently gorgeous, and the room set aside for Mira was perfect. She got to eat the same meals as King Solomon himself, and the castle maids were handpicked elites. Mira's personal maid, Lily, was especially skilled.

Still, that wasn't quite the same as an inn. Mira entered, ready to experience just what kind of service this world offered first-class adventurers.

There was actually one problem: the treasures she'd brought back were *so* valuable, she'd have difficulty finding a buyer. But Mira didn't realize that; she simply pressed on, blinded by her experience thirty years prior.

Like the exterior, the lobby was dazzling and resplendent: a chandelier above, a soft carpet underfoot, elegant furniture here and there. It was luxurious in a clichéd way, but that made the opulence easy to recognize and solidified one's first impressions.

Hrmm, it's packed here. And these people don't quite look like adventurers...

The lobby practically oozed dignity and class, but it was a fair bit noisier than Mira expected. In that regard, it wasn't much different from other inns. On a quick look around, she saw that the clientele included not just adventurers but major merchants and apparent tourists. The inn seemed very safe, and memorable to boot.

As she went to reception, she started to worry that the inn wouldn't have a vacancy. Owing to its sheer size, it *did* have open rooms. But the cheapest ones—priced at fifty thousand ducats per night—were fully booked. The only rooms remaining were seventy thousand ducats or a hundred to a hundred fifty thousand ducats.

Mira immediately picked the most expensive. "I'll take the one hundred fifty thousand ducat room, then."

She feigned indifference as she accepted the gold key. Apparently, only the priciest room's key was golden; she twirled it around her finger, showing it off, as she headed to the grand staircase.

Then a familiar name reached her ears.

"Hey, have you heard? They say Fuzzy Dice appeared in Haxthausen!"

"I heard that too! I guess he sent his calling card to the Dorres Company!"

"Yeah! That company got big out of nowhere, right? None of the rumors about them are good."

"Nope. Apparently, they were investigated because of their ties to Chimera Clausen, but the investigation came up short. They couldn't find any evidence."

"So it seemed. But it'll be fine now! Fuzzy Dice is there, after all. I'm sure he'll find evidence—of their criminal profits, and more!"

A group of female adventurers Mira had noticed relaxing in the lobby were chatting about Fuzzy Dice while their friend reserved a room. Excited squeals of "Oh, he's so cool!" punctuated their conversation.

They were discussing a famous phantom thief. When Mira splurged on trading card packs a long time ago, "Fuzzy Dice" was the single RRR card she'd pulled. She'd learned more about the man from a woman named Theresa on a train home from

Alisfarius. Fuzzy Dice only went after those who did bad deeds. In a way, he was like a Robin Hood character.

As Mira remembered that, the girls continued talking. The phantom thief would evidently appear five nights from now. The location: the Dorres Company mansion in Haxthausen. His target: all the company's ill-gotten assets.

Ill-gotten assets, hm? I wonder where this Fuzzy Dice character comes upon such information. Also...I think he donates to an orphanage, right?

Climbing the stairs and eavesdropping, Mira remembered a few things about Fuzzy Dice. She recalled a story connected to orphanages that had come up during that same train ride. She'd heard it from the bard Emilio, who'd sat with her after Theresa. He'd traveled with a blind woman, Lianna.

In his journeys through various places, he'd picked up a lot of knowledge. One thing he'd learned of was an orphanage in a nameless village. It had been built eight years ago to handle the overflow of orphans caused by the Defense of the Three Great Kingdoms. From what Mira heard, Wise Man Artesia was involved in that.

It was...in the mountains of northeastern Grimdart, as I recall? Hrmm... Garuda could get me there in a day or two.

According to Emilio, there were rumors of a village in that mountain range. The problem was *where* in the mountains the village was. However, Mira had a flash of inspiration.

Orphanage, phantom thief... Phantom thief, orphanage... Hrmm. Maybe I could question him.

If Fuzzy Dice donated to that orphanage, he must know its location. In that case, going after him might just be the best idea, Mira thought to herself as she finally opened the door to her exorbitantly expensive room.

**She
Professed
Herself
Pupil of the
Wise Man**

30

IRINA THE BUTCHER was a legendary figure in the modern day. Long ago, however, she'd served as vice-captain of a famous mercenary group during a war.

The Black Lion Mercenaries, an elite group of thirty, was led by the Fiend Slayer Beowulf. Their exploits took them across the continent. Only Beowulf had the power to cut fiends down on his own, but he wasn't arrogant. He cared deeply for his comrades, and all—including his clients—trusted him in turn.

He was the object of Irina's secret love.

Given Beowulf's title, most jobs that came to the mercenary group were fiend-extermination requests. Everyone in the group gradually specialized in hunting fiends, and they became well-known as fiend exterminators rather than proper mercenaries.

One day, the Black Lion Mercenaries received an extermination request from a major nation's duke. The duke asked that they swiftly defeat a fiend that had suddenly appeared in the holy tomb where an ancient king lay. Left alone, the creature would disrupt a ritual held every four years. The reward was, in a word, exceptional.

Beowulf accepted the request. After getting the details, he had the Black Lion Mercenaries, including Irina, head to the holy tomb fully armed. The fiend they saw there was a silver wolf that almost looked...divine. It was the most ferocious enemy they'd fought by far, but the mercenaries didn't retreat. Although it was a long battle, they found a way to victory. While they used Beowulf—whom the wolf feared most—as a decoy, Irina successfully cut off its head with her battle-ax.

Though several mercenaries were injured, they'd managed to defeat their strongest foe ever without casualties. Since the group prided themselves on exterminating fiends, they cheered joyfully at the victory.

In the next instant, something happened. White mist spewed from the wolf's severed head and engulfed Irina. She screamed in agony.

Beowulf tried to save her, but the other mercenaries stopped him, telling him it was too dangerous to run into that mist; they didn't know what it was.

He shook off their warnings and dashed to Irina. He *didn't* know what the mist was—and that was exactly why he needed to rescue her right away. He loved Irina, so he couldn't stop himself.

Irina's own battle-ax cut him in two immediately.

Everybody watched breathlessly as Irina stepped from the thinning white mist. She was expressionless, and her eyes were lifeless. They looked at her. Then at Beowulf's corpse, halved at the waist. Then at Irina's battle-ax, covered in his blood.

The mercenaries' first reaction was confusion. They all knew the love Irina harbored for Beowulf; they all knew he felt the same.

Irina's face—which blushed when they teased her about that—was now icy pale. Beowulf's eyes, which narrowed when he asked the others when he should confess to her, were frozen open.

"How could you?!" someone screamed.

That only provoked Irina to swing her axe, turning yet another comrade into a corpse.

Screams and shouts echoed through the holy tomb as Irina lunged. In the chaos, every mercenary but her was killed.

One person witnessed this tragedy from afar: a servant of the duke who'd approached the mercenaries. The moniker "Irina the Butcher" came from his ensuing report.

After the tragedy, Irina remained at that holy tomb, attacking all who approached. The silver wolf's rotting corpse at her side, she became an even more formidable enemy than that fiend itself had been. It didn't take long for the tomb to be sealed away.

Centuries later, someone stepped into that sealed location: Soul Howl. He'd come running after hearing rumors of an undead maiden.

Naturally, that undead maiden was Irina herself. The legend surrounding her buttressed her reputation as a butcher.

Writings on the holy tomb claimed that a group of bandits once broke in to plunder it, then killed each other over the loot. After Irina slayed all her former friends, their residual grudge killed her and turned her into an undead being. Even now, those documents claimed, Irina awaited more sacrifices in the holy tomb.

Soul Howl found the tomb based on a description and various other documents. Just as he hoped, he located the undead Irina in its depths.

Irina was strong, swinging that massive battle-ax around easily. Nonetheless, Soul Howl was already a famous Wise Man by that point, so he trounced her mercilessly.

After that, he tried to use a spell to purify her and make her his pawn, but his spell failed.

If undead were too strong, Soul Howl needed to weaken them before casting the spell. He'd expected it to work just fine at first, but then he realized that he needed to drain Irina further. Depriving her of more stamina, he tried the spell again. Once more, it failed. A special condition apparently needed to be met.

Realizing this, Soul Howl left and researched both the tomb and Irina further. One thing became clear: Irina was no thief. She'd been a mercenary with the Black Lions.

From that, Soul Howl realized that the literature about the holy tomb was all lies. He returned to the tomb and investigated a corner full of scattered skeletons. They were the Black Lion Mercenaries' corpses. Tattered weapons and equipment remained there as well, though they were decayed and unusable.

One sword alone retained its shape and some sheen. A skeleton with only its upper half left wielded the blade, within which Soul Howl noticed a faint, wishful emotion still flickered. He picked up the sword and used necromancy to unravel that desire. It was weak, so he only managed to comprehend a bit, but it broke through his dilemma.

With that sword in hand, Soul Howl confronted Irina the Butcher again. At the end of their battle, he pierced her heart with the sword. Light poured from the blade and gently enveloped Irina, driving some kind of white mist out of her. It was almost miraculous.

After that, two phantoms appeared before Soul Howl. One was Irina, and the other introduced himself as Beowulf. From them, he heard the truth of what had happened at the holy tomb.

The Black Lion Mercenaries had received a request to defeat a fiend. However, the silver wolf wasn't a fiend; it was a holy beast protecting the tomb. When they killed it, the person closest to the corpse was chosen as the new keeper of the tomb and cursed to be undead for all eternity. Designated the tomb's new protector, Irina was deprived of her free will, and she attacked the intruders—the Black Lions. Ever since, she'd continued to slaughter all intruders.

After sharing the truth of what had happened there, Irina and Beowulf entrusted their honor to Soul Howl, then finally became light and disappeared. The sword stabbed into Irina's corpse crumbled and disappeared as well, having completed its mission.

The desire Soul Howl sensed remaining in the sword had essentially been adoration of Irina. Beowulf's deep love had, after so many years, finally released her from her suffering. Not that any of that mattered to Soul Howl; he was just excited to have her corpse.

Then a silver wolf appeared. It wasn't the giant creature Beowulf and Irina had described, just a rather large dog. Was it the sacred beast's pup? Regardless of its size, it exuded divinity.

"Are you one of the scoundrels who would defile this holy tomb?" the silver wolf asked Soul Howl.

Of course, he answered no.

"Then why have you come?" it pressed him.

He told the wolf that his objective was to obtain the nonpareil corpse of Irina the Butcher. His words seemed to get through to the wolf. Its sharp gaze softened. Then it quietly told him to leave at once.

Soul Howl didn't leave right away, however. He asked about some things that had been on his mind: what did this holy tomb hold, and who were the scoundrels the silver wolf spoke of?

The wolf couldn't answer the former. The latter, it explained, were a nobleman's private army. Having said as much, the wolf approached Soul Howl with a scrap of old armor in its mouth that bore the emblem of said nobleman. Then the wolf once again demanded that the necromancer leave.

Soul Howl thus exited the holy tomb with Irina's corpse in tow. As he did so, many specters revealed themselves to him. They harbored no malice, for they were Irina's former comrades.

Each specter thanked him for releasing Irina and Beowulf, then returned to heaven. However, one remained. From that specter, Soul Howl learned about the duke who'd had the mercenaries kill the holy beast under the auspices of fiend extermination.

Stating that she was Beowulf's mother, the specter asked that Soul Howl relieve her residual grudge. She promised that, if he granted this final wish, she would reward him by sharing the location of the Black Lion Mercenaries' secret hideout. It supposedly housed many of the mercenaries' personal valuables.

Beowulf's mother said that a memento of Irina's was sure to be among those belongings. She mentioned that because she recognized Soul Howl's profession and desire to have Irina's corpse. She seemingly knew quite a bit about necromancy.

Mementos were vital for Martyr's Rebirth. They could be stored inside the Martyr's Coffin, providing various unique effects, without the restrictions that applied to grave goods.

Soul Howl graciously accepted this unexpectedly useful request.

His only clue was an emblem on a piece of old armor, but Soul Howl spent time researching the duke's family. He scoured literature, wandered through cities, and even got help from a friend who loved history.

This acquaintance was very eager to give him a hand. They enjoyed history even more than Soul Howl, and the hidden truth about Irina the Butcher seemed to pique their curiosity. Thanks to their efforts, Soul Howl finally identified the duke's family.

How to clear up Beowulf's mother's grudge, then? Soul Howl had considered that along the way. Faced with the truth as it was, though, he was at a loss. The lineage of the duke who'd deceived the Black Lion Mercenaries had ended over two centuries ago. How could Soul Howl clear up the specter's grudge when all the duke's relatives were long dead? That was surely impossible.

Still, Soul Howl couldn't give up this late, so he looked around the family's ruined former home. In a well-secured library, he found a document on the duke's lineage.

Its end had been caused by no less than a curse. At one point, everyone related by blood to the duke began dying untimely deaths one after another. Was that retribution for killing the sacred beast and defiling the holy tomb? Soul Howl thought so at first, but the text that followed changed his mind. It explained that the duke needed to obtain an artifact within that holy tomb by any means necessary to *lift* that curse.

In other words, the duke had done it to save himself and his bloodline. He couldn't reach the artifact due to the sacred beast in his way, and while he was at loose ends, his relatives were dying.

Hiring the Black Lions was surely his last ray of hope, and it had ended in tragedy. A painful revelation, to be sure.

However Soul Howl searched after that, he found nothing more; there was no way to relieve the specter's grudge, ultimately. That was the truth, however, so he shared the facts with her. Amazingly, her expression lightened, as if a weight was lifted off her shoulders.

Beowulf's mother couldn't forgive what the duke had done, but the fact that he did it for his family resonated with her maternal heart. In turn, she gave Soul Howl information on the Black Lion Mercenaries' roost. The necromancer impatiently wrapped up the part where the specter went to heaven so that he could rush off and find the mercenaries' hoard.

But many years had passed since the specter's time. The treasure had already been cleaned out, and the hideout vandalized.

Just before he lost his will to continue with this string of disappointments, Soul Howl found something on the floor. It was a simple item carved from wood, seemingly some kind of hair ornament. No doubt it seemed like nothing but junk to those pillaging the hideout for treasure.

But Soul Howl sensed the adoration in that hair ornament. He didn't know whose love it was, but he knew who the item belonged to.

It was the memento of Irina's that he'd been searching for.

"You're as beautiful as ever, Irina." Soul Howl stroked her hair as she lay in the coffin, showering her with pure love.

Not many people could understand his wicked love. Most would find it creepy and keep a wide berth. But he had friends he could be proud of.

And there was one other person who didn't hate him, despite his unusual tastes. Far from it—that pushy woman openly pried into his business.

Soul Howl continued facing his many trials and tribulations, all to see that woman infuriated again.

AFTERWORD

TIME SURE FLIES. Look, it's Volume 11!

We only made it this far thanks to fuzichoco, my editors, dicca*suemitsu, and many more—not to mention all of you, my readers. Thank you so much!

Quick change of subject. Remember how, in the last volume, I mentioned needing to move out by April? It turns out the construction company is busy, and the rebuilding work will be delayed.

My moving deadline was extended! I can stay here till the end of June now.

I'm writing this at the end of April, but forget moving—I haven't even found a spot to move *to* yet!

When this eleventh volume is released, how will I be doing? Will I have found an ideal place within my budget? Will I even make the deadline?

The answers to these questions will...hopefully...come next volume!

I hope you'll be there to see them.